STORM DIVERS

TERRY MIXON

YOWLING
CAT PRESS

Published by Yowling Cat Press ®

Digital edition date: 6/21/2023

Print ISBN: 978-1947376038

Large Print ISBN: 978-1947376618

Cover art - image copyrights as follows:

Depositphotos.com/Kirschner

Depositphotos.com/Maxmag97.mail.ru

Depositphotos.com/Mode-List

NASA

Donna Mixon

Cover design and composition by Donna Mixon

Print edition design and layout by Terry Mixon

ALSO BY TERRY MIXON

You can always find the most up to date listing of Terry's titles on his Amazon Author Page.

Note: the links below (ebook only, obviously) redirect you to my website where you can click a button to go to Amazon. This allows me to participate in Amazon's associates program and earn a little more. Sorry for any inconvenience.

The Last Hunter

The Last Hunter

Bonds of Blood

Alpha Strike

The Enemy Revealed

Command Authority

The Grand Conspiracy

Shield of Humanity

Fog of War

Ships of the Line

Operation Liberty

The Empire of Bones Saga

Empire of Bones

Veil of Shadows

Command Decisions

Ghosts of Empire

Paying the Price

Recon in Force

Behind Enemy Lines

The Terra Gambit

Hidden Enemies

Race to Terra

Ruined Terra

Victory on Terra

When Luck Runs Out

Gunboat Diplomacy

The Imperial Marines Saga

Spoils of War

Imperial Recruit

Enemy Action

The Humanity Unlimited Saga

Liberty Station

Freedom Express

Tree of Liberty

Blood of Patriots

Single Novels

Scorched Earth

Storm Divers

The Vigilante Series with Glynn Stewart

Heart of Vengeance

Oath of Vengeance

Bound By Law

Bound By Honor

Bound By Blood

Box Sets

The Empire of Bones Saga Volume 1

The Empire of Bones Saga Volume 2

The Empire of Bones Saga Volume 3

The Empire of Bones Saga Volume 4

Humanity Unlimited Publisher's Pack 1

Humanity Unlimited Publisher's Pack 2

Want to get updates from Terry about new books and other general nonsense going on in his life? He promises there will be cats. Go to TerryMixon.com/Mailing-List and sign up.

DEDICATION

This book would not be possible without the love and support of my beautiful wife. Donna, I love you more than life itself.

ACKNOWLEDGMENTS

Once again, the people who read my books before you see them have saved me. Thanks to Alan Barnes, Tracy Bodine, Michael Falkner, Michael Goad, Cain Hopwood, Kristopher Neidecker, John Naiser, Bob Noble, Andrew Olivier, Jon Paul Olivier, Bill Smith, Tom Stoecklein, Dale Thompson, and Jason Young for making me look good.

I also want to thank my readers for putting up with me. You guys are great.

1

"**I** said no."

Rachel Price plucked her seatmate's hand from her leg for the third time in five minutes. That was enough. She decided she was going to make him regret being a pig in ways most men never even dreamed possible.

The man just smiled smugly. The same as the last two times she'd warned him.

She wanted to rip his genitals off and jettison them out the shuttle's airlock. The frozen remnants of his manhood would eventually enter Jupiter's atmosphere and burn up. That felt fitting.

Alas, she couldn't afford to draw any attention to herself, especially now. Even when provoked like this. She was on a mission, even if it was unsanctioned.

Mister Fingers was an arrogant businessman from one of the Mediterranean Sea domes. He claimed he was sponsoring a team in some sporting event. As if that was supposed to mean something to her.

She knew this because she'd had to listen to his nasal bragging through every meal for the last month. It made her wish she'd taken something other than a slow passenger freighter like *Calypso* for the trip from Earth to Jupiter.

Oh, well. It was water under the bridge at this point. Time to make the magic happen.

Rachel smiled sweetly at Mister Fingers and made sure to pass her breasts right in front of his face as she got out of her seat. His eyes followed.

Creep.

She floated back to the head quickly. If the pilot called everyone to their seats too soon, he'd ruin her plan.

The real purpose of the trip was to get into her carry-on bag when she got back to her seat without arousing suspicion. She didn't have to go, but washed her hands anyway, just in case anyone was listening.

Rachel opened the bin when she was done, shielding her bag with her body. Under the folded clothes sat her service weapon, safely secured under mesh.

That was only the beginning. The bag had her full kit. All the tools a spy working for the Republican Intelligence Service might need while defending the Republic.

She pulled a pressurized spray can out of her kit. The label indicated it was deodorant—the kind specially made for a woman, of course—but that was a crock. It was something cooked up by the geeks down in the RIS labs.

Something that was going to ruin Mister Fingers's day.

She misted just a bit on his bag before putting the can away and closing her things back up.

Thankfully, they entered the station's landing bay a few minutes later. She only had to endure two more gropes.

Disembarkation generated some well-deserved distance between her and her seatmate. The perceived gravity once they went down to the customs level was about Mars normal. It felt like home.

Not that the corporate reception and customs area was anything to cheer a weary traveler. They were the same all across the solar system, filled with industrial beige walls, crappy furniture, and suspicious customs officials.

The one on Mercury's Shadow Station was almost identical to this one, as a matter of fact. She had no doubt that the ones the recluses on Pluto used to keep the rest of civilization at bay would be substantially similar.

She'd never had a chance to see what things were like in any of the extra-solar colonies, but those were undoubtedly the same. It seemed a universal constant.

Rachel stayed close to Mister Fingers as they lined up for the inevitable customs inspection. No doubt, he thought that was due to his manly charms. In reality, she wanted to be close when things hit the fan.

Each planet was part of the Republic, like it or not, but all guarded their tax bases well. They wanted a cut of anything coming in, so smuggling was something of a system-wide sporting event.

The rules were simple: don't let them catch you, or find someone willing to look the other way for a price. If you failed, you'd get a whopping fine and a court date to explain everything to a stern-faced magistrate.

Getting minor things by wasn't usually a problem. Most customs agents were willing to take cash to look the other way for harmless stuff.

That all changed if they suspected you were a Disruptor. Everyone took those terrorist nutjobs seriously. They blew things up and killed people.

The customs agent in Rachel's line examined her readout as Rachel stepped forward, held her arms out, and let the scanner examine her for weapons or other proscribed items. A similar system checked her bag.

Rachel wasn't worried about the agent spotting her weapons or other gear. A tag in her kit triggered a hidden subroutine in the scanner. It wouldn't have mattered if she'd been carrying a nuke. All the woman saw was a normal bag and its mundane contents.

The only risk was if the woman wanted to perform a closer inspection. If so, it would be embarrassing when customs detained her. Nothing more. She had a RIS get-out-of-jail-free card.

Still, there was her professional reputation to think of. If they caught her, she'd never hear the end of it from Zane Hale, her partner.

That brought back a stab of worry that she quickly suppressed. He'd come to Jove Station to visit his brother. When he'd missed his return flight, she'd sent him a message.

One that had gone unreturned.

She'd contacted security, but their investigation had gone nowhere. Her partner had vanished.

Keeping her worry about Zane under control for the month-long trip out from Earth had been a form of torture. Even though their boss had tacitly authorized this trip, she was still on her own time.

Which was fine. Like most workaholics, she had vacation time to burn.

A low buzz from the machine in the next aisle got the attention of all the customs agents. Rachel heard the man in Mister Fingers's line tell the bastard to move aside for a closer inspection.

That sounded relatively benign, but Rachel saw the agent in her line put her hand onto the grip of her sidearm and partly turn to watch the annoyed businessman. A scanner detecting explosive residue was something everyone took seriously.

"Move along, ma'am," the agent said. "Everyone else, please back up. We might have an equipment glitch."

A convenient story to get innocent bystanders away from a possibly explosive situation.

Rachel had the pleasure of watching the agents subtly herd Mister Fingers into an exam room. Behind the closed doors, she heard muffled shouting, so he was going to get some roaming hands of his own very shortly.

Revenge was sweet.

They wouldn't find anything, of course. The spray wasn't actually explosive, and it evaporated quickly. They'd mark it down as a false positive. But not until they put the bastard through the wringer.

Rachel smiled, grabbed her bag, and walked out of the port.

Jove Station was huge, a spinning wheel and hub almost a mile across, so she'd want to get a ride to her hotel. Not only did the station serve as a major construction center for ships of all kinds, it was the jump-off point for the entire outer system and FTL ships from deep space. The Republic required the latter.

Faster-than-light drives created some kind of shockwave when they decelerated from superluminal speed, akin to a sonic boom in atmosphere. Whatever was in front of them when they dropped below the observed speed of light caught the most energetic particles. A nonsurvivable event, she understood.

She wasn't sure how far out that extended, but no one wanted to take chances with an off-course FTL ship causing devastation in the inner system.

It was local evening, so she'd check in and then go look up her partner's brother. Adam Hale might be more forthcoming in person.

Based on his uncooperative reaction to security when they'd asked him about his brother, she'd already decided to make a covert approach. She'd pretend to be Zane's girlfriend. A role the two of them had played a number of times over the years.

They'd tried being lovers, but that hadn't worked out. Zane was excellent in bed, but there wasn't any fire between them. So, they'd gone back to the way things had been. Mostly.

In any case, Rachel had a seemingly valid reason that she could share with Hale. One she'd use to pry the real story out of him about why her partner had come to see him.

She'd run his background, of course. Ex-Republican Army. He'd served as an officer for five years, rising to the rank of captain.

Her stomach had churned when she'd discovered he'd been involved in the fighting on Mars a decade ago. As a native, she was intimately familiar with the Free Mars movement. The name came from an Earth novel, but the organization wasn't fictional.

She should know. She'd been a member on the political side.

It had been a harmless pastime until the Free Mars action wing had crossed the line and bombed the Keller Dome.

As the seat of the Republican government on Mars, security had protected it very well, but the movement's idiots had smuggled explosives in somehow.

The dome had survived. The governor and his staff hadn't.

The Republican Army had struck back quickly. She understood

why they had to, but that didn't excuse the indiscriminate use of force against civilians.

Oh, they'd claimed the people they'd killed had been armed resistance fighters, but Rachel knew better. Many of her friends died when they raided the movement's offices. It had been a slaughter.

She'd been off on Vesta at the time, but she'd known there was no way those people would hurt a fly. It had been a cover-up. A smear campaign against the movement.

One Hale had been involved in. He'd led the forces that had attacked the movement's offices.

Back then, she hadn't had any way to learn more. And if she was honest with herself, she didn't have the training for it. Once she'd applied for and joined the RIS, they'd kept her away from working any cases on Mars, but eventually granted her access to the sensitive files dealing with the operations there. Some of them, anyway.

Frankly, she hadn't expected them to accept her application. It was her half-assed idea of digging up the truth. Apparently, the RIS didn't care. Or they wanted her data on the movement. Not that she knew much. They'd killed off all her contacts.

Years later, that little tidbit about Hale had only come to light when she'd looked at Zane's private papers. Adam Hale was the beneficiary of her partner's life insurance policy. It had his service ID number beside his name.

The same number that she'd found in a report on the Mars incident a number of years earlier, but with the names redacted.

If she were lucky, she'd dig up something interesting to pass on to the authorities here on Jove Station. It wouldn't make up for the deaths of her friends all those years ago, but putting Adam Hale in detention for the rest of his life would feel very good indeed.

2

———

"**Y**o! You in here, bro?"

Adam Hale looked up from the thruster he had disassembled on his workbench. "In back."

Jason Chang sauntered in. "I figured I'd find you here. There's a party on, you know. People are expecting to see the one and only Adam Hale there."

He'd figured that was what this was about. "I don't feel like being around other people. And I have nothing to wear."

"With the qualification dives starting tomorrow, there are a lot of new people on the station and they want to see the local favorites." The smaller man waggled his eyebrows. "I can think of a few ladies that wouldn't mind the fact you have nothing to wear."

Adam dropped his wrench and grunted sourly. "You're an irritating little Asian man. Has anyone ever told you that?"

"Almost every day," Jason said with a wide grin. "Just think, my branch of the family hasn't seen China in something like a hundred and twenty years. I'm not sure we're actually Asian anymore."

"Don't let your grandmother hear you say that."

Jason's eyes darkened. "Come on. We'll be early for a change."

His friend's reaction wasn't a surprise. He didn't like talking about his family. Adam knew that was because some of them were involved in things that might not exactly be legal. He let it go like he always did.

Adam held up a grease-covered hand. "Shouldn't I go shower?"

"Just wash up. Girls like clean hands. Keep the scruffy look, though. It works for you."

He had to admit his oldest friend was right. The casually unshaven, rough-and-ready look seemed to attract women like moths to a flame. That was good, sometimes. Most times not. He had to be in the mood for feminine companionship.

Adam dispensed some specialized soap on his hands and started rubbing the grease off. "Kira went on a tear today. She's not happy about the delay with *Javelin*. She made third shift stay late and redo some buildup around the faster-than-light drive container."

Jason snorted. "Kira Houston is always on a tear. That's how she took Ramirez's position away from him. Ramirez was a racist. How he ever got put in charge of anything is beyond me. I'll look over the FTL work myself."

"Are you sure you should be calling people racist? I seem to recall you giving me crap for being vanilla ice cream?"

"Yes, but I only say that to try and change your misguided ways. You can be such a stick in the mud."

Adam considered changing out of his work clothes, but decided against it. All he added was a leather jacket with patches representing his various dives.

That's what really drew the women, he knew. Him being a storm diver. It was the new extreme sports craze to grip the system. A decade ago, it had been cross-country on Mercury's bright face. God only knew what it would be a decade from now.

For now, it was hot, with the coverage being even more frenzied than usual this week. The Republican Sporting Association had sponsored the first annual storm diving competition this week. Would-be divers and corporate teams had flocked to Jove Station. It was a zoo.

It amused Adam how these people thought they could do better than the local talent. He and his friends had been doing this for years.

Even decades in some cases. They'd honed their equipment to the bleeding edge and lived for the adrenaline rush. They craved it.

No way they'd let some off-station hotshots break any of their records.

One bonus for the locals was that they'd already qualified. The RSA rules stated that to compete a diver had to hit the base of Jupiter's troposphere and remain for at least ten minutes.

They'd all managed that plenty of times. Their ships already carried the telemetry recorders the RSA mandated for officially recording the depth, speed, and duration of dives. They'd pioneered them.

Those would be the records everyone would be striving to beat. The ones set by Adam and his friendly—or in some cases, not so friendly—competitors. The games would award medals for fastest entry, deepest dive, most intense weather event endured, and longest duration in the fluid area of Jupiter's atmosphere.

Adam held the speed record, and he intended to keep it.

Divers could make as many as three dives over the next week. In some cases, the newcomers had different ships with profiles tailored to different goals. That was all fine with the RSA. The diver was competing, not the equipment. As long as a ship had telemetry, it was a valid dive.

Even before the announcement of the games, he and the rest had built loyal followings in this extreme sport. The vids Jason put together netted both of them more than the construction work they officially did, and that paid very well indeed.

A lot of people in the sport blew through money as if it were infinite. Sometimes, when they failed to put enough back into their ships, they died.

Not that storm diving on Jupiter was safe. The king of the solar system was unforgiving of those who trifled with him.

Even here in orbit, the gravity was heavy. The station was in freefall around the massive gas giant, but if it hadn't been, almost three times Earth's gravity would crush them all. That made boosting back out of the depths a herculean task.

Jove Station fell around the giant world and escaped the press of gravity, except for the times when they had to use the fusion drives to boost their orbit. Those moments gave everyone a little taste of what he felt on dives.

The radiation was hellish. An intense magnetic field and buffer compartments of water kept the station inhabitants safe.

Those like him who worked on the exposed FTL ships in the shipyards only had magnetics to protect them. If they failed, death would quickly follow. Not that the workers would die immediately. They'd fade away, painfully, into oblivion. He thought of it as rotting from the inside out.

It had happened once before. When the Disruptors had bombed the station's magnetic shield controls. The water buffer protected the station until the techs got everything online again. The construction crew on duty that day wasn't so lucky.

Far too many of them died in terrible agony over the next week. Anti-radiation meds were good, but not when someone got multiple lethal doses. Shit like that made him wish he were still in the Army.

Until he remembered what had happened on Mars.

"You hear about the excitement at customs?"

Adam zipped his jacket. "No. They catch someone smuggling in live iguanas in their pants again?"

"Alas, no. Some guy set off the explosive detectors. No bomb, but they gave him the full tour, if you know what I mean."

"Did they at least buy the poor bastard dinner first?"

"Nope. And, boy was he mad. Frothing, actually. Threatened everyone in sight for denying him his rights and tried to call a lawyer. Says he'll sue."

Adam shook his head. "Good luck to him with that. Not after the last time the Disruptors got onto the station."

"I think they explained that in great detail as they probed him. I hear it took four of them to hold him down."

"So, how'd the idiot set off the detectors?"

Jason shrugged. "They have no idea. The leading thought is some type of detector failure. They're ripping into the systems now."

The two of them exited the shop they rented from the port and started walking down the street. The name of the club they frequented was almost a given, considering. The glowing red spot over the door was unnecessary, unless you were a newbie that had no idea where the Great Red Spot was.

The artfully placed red lights inside kept up the atmosphere. Not that everything was red. It was mostly just dim.

Writhing bodies packed the dance floor, weaving to the industrial beat playing at near ear-damaging volume from the speakers. The DJ stood over his console above them, dressed in what looked like tin foil and a miner's lamp.

Adam shook his head. He'd never understand some people.

They made their way to the back and through an unmarked door. The music dropped to manageable levels. Soundproof it wasn't, but it was good enough.

This was more to his taste. Still as hectic as out front, but less frantic. Local storm divers and their friends made up the crowd. And groupies. You couldn't escape them. Not everyone wanted to.

"I'll leave you to wander while I check out the buffet," Jason said.

"What about Cindy?"

"Who do you think sent me for takeout?" his friend asked with another waggle of his eyebrows. "She keeps asking about you coming over, bro."

"And see you naked? No way?"

His friend laughed and headed into the crowd. He'd probably charm some groupie into going home with him for a night of wild sex with his adventurous girlfriend.

Adam knew for a fact that Cindy had no interest in him. She'd told him so when she'd started seeing Jason. She was monogamous when it came to men and only saw women when in the company of her steady. Not that Jason would complain about that.

He decided he'd have a drink, make one pass through, and then head back to the shop. That would satisfy his friend and let Adam get back to work. Dive time would come early, and he had that thruster to finish.

The various members of the other local dive teams nodded his way as he walked past. Some tried to draw him over, others shot him the finger. Okay, only Double Dick flipped him off. Richard

Dickerson—Double Dick to friend and foe alike—was just that kind of guy.

Adam and he didn't get along that well. Of course, Double Dick didn't like anyone any better. The man was an asshole.

The bartender knew what a raised finger—index—meant for Adam. One ice-cold beer rapidly came sliding down the bar. Adam replaced the bottle with cash and turned to face the crowd.

It was a busy night. And that was without all the out-of-towners flocking the station. He wondered what the party was really for. No one had died this week, so this wasn't a wake. It wasn't somber enough to be a wake, anyway.

Everyone was probably just getting things out of their systems before the dive. They always said, live today as if you'd die tomorrow. For storm divers, that was truer than any of them would care to admit.

Storm diving was the ultimate ride, but that had a ridiculous amount of danger attached to it. The thrill came from knowing the king would kill you if he could. And he could.

No matter how careful they were, Jupiter claimed blood every year. The far side of the club had a wall with pictures of the men and women who'd never come back. Lost forever in the depths when their ships failed. Or their nerve.

Divers rarely talked about that. Other than the random drunken salute to the fallen.

Adam happened to be facing the entrance to the room when the door opened. He didn't recognize the woman, but she was a looker. Tall, muscular, and confident. She moved with the kind of grace he'd only seen in people that practiced one of the various martial arts. Kind of a coiled readiness.

He could thank the Army for that kind of eye. In his day, he'd led many people who moved with just that assurance.

She swept the crowd with her gaze. Their eyes only locked for an instant, but he knew she'd found what she was looking for.

Him.

This didn't bode well. The only people that sought him out—other than his friends—were either groupies or people with scores to settle. He'd made a fair amount of enemies in his lifetime. He didn't recognize the woman, but that didn't mean she wasn't out to do him mischief.

He took a drink and headed directly toward her. If there was going to be trouble, he'd settle it right now. He'd never been the kind to tug at a stuck bandage. Rip it off, he'd always said. Besides, he might be dead tomorrow.

She zeroed in on him as he dodged through the crowd, giving up the pretense of looking for someone else. Good. Lies only slowed things down.

Adam stopped a few feet in front of her. "You're looking for me. I don't suppose I won the system lottery."

"What makes you think I have any interest in you?"

Her voice was deeper than he'd expected. And guarded.

He smiled. "I've got a superpower."

That got a grudging smile out of her. "I had everything all worked out in my head, but you have a better eye than I expected, Mister Hale. Or you got lucky."

"Trust me, things rarely go as you plan. You don't look like a groupie, so what brings you calling?"

"Zane."

Adam felt his expression close up. "I haven't seen him in ten years and I don't expect that to change. Go back to security and tell them that. He's not here. They should know that already, but some of you people are slow."

"You're wrong, Mister Hale. I know Zane came here. He told me he was going to before he left Earth. He went through customs on this station and vanished. I'm going to find him, and you're going to help me."

That brought a slightly sneering smile to his face. He hated the expression, but sometimes couldn't stop himself.

"What are you to my brother? A girlfriend? Don't try wife. He's not the marrying type. Or maybe a coworker. Are you a spook?"

"My name is Rachel Price. All you need to know is that I care about Zane. I don't give a shit what problems you have with him. He came to see you and vanished. I want to know where he is."

Adam put his fists on his hips and leaned into her personal space. To her credit, she stood firm.

"Then we can settle our business right now. I never saw him. He didn't come sniffing around or I'd have busted his chops. The two of us aren't close. You want to look for that worthless sack of crap, be my guest. Find him and get the hell off Jove Station."

He drained the beer and tossed the bottle into a bag by the door as he headed out.

The encounter had his blood up. Rage boiled behind his eyes, and it was a damned good thing the woman had let him go. He was in no mood to let her screw with him. Now he'd have trouble getting to sleep, and that would make tomorrow a pain in the ass.

3

Rachel returned to the hotel angry with herself. She'd blown the intro like an amateur. Hale had spotted her the moment she'd come through the door. Even before she'd seen him. That was unforgivable.

Worse yet, he'd closed up like a turtle when she'd mentioned Zane. The antipathy there was real, though she had no idea why he hated his brother so deeply.

Still, the two were family. One look made that clear to anyone with half a brain. They had the same features. Only where Zane was handsome in a sleek and sophisticated way, his brother was rugged and dangerous.

Not that Zane wasn't dangerous. Oh, she could attest to that. But Hale, he was a killer under the surface. His eyes told the tale. Cold and hard. Just the kind of eyes that could watch her friends be shot down in cold blood.

She'd expected that. The man had been one of the Republican Army's elite ground troops. A Mustang, an officer who'd come up through the ranks. She hadn't been able to access the classified portions of his record, but she suspected he'd been one of their most deadly men in his day.

That called to her in a way she hadn't counted on. Oh, had it ever.

Her body had reacted to his attempt to intimidate her by wanting to move in even closer. That kind of visceral reaction had no place on this mission. He was a contact she needed to persuade into helping her. Nothing more.

Rachel rode the elevator down to her floor, seething in silence, the gravity slowly becoming stronger as she descended. The well-to-do stayed on the higher floors, closer to the station center. Someone on a government paycheck had to make do with higher gravity.

As a Martian, she'd had to work hard to build and keep the muscle she had. At only 1/3 the gravity, Mars put many of the inhabitants at a disadvantage when compared to Earther muscles. It had taken her a year of intense workouts just to be ready for the trip to the mother world.

As a rule, her people were taller than average, but more slender. Gaining the muscle mass her ancestors had once possessed was doable, but hard work.

Getting rid of her accent was harder than gaining muscle, but the RIS had helped. Now she could fool most people into thinking she was from almost any part of the system. Her fallback accent was a kind of muddle that really didn't sound as though it was from any specific place.

The hotel was packed to capacity, but she'd managed to get a room on the underside of the station. It had a small window with a view of the massive gas giant spinning slowly below. It was grand, and she'd spent entirely too much time after checking in gazing down at the massive planet.

The station's magnetic shielding made the view possible, but if anything went wrong, a protective screen would close it off.

Rachel locked her door and stood in front of the window again, watching the atmospheric bands on the giant planet. So beautiful.

Hale was a bust for the moment, so she needed to focus on other angles. Like the hotel.

She'd reserved a room here because that's where Zane had

intended to stay. They'd told security that he hadn't checked in, but she wanted to verify that for herself.

Her kit had everything she needed to worm her way into the comp system of a commercial hotel. Even an expensive one like this. Oh, it wouldn't get her into the truly secure systems, but experience had taught her that most companies shied away from spending what it truly took to fortify their network.

The room had standard wireless, but that was almost certainly on an isolated guest system. They were smart enough to separate the business and guest sides, she was sure.

Her comp had a lot more range than average, though, when paired with her custom remotes. Such as the one she'd planted near the front desk. That would link to the guest services system. She'd eventually need to get into the business side, but this would be a good start.

* * *

ADAM WORKED on the thruster for another hour before he gave up in disgust. The woman in the bar had him too pissed off to focus.

He retreated to the room he kept in the rear of the shop. It wasn't much, but it had everything he needed: a place to sleep, a place to heat food, and a shower. The shop satisfied his other needs.

After a moment's consideration, he pulled a second beer from his fridge. He'd take some sober pills in the morning.

Why couldn't his brother leave him in peace? Even when he wasn't here, everyone seemed to think he was. That had to be bullshit.

The last time he'd seen Zane, they'd fought over the intel on the Mars operation. God, the RIS had royally screwed that up. Instead of a building full of terrorists, they'd found office workers.

Admittedly, some of them had been armed, but that was no excuse for the intelligence minders the RIS had forced on them to open fire on everyone. By the time he'd stopped the slaughter, far too many bystanders were dead.

To the general public, it hadn't mattered that he didn't order the slaughter. That the RIS agents had acted far outside any rules of engagement. The killing had taken place when he was in command and supposedly in control. The buck stopped with him.

The RIS agents had confiscated all the helmet recordings as soon as the dust had settled. Then they'd covered their own ass, blaming him and his men for the atrocity.

His superiors had fought for him, but they'd lost. Adam ended up resigning his commission in disgust.

When he'd returned to Earth and confronted his brother with the RIS's betrayal, their fight had been epic. They'd both said things they couldn't forgive or forget. The two hadn't spoken in the almost ten years since.

But that didn't mean the memories didn't hurt to this day. They'd been brothers. Closer than most. He'd looked up to his older sibling. Idolized him growing up. Then Zane had helped betray him.

Perhaps that was too harsh. His brother hadn't been part of what happened on Mars. But he'd defended the RIS and blamed the slaughter on the Army. On Adam. All the innocent lives taken that he couldn't atone for.

And now that woman was here looking for Zane. Adam knew deep in his heart that his brother wouldn't have come to see him. That part of their lives was over.

If his brother really had come to Jove Station, it was for some other purpose. Some spy shit. None of Adam's business.

He finished his beer and tried to get some sleep, but the woman haunted his dreams, too. She was probably a spook like Zane. That made her the worst of the worst in his mind, but his subconscious seemed to have a different impression.

Maybe he should've gone groupie surfing like Jason had. It had been too long. He finally took a knockout pill and let the darkness take him under.

* * *

It took Rachel longer than she'd have preferred to access the guest services network. Their security really was top-notch. Once she did, the first place she went was the registration log. A quick search located Zane's entry.

It said he'd failed to check in, but something looked a little off. Normally, this kind of place charged the guest who failed to show up, but this time they hadn't. Or rather, they had and then they'd refunded the money.

Even if he'd been on RIS business, that shouldn't have happened. Could the hotel have lied about it? What did they have to gain by doing so?

She sat back and considered her options. She needed more information.

The entry indicated what room the hotel had assigned to Zane. In this case, it was a suite. It had been months since he'd supposedly arrived. If he had actually checked in, he might have left some trace of his presence. It was a slim hope, but not an empty one.

The suite had a single guest. That complicated matters, but she'd crept past sleeping people before. She'd never searched a place thoroughly under those circumstances, though. This was going to take some finesse.

First, she needed to get in.

Her access to the front desk comps was sufficient to add her retinal pattern to the guest list for the suite. She'd scrub it back out once she'd finished.

Rachel extracted herself from the registration system, erasing her tracks from the logs. A dedicated security sweep might find traces of her activity, but that would mean she'd already blown it big time.

This was crossing the line, and she knew it. She wasn't on a mission, so this would be a real crime. As if hacking the hotel comps wasn't. If they caught her, she'd face detention. Maybe the RIS would intervene. Maybe not.

But it didn't matter. She wouldn't let her partner down. If that meant breaking every rule in the book, so be it.

It only took a moment to grab the gear she'd need on the intrusion. She hoped it wasn't necessary, but she stashed her pistol in a concealed holster at the small of her back, next to a compact shocker.

There were few guests up and about at this hour. She took the stairs up to the higher levels. The gravity dropped until it was almost Mars normal. Whoever was here had money to burn. Particularly since the hotel had jacked the rates for that sporting event.

The small camera over the target doorway noted her presence, verified her retinal pattern, and unlocked the door. It opened silently at her touch. Rachel slipped inside and closed it again using all due care.

The suite was larger than her room by a significant margin. Zane had really splurged to get a place like this. It had three bedrooms, a large common area, and a real kitchen. Probably stocked with all kinds of good stuff. Pretty fancy for just one person.

Zane had trained her, so she knew where he'd stash anything he wanted concealed while in a strange place. He wouldn't want the cleaning staff to find his kit.

He'd most likely use the air vents. On a station like this, there'd be lots of them. She'd have to search them all, but the areas where the current guests weren't sleeping would be a good place to start.

She checked at the various doors and figured out which room had the guest. Then she moved on to the unoccupied ones.

With a sleeping person so near, she had to be careful not to make any noise. She took the precaution of putting a proximity sensor on the doorway to the occupied room. If the guest started moving around, she'd get a warning in her earbud.

There was nothing in the air vents in the unoccupied rooms. A scan for fingerprints found more than a few, but not Zane's. The kitchen was a bust, too. Though, she did admit the food made her mouth water.

Maybe she'd steal a sandwich before she departed. That wouldn't add much to her sentence if security busted her.

Well, she'd have to take a more calculated risk and search the occupied room. That presented a lot more danger, but she could do it.

The earbud beeped at her. The guest was up.

Rachel killed her hand light and slipped back into the bedroom she'd just searched. The guest walked over to the bar, picked up the bottle sitting on top, and headed out into the hall.

That was odd. Where would they be going at this hour? A late date? Did she have time to toss the main bedroom while they were out? She hoped so.

She recovered the sensor from the doorway and slipped into the darkened room. The vent would be on the left side of the bed.

Rachel took the collapsible stool she'd been using and headed over there, using her feet to feel for obstacles. If the guest was a man, he might have left his shoes beside the bed. And she found them. Messy bastard.

She'd just started undoing the vent when a male-sounding grunt from the bed told her she wasn't alone.

Dammit. She'd been sloppy. Either the guest had snuck someone else into the room or he'd had a late-night friend come over. If he turned the lights on, it would be an ugly scene.

Rachel dropped to the floor and hugged the bottom of the bed just before the lamp came on. She could see bare male feet stumbling toward the bathroom. He didn't bother closing the door before stinking up the air.

It was risky, but she had a very brief window to act. She jumped back onto the stool and removed the vent cover as quietly as she could. Damn it. There was nothing there but dust bunnies.

If her partner had left anything behind, it would be in the bathroom. The now contaminated bathroom.

She put the cover back into place and slipped into the closet as even worse sounds began coming from the bathroom. This was going to be fabulous.

As she was closing the sliding door, she spotted the man's wallet on the dresser, just within arm's reach. She snagged it and gave it a quick search.

Just her luck. It was Mister Fingers. Or, as his Republican ID card said, Damalis Stavros of Biros Dome. Annoyingly, his image actually looked like him.

Hers looked as though the bored woman at the bureau had waited until she blinked to snap the shot. She'd considered taking her own and forging herself a new ID, but that might be awkward to explain.

The wallet was empty of cash and credit chips. She doubted the man went anywhere without piles of money, so Rachel suspected he'd leased a woman for the night and that she'd robbed him blind.

The thought amused her. Rachel had worn gloves, so there'd be no identifying fingerprints for security to scan. She'd need to scrub the access logs so they didn't come looking for her, but she'd already planned to do that.

She put the wallet back in place as the man flushed. With the closet closed, he wouldn't see her there. Caution made her slide back behind the hung clothes where the luggage hid her legs. Even if he opened the door, she'd be out of plain sight. Mostly.

He came out of the bathroom and muttered something unintelligible. Perhaps he'd just noticed that his companion had departed. That could be good or bad.

She heard him curse and stomp toward the dresser. He must be after his wallet. The cursing went up significantly in volume. He knew the woman had robbed him.

Rachel didn't object to any of that, but she'd have rather he figured it out the next morning. The question now was whether he'd go to security now or wait.

The door to the closet slid open, and he grabbed a suit from the hanger right in front of her face. She had just enough time to lean to the right before he created an opening.

She took calming breaths as he dressed. Slow and deep. Trying to ignore the stench from the bathroom.

If he called security to come here, she'd have to knock him out, and that would set events in motion. She'd rather avoid that kind of attention. Her only hope was that Mister Fingers seemed the kind of man who loved to go yell at people where others could listen in.

If so, he'd go to the front desk and create a humiliating scene for the poor bastard on duty. She could only hope he ran true to form.

Her luck turned good, and she heard him leaving the suite. Once she was sure he wasn't coming back for something, she came out of the closet and headed for the bathroom. The clock was running down, and she only had a few minutes left.

The smell was nauseating, but she couldn't turn on a vent or spray any freshener. Someone might notice. The foul air made her eyes water.

The tub seemed big enough for her to swim in. Well, to do laps, at least. The shower had multiple heads and was probably divine. She was jealous.

Rachel pulled the cover off the vent, and her breath caught. A kit just like hers sat there. Zane had made it to the hotel. Someone had erased the record of his arrival and lied to security about it.

She took the kit and put everything back the way she'd found it. Once she'd made a quick pass to verify nothing was out of place, she started for the door and stopped by the bar. Since security would blame it on someone else, she might as well get some of the good stuff.

Most of the bottles inside the cabinet were small and sourced locally, but she found an imported red wine in the back. She also grabbed the expensive single malt beside it.

That might make for a decent peace offering, if she had to make nice with Hale. This was going to cost Mister Fingers a pretty penny when the bill came due. It couldn't have happened to a nicer guy.

She took a chance by raiding the refrigerator for some of the high-class meats and cheeses. They would go very nicely with the booze while she sifted through Zane's kit. A handy canvas bag with the hotel logo held the bottles, food, and a loaf of nice bread for her.

Rachel slipped out of the suite and headed for the stairs. She made it just as the elevator doors slid open, and she ducked inside the doorway, pulling the door almost closed as Mister Fingers followed a harried-looking security man down the hall.

Maybe she shouldn't have taken as much time as she had, but it had worked out. This time.

Once she'd gotten back to her room, a few minutes' work erased all electronic evidence of her visit to Mister Fingers' suite. The camera above the door didn't record images. It only provided room access, so she was safe there.

The hotel entrance would provide an image of the prostitute the man had brought in for the evening. She'd take the hit for the booze and food, which wasn't fair, but Rachel didn't feel too bad framing a thief for robbery. Well, technically burglary, but close enough. It was certainly a grand theft.

She set the kit on the coffee table while she ate a sandwich made from that divine food. The implications of this situation had changed. There was a cover-up going on. She'd have to be a lot more careful in how she approached finding her partner.

Logically, the next thing she should do is report the change in status to her boss, but she wanted to get a better feel for what was going on first. Something smelled. Zane had come here without telling them the truth, and she trusted his judgment.

For now, she'd keep this to herself.

4

Adam woke with a stab of pain between his eyebrows. Knockout pills did that to him. He took a pill for the pain and another to sober him up. He didn't need the slightest trace of alcohol in his system today. Storm diving could kill him without any help.

Some of his friends on the construction crew asked why he did such crazy shit. He really didn't know how to answer the question. Honestly, it was the only time he felt alive anymore.

The money Janus paid for the technology he and others developed was a factor, too. That was why they tacitly allowed the divers to do their thing. What they did with it, he had no idea.

In any case, if he made it deeper or faster, safer or easier, the corporation was happy to deposit large sums of cash into his account. The videos from the dive would generate a lot of attention and money from the fans across the system. Outside it, too.

With the added prominence of the games, the market for fresh material was hot right now. Hence his plans for the day. Since he didn't need to qualify, he could feed the fans' hunger. He wouldn't be going deep. He'd go for the most awesome visuals.

Jason was looking over their dive ship when he arrived at the bay they rented. He seemed rested, which had to be a lie. Or he hadn't found a new lady friend to share with his girl.

Adam clapped Jason on the shoulder. "You look like you struck out, bro."

The other man grinned. "Never. I took a wake-up pill. I can do that. One of the benefits of being the mechanic instead of the pilot."

"How's she look?" Adam patted the side of his custom dive ship. She was sleek and had only the most vestigial of wings. They'd gone with a bright-blue paint job this time. It looked good.

"I tweaked the magnetic field generator just as we discussed," Jason said. "I think it'll reduce the leakage by maybe half a percent. Janus will like that. Port thruster three looked hinky, so I swapped it out."

Adam nodded. "I was going to do that, but didn't have enough time to build the spare in the shop."

"Would the tall lady with the dark-brown hair be the reason you couldn't wrap it up? I saw the two of you talking last night."

He shook his head. "No way. I sent her packing."

"It sure seemed as though she sent *you* packing," his friend teased. "You left and she was right behind you. I was giving you credit for angry sex. If she comes back, can I make a run at her?"

"She's all yours."

The first thing they did was go over every aspect of the dive plan. Everyone thought that he and his comrades were suicidal fools that rode off like cowboys seeking thrills no matter the cost. Nothing could be further from the truth.

They planned every dive in meticulous detail. Each aspect of it was isolated and steps taken to mitigate risk. Safety first, last, and always.

The external preflight involved them both going over each of the systems closely and then double-checking one another. Only once they were both satisfied did he go inside the ship to start the instrument checks.

Adam slid into the narrow cockpit and ran the ship through the normal preflight tests. All systems green. With the hellish environment in Jupiter's atmosphere, the ship had to be in top condition. The slightest flaw meant death.

Once he was satisfied, he climbed out. "We have a big crowd today?"

"With the games starting? Hell, yes. Eight other divers are making runs today and the gallery is packed. Some guy called trying to set up an appointment for an interview. I think he was a reporter."

"He can wait," Adam said.

Those were serious numbers. Normally, they had around six divers take a run during any given week. Sometimes as few as two or three. Occasionally none.

There weren't that many people crazy enough to plunge into the king's atmosphere. The biggest pack they'd ever had was an even dozen. Two of whom had died. One with a failed thruster and one because she'd gone too deep and the pressure ruptured her hull.

Each of the dive ships had a telemetry package that came free in a worst-case scenario. Its powerful thrusters brought all the data back to Jove Station. That allowed them to find out what had happened and to help guard against it in the future.

However, there was a gruesome side as well. Included in the retrieved data was the pilot video, which meant they got to watch their friends die.

Occasionally, a copy of one of the cockpit recordings got out. Then it made the rounds all across the system. There was no accounting for some people.

He sighed. If it happened to him, he supposed it didn't matter. He'd be dead.

The last thing he checked was his suit. It wasn't anything like what normal spacers wore. The G-forces he'd hit diving into the Jovian atmosphere were much harsher than on a normal planet.

His suit helped him breathe and made speaking possible. It also gave him extra strength to force the controls if he had to.

Unlike other ships, the dive vessels all used mechanical linkages and hardwires. It was almost like going back in time. If too much radiation got through the protective magnetic fields, it would crash any electronic relays.

Today's dive wouldn't be anything to write home about. Well, at least not for him anyway.

Most of the excitement came when they dove on the Great Red Spot, the massive anticyclone that circled Jupiter south of the equator, but that wasn't where the most danger lurked. The winds encountered there only rose to just over four hundred kilometers per hour.

His plan for the day was to go for the visuals rather than push the limits of his ship and body. The king's atmosphere was over five thousand kilometers deep, so there was a large canvas for him to choose from.

The base of the atmosphere wasn't actually the planetary core. Scientists had designated that at the one bar mark, where the atmospheric pressure was just a little less than at sea level on Earth.

At about 12 bars, hydrogen became a supercritical fluid. Divers treated 10 bars as the bottom of the atmosphere. The drop from 1 bar to 10 bars was about ninety kilometers.

He'd ventured lower, of course. They all had. The pressure and temperature went up dramatically the deeper one went, but they could do it if they were prepared.

The visible clouds started about 0.6-0.9 bar and went down about fifty kilometers. Ammonia ice made up the uppermost level. Below that were denser clouds of ammonium hydrosulfide and ammonium sulfide. Those were at 2-3 bars. At 7 bars, he'd find water clouds.

And with water came lightning.

That was his goal today. He wanted to capture a massive thunderstorm on video. He'd target one in the northern hemisphere. He had a bright-white one in mind. It would be a turbulent ride, but well worth it, if the light show was half as good as he expected.

Of course, that risked running into the impressive deep winds. Advanced probes had revealed roaring wind speeds over six hundred kilometers an hour in some cases before the king killed them.

Scientists believed those only hinted at what might exist even further down. Some of the jets and bands occasionally produced storms that moved that fast.

Not as sexy to the uninitiated, but a far more dangerous aspect to the sport. He'd done a few of the powerful northern storms before, and that had padded his bank account while getting him a lot of cred in the diving community.

Depth was one of the milestones divers used to compete against one another. His accomplishments weren't too shabby, but Double Dick held that record at 250 bar, a damned impressive achievement.

Others had gone deeper, but they'd died in the attempt. Only their data recorders made it back out. Divers only counted a record if you lived.

They also used wind speed and atmospheric pressure for records. Plus, the fans valued the wildest rides.

Public opinion was more than raw statistics, though. It was a combination of risk, daring, and panache. Adam thought he had Double Dick beat when it came to showmanship. The fans seemed to agree.

Once he had everything checked, Adam stretched his back. "Time to make the donuts."

* * *

RACHEL ARRIVED in the launch bay she'd tracked Hale to tired and confused. Sleep hadn't come easily, and Zane's kit had been maddeningly short on answers to her pressing questions.

He'd brought along some encrypted data chips, but none of the normal passwords they'd shared worked. Either he hadn't wanted her to know what was on them, or he'd been extra paranoid.

She'd gone by the rooms that the station had Hale listed as living in, but he hadn't answered the door. Frankly, the place looked semi-industrial. A passerby had sent her here.

The bay looked nothing like what she'd expected. It covered a lot more room than she thought and had far too many people milling around.

There were at least a dozen work bays, about half of them occupied. She spotted Hale and another man in one of them looking over a sleek blue ship. Well, it really looked more like a weapon, but she was sure the station wouldn't let them build something like that.

The thing was too small to go anywhere meaningful. Hell, she wasn't sure it really held a person at all. Time to gather some more information.

She made her way to where most of the people were talking and drinking. There were large screens mounted on the walls, but they weren't on. The chatter was all about pressures and temperatures, radiation and depths. It made no sense to her.

Giving up on figuring it out on her own, she found a likely looking guy off by himself and played tourist.

"Excuse me?" She smiled brightly at him. "I'm new. What's going on?"

The young man looked up from his tablet. "They're almost ready. Give them another ten or fifteen minutes and they'll begin heading out one by one."

"Doing what?"

His smile grew quizzical. "You really *are* new. They're going storm diving."

She heard the words, but drew a blank on what he meant. It must've showed, because he continued.

"They're going to take their ships down into Jupiter and ride the storms."

Rachel considered what she knew of the massive planet and shook her head. "I must be misunderstanding something. That's suicide. Why would anyone even consider that?"

He shrugged. "For the rush? And, yeah, they sometimes don't make it. That's what makes it exciting."

That wasn't exciting. That was *insane*.

Rachel thanked the man and stepped back against the metal wall. She used her com to bring up information on storm diving and discovered it really was a sport. One for the crazed and deranged.

They took those little ships and drove them deep into the Jovian atmosphere where the incredible winds and pressure killed a number of them every year.

She looked into the bay where Hale and his companion were lifting the ship on a hoist. They intended to dive into something like the Great Red Spot.

Any doubts she might have had about Hale's personal bravery

evaporated. If he could do this, he had no fear at all. And absolutely no common sense.

It took her a few minutes to discover there was a huge following for these storm divers. They apparently recorded their feats of crazed bravado and beamed them all across the system.

She'd thought the people doing the long drives across the face of Mercury were nuts.

Hale even had a page for fans to track his dives. Holy crap. He really had dived into the Great Red Spot. He'd dropped down to where the atmosphere changed into a liquid and then went into that like a submarine.

A few clips showed his ship skimming along through storms in the ammonia clouds where he was fighting the ship for control. His incredible stupidity stunned her. What would make anyone risk death so cavalierly?

She put her com away and watched Hale come out of his bay in a mechanically enhanced flight suit. How could that thin metal protect him from the lethal radiation?

Not that she'd cry about it if he died, but he might have critical information about Zane. If he killed himself before she got it out of him, she might never see her partner again.

Well, she certainly couldn't walk up to him and tell him what an idiot he was being right now. She had to hope for the best and try other angles to figure out where Zane was.

She watched Hale climb into his ship, and several of the monitors in front of her came to life. It dawned on her that all these people were here to watch the dive as it happened. They were vultures, waiting to see if someone died today.

It was sick.

And so very much like humanity. Some people would go out of their way to see someone crash and burn. The kind of people that got some kind of vicarious thrill watching an accident where someone died.

Three of the monitors showed the outside of Hale's ship. One faced aft and two forward, angling off to the right and left. A fourth monitor showed Hale inside at his controls. The damned thing was so tight he barely fit.

She'd seen videos of people skiing down mountains after dropping from helicopters. That had always seemed crazed to her. This was beyond the pale. Yet his page said he'd made over seventy dives. Was it really as dangerous as it seemed?

A search said divers on average either retired or died before fifty drops. Rachel guessed that answered her question. Well, she wasn't here to save him. She had a mission to accomplish, and his absence gave her a chance to get some work done.

5

Adam completed the internal check on his ship again. All still green. He was the first up today, so he called traffic control as soon as Jason moved him into the lock and drained the atmosphere.

"Jove Control, this is Alpha Delta One Five. Request permission to depart Jupiter inbound."

A woman's voice came back promptly. "Alpha Delta One Five, you are third in the queue. There's a freighter south of the station going retrograde. A repair tender is right behind it. Two minutes until your window."

"Copy that, Control. Standing by."

"Have a good dive, Alpha Delta One Five. Come back safe."

"That's the plan. Out."

He knew the controllers thought he and his friends were madmen, but they'd be there for him if something bad went down. He respected the men and women at Jove Control more than almost anyone else in the universe.

Of course, their best wasn't good enough to save anyone deep in the Jovian atmosphere, but they'd managed to direct help to a few divers that had made it out with some kind of problem. They'd saved more of the construction crew when the Disruptors struck than seemed possible.

Two minutes later, almost to the second, Control gave him the green light. He gave the internal camera a thumbs-up and hit the hatch activator. The plate under his ship split in two and his ship fell free as it opened on either side.

The small screens ahead of him showed the view from the ship as he fell away. This part wasn't exciting for the fans, but he found it thrilling. Jupiter filled the sky below him, magnificent and terrifying. He was an ant daring the king's boot.

Small bursts from his thrusters slowed his orbit, and his ship started falling. He'd already laid in a rough course, but the king's storms and winds were not the easiest thing to forecast. He'd have to make some adjustments as he went. Once he was in the fray, he'd be flying by the seat of his pants.

Somewhere behind him, a series of probes would take his feed back to the station. For a while, at least. It wasn't in as high a resolution as his ship was recording, though. That was for the subscribers once he made it back out. Assuming he did.

As his ship plunged toward the gas giant and the protective tiles began absorbing the punishment, the pressure on him grew stronger, climbing to the point where only his suit kept him conscious. It was worst during the blazing descent and the eventual flight back up to the station.

His vision narrowed, and he fought to keep all the data in his head as the ship transitioned from being an object above the planet to one coasting toward a red sea of clouds below him. A small white oval just to one side was quickly growing larger.

He dropped into the red, flying blind at this point. It wouldn't clear until he fell below the clouds.

Adam edged the ship over until it entered the swirling storm he'd targeted. He was going with the winds. Fighting them directly was a recipe for disaster. He'd work with them as much as possible. On a crazier day, he'd go the other way.

It took a while, but he finally dropped below the ammonia clouds and into the water zone. Lightning was rarer on Jupiter, but each strike was several times more powerful than their tiny cousins on Earth.

They would make a good show, if he found any. The sky was boringly dark, not showing a hint of the flashes he wanted.

He nosed the ship deeper into the atmosphere and closer to the storm. It shuddered as crosswinds tried to rip it from the sky. The G-forces had finally dropped down to manageable levels.

There! Off to the left, a small flash hinted at the action he wanted. He arrowed closer, upping the thrust. He broke into a clear zone. It was probably a storm band. It allowed his cameras to catch some amazing images from the clouds ahead.

They swirled angrily, with bright flashes illuminating them from within. Excellent.

"Here we go." The microphones would pick up everything he said, saving it for the fans. He was too deep for the folks on the station to receive him at all. Jupiter put out some surprisingly strong radio noise.

A massive lightning strike shot out of the clouds and off to his right. His eyes closed for a moment, far too late to block the glare. The screens dimmed the worst of it, but he still blinked away the afterimages.

"That was a nice one. I hope you folks are enjoying the show as much as I am."

He'd fly along in the open for as long as he could. That would get some great shots.

Everything went according to plan, too. Surprisingly. The clear area stretched along for further than he'd hoped, and the storm cooperated by shooting some damned nice blasts all around him.

He checked the clock. He'd need to start up soon if he intended to catch Jove Station on this orbit. He had fuel for a longer run, but he liked having margin.

That's when the holographic monitors blanked and he jerked as though he'd touched a live wire. It only lasted a moment, but he knew he'd taken a lightning strike.

They'd designed the ship to conduct any hits along the outer hull, safely allowing them to dissipate, but the ship hadn't been able to handle this one as cleanly as they'd hoped. Obviously.

The screens came back on, and he began a systems check. A loud tone sounded in his ear even as a warning began flashing luridly on the caution and warning panel.

Dammit. Port thruster two had failed. Thankfully, they'd built a lot of extra margin into the ship.

"Well, this was a little more excitement than I expected, folks. Looks like the storm knocked out one of my thrusters. Time to call it a day."

He brought the nose up and increased the thrust until it pressed him painfully back into the seat.

The screens blanked a second time, and this time they didn't come back on. Louder warnings echoed in his ears. He'd taken another hit and lost the primary electronics as well as starboard thruster two.

Now he was in real trouble.

* * *

GETTING into Hale's place was as simple as bypassing his rather upscale lock and his uninspired alarm system. She figured Hale's friend would be back at the bay while the dive was taking place, so she had at least a few hours.

Waste not, want not.

Rachel activated a highly illegal com jammer and went in. If there was an alarm system, she didn't want any signals getting out. These days, hardwired com lines were rare, thank God.

The interior wasn't the quarters she'd expected. It was a workshop. Parts—presumably from Hale's ship—sat on benches and hung from the walls. While he no doubt considered them important, she needed to find his personal belongings.

She found them in a rat's nest in back. It wasn't dirty, but it certainly wasn't where he brought women. Or men, if that was his thing.

It consisted of a cramped bedroom with only enough space for a thin mattress and a closet. The room beside it was a kitchenette, if one stretched the definition enough. It might be capable of reheating leftovers or cooking pre-prepared meals on a good day.

A check of the mini-fridge confirmed her suspicions. He ate those cheap-ass meals one bought frozen. His taste in beer was better, but not terrifically so.

Rachel found the high-class liquor in one of the cabinets. The bottle was dusty and mostly empty, but at least worthy of the name. It wasn't in the same league as the bottle she'd filched from Mister Fingers, but hardly anything out here was.

Hale's bathroom was a horror show. She held up a razor he should've tossed out a few months back and shuddered. She'd wash up when she was done. Somewhere else. With something more potent than soap.

She planted her hands on her hips and curled her lips in distaste. What a pigsty. She'd expected better of Hale.

Hell, he didn't even have any pictures up in the bedroom. Not any Army awards, either. The kind one earned for slaughtering helpless civilians. Maybe that was why.

He might pass out in this hole, but he didn't keep his important things here. She'd have to do some more digging.

First up, she decided to plant a few bugs. It wouldn't hurt to see and hear what he was up to. If she poked at him again later, he might reveal something when he thought he was alone.

That turned up the first interesting thing about this dump. She found a bug in the kitchen. It didn't look like the ones used by the RIS.

It was a good thing she'd been jamming the coms. That would keep her intrusion a secret. She examined the device under a magnifier. It was short range and had no memory. There'd be a central unit in here somewhere.

Who the hell was spying on Hale? It wasn't as if he had anything worth overhearing. Unless it was about his brother.

Would station security have bugged him? That seemed a trifle extreme for a missing persons case. Except for *her* investigation, of course.

Rachel went over every centimeter of the place. She found a

dozen bugs of the same style. She left them just as they were. The central unit turned up behind his wall screen. It, too, was an unfamiliar model.

Hacking it wasn't a straightforward task, but she managed to worm her way in. The central unit sent out the recorded data every day or when triggered, so she had time to finish up and erase her presence from the stream.

No need to get someone all excited. The timer said she had another three hours before the scheduled data dump. Then it would erase what it had recorded.

Too bad it didn't have more memory. The history would've been useful. She copied what there was before she put the unit back into its hiding place.

She planted her own bugs, leaving one where she could see who came for the central unit. Hers had enough range that she could collect their take with a casual pass outside the shop. Once she was done here, she'd remotely fry them.

Now, she still needed to find his stash of private papers. They turned up in the shop, hidden inside a large piece of equipment. It held the usual things: important documents, spare cash, and mementos.

She took pictures of everything. There'd be time to parse it all out later.

Some of the pictures caught her eye, though. Zane and Hale, standing shoulder to shoulder, grinning like fiends. They looked happy. Hale was in his Army uniform, so it had to have been from a few years before Mars.

She'd thought they'd always had a bad relationship. Apparently not. Something had driven them apart. Based on how they looked, something horrible. The Mars massacre, probably.

Well, nothing here would tell her any more about Hale until she'd studied the documents.

She started to close the hiding place back up, but a strand of loose wire at the bottom of the machine caught her eye. It seemed like a piece of scrap, but the color was different from all the other bits like it.

It sat over a seam, so there might be a secret compartment down there.

Rachel carefully removed everything and examined the area. She'd put everything back exactly as he'd left it.

The hidden compartment was similar to the kind Zane favored, so opening it was easy enough. The first thing she saw was a leather book. A woman would call it a diary, so she supposed it was his journal.

She smiled. This was priceless. If he'd seen Zane, he'd have written it down.

The compartment also contained enough illegal weaponry and ammunition to send station security into a seizure. Military-grade stuff. How the hell had he smuggled them onto the station? Was he a Disruptor?

He didn't seem the type, but she'd have to be cautious. If he didn't play ball, she now had a way to take him out of play.

Even if he did, come to think of it. One call to station security and he'd be locked up for the rest of his life.

Rachel's smile turned vindictive. Now she'd get the answers she wanted, and she'd make the bastard pay for what he'd done to her friends. Today was looking up.

She quickly captured the contents of the journal with her com and then put everything back precisely as she'd found it. She made one last pass through the shop and quarters to be sure she'd left no trace.

Satisfied, she erased her presence from the other bug's central unit and paused the recording long enough for her to slip out. The people monitoring the stream wouldn't know, because the unit only recorded movement and noise. Blank times were expected.

She locked the shop, rearmed the security system, and killed her jammer. Now he'd be none the wiser.

"Excuse me."

Rachel put a smile on her face and turned around. Two men in station security uniforms had just come out of a building across the street and were heading toward her.

Oh, hell. This might be awkward.

6

Adam wanted to be conservative, but with two units gone, he'd have to go for broke. He pushed his remaining thrusters as hard as he dared and rose into the stormy clouds. The gravity was punishing, but less than it should've been.

"Well, folks," he said for the camera, struggling to form coherent words under the pressure. "It looks like... my luck has... turned bad. I'm heading... back up with... two failed thrusters.

"It's a toss-up. If I... make it back, this... might be my most... exciting video yet. If I don't, let that... be a lesson to you... that you can never... have too much... of a... safety margin."

He cut to the private channel. Under normal circumstances, he'd use it to talk with Jason when he was in range of the station. In this case, he could record a private message that only his friend would get if he didn't make it.

"I'm not sure... what happened, bro, but you... can't blame yourself. That was... some damned... powerful lightning. Two separate hits. I'm lucky... anything still works."

He stared into the camera, which had gone private with the channel switch. "I'm serious here, man. I don't want you... blaming yourself. I made the choices… that got me here today… and I have… no regrets."

Adam grinned. "Now, if you'll… excuse me, I need… to see about… making it home… alive."

He switched the system back to public mode and checked his caution and warning panel. The two thrusters were red, and so were his monitors. He hoped the external cameras were still recording. They should be. The damned things were nearly indestructible.

There was something new. He had a yellow on the magnetic shield. It was still operating, but there was no telling how long it would last. Without his main screens, he couldn't see exactly what had gone wrong. If it failed, he might make it back to the station, but he'd still die.

"Looks like my… magnetic shield is… futzed," he told the fans. "I might be… up the creek… if it goes… down entirely. This is definitely… not my day."

The ship fought its way above the clouds, and he began to see the sky darken. He was making it. He couldn't set a course to the station if he couldn't see it, though. His only hope was the repeaters they were dropping.

The units fell into the atmosphere and burned up, but there were always supposed to be a few in range to transmit when the ships popped back up. They'd also retransmit his radio signals.

"Jove Control, this is Alpha Delta One Five. Do you read?"

A few seconds went by with no response. He must still be out of range. Or his antenna was fried. Wouldn't that be great?

He could test that theory, though. He made the manual switch to the antenna on the emergency telemetry package. It wasn't as powerful, but nothing short of the destruction of the ship could break it.

"Jove Control, this is Alpha Delta One Five. Do you read?"

"Alpha Delta One Five, this is Jove Control. Go ahead." The transmission was fading in and out, but it sounded like the same woman he'd spoken to before the drop. The lightning must've fried his main antenna.

"Control, I'm declaring an emergency. I've lost two thrusters and my main electronics. I can't see the station and I'm not sure I won't lose another unit."

"Copy, Alpha Delta One Five," the woman said briskly. "Come port three degrees and raise your nose a little. We're scrambling a rescue unit, but you'll need to get further out of the atmosphere before it can get to you."

He changed course as indicated, and the private circuit cut in. "You broke my ship, didn't you?" Jason demanded. "Dammit, boy. Do you know how much that thing cost?"

"You know how it is," Adam said wryly. The G forces were coming down as he made it into orbit. "I've lost two thrusters, my main electronics, and the magnetic shield is having some kind of issue. I think it's still working, but I can't do any measurements to be sure how well."

"Crap. Let me see if I can get in remotely. Hmm. The magnetics are still online, but the primary cooling loop is compromised. It's heating up past the safety point."

The light for it on the caution and warning console went red. "I see that. It's critical now."

"That's me boosting the backup past the safety margin. It won't hold long, so you need to get back in here soon, man."

"Working on it."

The G-forces dropped off completely as he made it into orbit. "Jove Control, this is Alpha Delta One Five. Be advised that my magnetic shielding is failing. I'm on the clock."

"Copy that, Alpha Delta One Five. We have a rescue tug almost to your location. If you have a complete failure, it will be able to bring you aboard."

That would save him, but not his ship. They had a lot invested in it, so he'd rather not abandon the damned thing to fall back into the king's atmosphere.

"Alpha Delta One Five, this is *Cricket*," a male voice said. "I'm matching speed now. Man, you messed up that pretty blue paint job."

"It's been that kind of day. How far off course am I?"

The ship jolted as the tug grappled it. "Don't you worry your pretty little head about it. I'll do the driving from here on in. We're about ten minutes out and Control has cleared the traffic for us to come in hot. Here's the game plan. If you lose magnetics, you eject. I'll pick you up faster than a hot lady in a bar."

Adam smiled. The man would get along great with Jason. "Copy that, but I'd rather not lose my ship."

"You can build another one."

If he ejected, the missing panels would compromise the integrity of the hull and the tug would crush his ship. That was the very last resort. "Roger, *Cricket*. We'll do this your way."

"Just what I like to hear."

Things went smoothly enough until about a minute out. Then the caution and warning panel lit up again. The magnetic shielding unit had just failed.

"You just lost the magnetics," Jason said on the private channel. "Time to eject and let the man bring you home."

"Negative," Adam said firmly. "We're almost there. I'm not losing our ship now."

"Dammit! A minute of exposure—"

"Isn't fatal. They'll give me some meds and I'll be sick for a day or two. I am *not* losing our ship."

"Stubborn bastard," Jason muttered. "You're going to get yourself killed or sterilized."

"I'm never having kids and I storm dive. I'll never even notice."

The general circuit came to life. "We're almost ready to dock. How're you doing in there?"

"Just peachy. Be advised that my magnetics just failed."

"I'll pass that on to the medical team we have on standby. We're close enough to get you in alive. The king is being lenient today."

Adam smiled. "You know how it is. Some days you get the bear. Other days the bear gets you."

"Well, sit back and relax. *Cricket* out."

He'd relax when he was dead. They'd need to tear the ship down and find out why so many major systems failed all at once. Even two lightning strikes shouldn't have been this devastating. There had to be something else going on.

* * *

RACHEL SMILED at the security men as she slung her bag over her shoulder. "Morning. Can I help you?"

The two men stopped beside her, one stepping off to the side and looking at his com. The taller man tipped his hat back on his head a little and looked pointedly at the door behind her. "This your place?"

"No, it belongs to Adam Hale. I was just checking to see if he was home. Why?"

"No specific reason. We're looking for an illegal com jammer. The neighbors complained and we're trying to localize the signal."

She made a minor show of checking her com. "I seem to have signal. I wasn't looking earlier."

The shorter man looked up. "The jammer is offline. Dammit, just when we were starting to close in on it."

The first man gave her a longer look. "Funny how that happened. Do you know anything about it, miss? I'll need to see some ID."

"Certainly." She smiled as she handed him her ID.

Inside, she cursed. Now they'd have a link to tie her to Hale. She'd lie, if necessary. Say that she hadn't gone inside. The door was in a small alcove, so they wouldn't know for sure.

The security man checked her ID against something on his com. Perhaps a list of wanted individuals. Most other places, she'd use a burner ID. Real, but not her data. Here, they had a record of everyone on the station. A person without a valid entry stamp would get a lot of attention.

He handed her ID back. "Thank you for your time, Miss Price. Have a good day."

"Thank you. Good luck finding the jammer. Those damned things are a pain in the ass."

He smiled. "We'll get that settled soon enough."

They headed one direction, and she sauntered off in the other. Once she was clear of the area, she decided she'd best go to the launch bay. If word of her hanging around his shop did turn up, she wanted to lower Hale's suspicions by actually asking around after him.

She arrived to find everyone glued to the screens and chattering as though something significant had happened. She heard Hale's name and perked up.

He'd had some kind of accident. Lightning strikes and thruster failures. It sounded like hair-raising stuff. Part of her was saddened to hear that he'd survived.

Rachel spotted the same guy she'd spoken with earlier and cornered him for a more detailed explanation. One he seemed happy to provide.

He ran down the events and pointed out some of the replays on the screens. She had to admit the lightning was impressive, and the angles of the flight versus the storm looked sharp.

"They took him into the main landing bay, and I hear he's off to medical with radiation exposure," the man concluded. "Probably not a fatal dose, but it'll make the fans go nuts when the official video goes out. The sponsors will go crazy, too."

"Storm divers have sponsors? Like a regular sport?"

The man nodded. "Sure. They've gotta pay the bills. After this, a pile of companies will be fighting to get him to sign on with them. He'll be an even bigger star."

She shook her head, bemused. "I guess I'll never get it. Well, since I'm not going to catch him, I'll head off. Thanks."

Rachel made her way back to the hotel. With her alibi as well seeded as she could make it, she needed to dig into the data she'd picked up. Perhaps his journal had some information about Zane. Or the men who'd bugged him.

She ordered lunch while she put her gear away. Good thing security hadn't searched her. This case was too full of close calls for her liking. She needed to slow down and do the job right. It wouldn't help Zane if they tossed her into the detention center.

Hale's journal was handwritten, of course. Tight, neat script filled the lined pages. All dated for clarity. The earliest entry was almost fifteen years ago. When he'd joined the Army.

Interesting. That meant he'd probably made an entry for the Mars attack.

She really had no business worrying about it now, but she wanted to know what the bastard had to say for himself.

Apparently, he was the kind of man who lied even to himself. His journal entries mirrored what he'd claimed had happened at the time.

Why he'd lie to himself about there being a rogue RIS element, she had no idea. His personal notes still claimed that the intelligence service had perpetrated the atrocity against his orders. He also claimed the people in the office building had opened fire first. A base lie.

Well, it didn't matter. He could do whatever it took to sleep at night. She was here to find Zane. When Hale got out of the hospital, she'd press him again.

He'd help her whether he wanted to or not. Then he'd pay for what he'd done.

7

The medical team gave Adam anti-radiation shots as they rushed him to the hospital and told him there were sophisticated methods of treatment awaiting him there. Which they rushed him to.

He didn't fight them. Radiation poisoning was serious shit.

After they treated him and put him to bed, he spoke with the port authorities. He gave them a rundown of exactly what had happened. They already had the low-resolution video and the telemetry information from Jason. Based on how they acted, the investigation would be pro forma.

The rescue bill wouldn't be cheap and neither would the hospital bill. He'd find out the details when they tallied it up, but it would probably match the earnings from this little outing. If they were lucky.

Once the doctors were sure the meds had successfully gone to work, they released him. If he had trouble, he could come back. The prognosis was for some nausea and a bit of fatigue. They'd gotten to him in time.

Rather than head home, Adam went to their bay. Jason had come to see him at the hospital, but he knew his friend really wanted to dig into what had gone wrong.

He found Jason disassembling a thruster when he walked into the bay. "That port thruster two?"

Jason looked up, tossed his goggles onto the bench, and pulled him into a hug. "Damn, bro. Stop scaring me like that."

"Sure thing. I'll give this up and learn knitting."

The other man snorted. "I can just see that now. You'll need a few cats, too."

"Cats are cool. I need some for the rodent infestation."

The station had plenty of bugs and rats. Once they'd made it out here, humans couldn't easily exterminate them. Roaches would probably survive the apocalypse.

"Tell me what you've found."

"I'm still digging into it, but something isn't right. That lightning was powerful, but the ship should've shrugged it off. It should've flowed around the hull without causing any damage."

Adam picked up part of the unit. "I can tell you now that didn't happen. I felt the charge when it zapped me."

"That's why I'm not sure what went wrong. It might not have been the thruster at all. It'll take me a while to trace everything down, but I'll find out what happened. It won't happen again."

Adam clapped his hand onto his friend's shoulder. "I know you'll do everything possible. Let's check it out together."

Jason frowned. "You should rest. You almost died today."

"I've got time enough to rest when I'm dead. I won't be able to sleep until we figure this out. Let me look at the thruster while you check the ship to see why the lightning got through the shielding."

Adam finished tearing the thruster down and started examining the parts. The current had almost fused the electrical components. That seriously shouldn't have happened.

"I've got something funny here," Jason said.

Adam knelt by where his friend was looking at the thruster mount. "What?"

"See this bright line? That shouldn't be here. It's the remains of a wire, I think. Where one had no business being. It melted fast, but not before the lightning fried the thruster."

"Let's check the other unit and the magnetic array."

They pulled the other failed thruster and found a similar smudge. It was a miracle they hadn't both failed during the first strike.

Adam felt his jaws tighten. Someone had tried to kill him. That hadn't happened since his stint in the Army.

The magnetics didn't have anything like that, but it could've taken damage when the jolts ran through the ship.

"What the hell?" Jason asked, scratching his head. "No way I'd let two wires hang like that."

Adam kept his face neutral. "Let me check one other thing."

He went back to the emergency telemetry package. It came out easily enough, and he took it to the bench. He knew it worked, but he had a suspicion. One that a few minutes of work confirmed.

"The thruster on this is shorted out in a way that didn't ping the caution and warning system. If the unit had fired, it would've dropped into Jupiter's atmosphere like a stone."

Jason scratched his head. "I repeat, what the hell? Someone sabotaged you. Why?"

"They wanted me to get into trouble down there and never come back up."

"Who have you pissed off that badly?"

Adam shrugged. "Nobody. Not recently, anyway. Though I know of at least one new face around here."

His friend's eyes widened. "That woman at the club? You sure you didn't piss her off?"

"Nothing in life is certain, but I'll find out. Until I do, I think I'll stay on the station. Go over the ship with a fine-toothed comb. If something else is buggered, I want to know about it."

Jason gestured at the telemetry package. "I'll report this to the port. They need to know."

"Hang off on that until I ask a few questions. I'll be back in a little bit."

* * *

RACHEL TRANSFERRED Hale's journal images to her comp and let it translate his handwriting into searchable text. The program wasn't perfect, but it was damned close. Especially with neat lettering like his.

Once it finished, she searched for Zane's name. There were a ton of hits before the attack on Mars, but not nearly as many since. None in the last eight years until Zane had come to Jove Station.

She brought up that latest entry and began reading. Hale wrote about security coming to talk to him about his brother. Not that he'd seen him.

Rachel sat back. He had no expectation that anyone would see this journal. That troubled her, particularly since his take on the Mars incident didn't tally.

What was really going on?

The buzzer on her door sounded. She hadn't ordered anything, so this was probably trouble. She locked her comp and looked through the viewer. Hale was standing in the hall.

She opened the door. "Well, this is unexpected."

"That's the theme for the day. We need to talk."

"Come in." She stepped back and closed the door behind him. "Can I offer you a drink?"

He shook his head. "I'll pass. Why did you try to kill me?"

That took her aback. "I haven't."

"And yet my ship is sabotaged right after you arrived. I'm not an idiot. There's a connection here. How did I piss in your Choc-O Puffs?"

She smiled a little in spite of herself. "You're a blunt man. I like that. I'm only here to find your brother."

Hale threw up his hands. "Christ. He never came to see me. I'm not sure how many ways I can tell people that."

"That doesn't mean he wasn't here. He checked into this hotel, even though they said he didn't. He left something very important here. Something he wouldn't have left behind if he'd had a choice."

Hale stopped pacing and stared at her. "That has nothing to do with me."

"Maybe. Maybe not. I'm your brother's partner. You guessed that.

It means we both work for the RIS. As you said, we're spies. That means we do spy shit."

She considered him a moment. "I'm starting to believe you're telling the truth, but you have other people that aren't so sure."

"What the hell does that mean?"

Rachel unlocked her comp, brought up the images of the bugs and central unit from his place, and spun the screen around so he could see it. "I found these in your shop and living quarters. Someone has been bugging you."

He stared at the images and then glared at her. "You broke into my place?" His voice dropped to a growl.

She kept her eyes locked on his. "Yes. I'd do even more if it meant finding my partner. These bugs are not RIS issue, so I'm not sure who is behind them."

"So, you never saw him? That worries me. Why would he come here, but not look you up?"

Hale stepped back from the table, visibly reining in his anger. "Because he's an asshole and I'd punch him in the face."

The corner of her mouth quirked up. "Succinctly put. Someone doesn't believe that. I need your help to find Zane, but it sounds like you've had a crappy day."

He turned back toward her. "Someone sabotaged my ship."

She felt her eyes narrow. "You're sure?"

"Oh, yeah. Someone worked real hard to make sure I died today. Was it you, spy lady?"

"Killing you isn't my style. I'd turn you in for all the illegal weapons in your shop and let you rot. Which, you'll notice, you aren't currently doing. Even though you deserve to die, it wasn't me."

"Is that what I deserve? That probably means you're a Martian. Interesting. You don't have the accent and you seem to get around just fine in normal gravity. Why should I believe you?"

She shrugged. "Let's have a race. You run back to your place to move your weapons and I'll call security. We'll see who gets done faster."

Hale shook his head. "You're a real piece of work."

Rachel allowed her wolf smile to creep onto her face. "You killed a lot of my friends on Mars. I want to see you bleed for it. The law says I can't, so I'll settle for putting your ass in detention for the rest of your miserable life.

"Before you get all manly, if you come at me, I'll put a bullet into your head. You might be all GI Joe, but I'm James Bond. Test me. I'd be really happy to kill you right here, right now."

He smiled without humor. "Looks like you have all the answers. Tell me, who bugged me and why did they presumably try to kill me?"

"Not my circus, not my monkeys."

They stared at one another for a moment before he spoke. "What makes you think Zane checked in to the hotel? Hell, what makes you think he actually arrived?"

"I searched his assigned room and found his kit hidden right where I'd expect. So the hotel lied to security about him checking in."

That brought the data chips she'd found in Zane's kit to mind. Maybe someone who'd known him longer had other passwords to try.

"He had some data chips that I can't hack," she said. "Maybe he meant them for you. Or maybe he used a password you'd know. None of the ones he shared with me worked."

"So he didn't trust you as much as you thought? Big surprise. He only trusts himself."

"Are you going to try to unlock them?"

He sat down on the couch, lowering the tension in the room. "That depends. If I do, will you stop trying to get me thrown into detention?"

Rachel considered his offer. She *really* wanted to see him rot. "If you try, I'll keep my mouth shut until I leave the station. If you actually open the chips, I won't say a word to anyone about the weapons."

"You drive a hard bargain. Why should I trust you?"

"I can call security now, if you'd like."

"Has anyone ever told you you're a bitch?"

"I can play nice if I want. Has anyone ever told you you're a mass murderer?"

The drop in tension reversed itself. The two of them stared at one another until he slowly nodded. "I guess I won't get a better deal. Give me the chips."

She moved her comp over to sit in front of him and retrieved the chips. Then she planted herself beside the door. It gave her a view of the screen and kept him from making a break with her only real clues about why Zane had come here.

Hale plugged the first chip in and started trying passwords at the prompt. "I'm running through some we shared back in the day. Then I'll try some of the older ones he kept to himself, but didn't hide well enough."

On the fifth try, the chip unlocked. "Hit it. Madeline Kramer. He called her Mad Red. She was nuts, but he wanted to ask her out real bad. Never did, though."

She edged closer and looked at the files. "Videos. What are they?"

Hale shrugged. "Damned if I know. The timestamp…"

He straightened abruptly. "The timestamps are from the Mars assault. These are the helmet cam recordings. The ones the RIS agents took away from us."

That wasn't what she'd expected. And it wasn't something she wanted to waste her time on, either. "Is there anything else?"

"Not on this chip. Here's the one with my armor tag. I'm surprised I still remember it."

He started it playing and began fast-forwarding through it. Even though she wanted to tell him to shut it off, she also wanted to see his lies with her own eyes.

Only that's not what happened. They came into the building ready to fight, but didn't start shooting indiscriminately. On the second floor, one man pulled a weapon and fired at them.

Hale took him out with a controlled burst and led his team past the fleeing civilians and into the movement's offices.

People were running every direction, and two men she didn't recognize opened fire on the troops. Two bursts took them down.

Then all hell broke loose. Someone began mowing everyone down. Several shooters. Hale's helmet cam gave her a good look at them as he tried to get them to stop, and she could tell they weren't

Republican Army. They didn't have the same kind of gear as the regular troops had. They looked like embedded RIS agents.

Hale and his men brought the rampaging shooters down physically, but it was far too late to save her friends.

She stared at Hale in shock. Everything he'd claimed from the beginning was true. Everything.

8

"You seem shocked," Adam said.

"Shut up and let me think."

She backed up the video and played it again slowly. "Holy shit," she muttered. "Someone else really did kill all those people."

"That's what I've been saying all this time. I didn't have the video to prove it because those RIS assholes took the recordings."

Part of him was infuriated, but the rest of him was pleased. He could finally make it clear that the RIS had framed him and his men.

Or could he? Doubters would just claim he'd faked it.

Did it really matter? People were going to think what they thought no matter what he did. He was never going back to the Army. So, how did this change anything?

Honestly, it didn't.

It didn't change things between him and Zane. Though he had to admit he was wondering why his brother had gone to all the trouble of getting these videos.

And why, once Zane had them, he hadn't come to him.

"Let me see if I can open any of the other data chips," Adam said. "There might be something on one of them that explains what the hell Zane came here for."

Price gestured for him to continue.

He picked up one of the remaining two chips and plugged it in. It also opened to the same password.

This one contained a variety of different file types. He didn't recognize most of them, but a few stood out. Like his military record.

He opened it and was shocked to see that it wasn't the sanitized version they released to other agencies. Much less, the heavily edited bits they occasionally allowed the general public to see.

This was the full meal deal.

"Is that your military record?" Price asked. "I had a hell of a time even getting the redacted version."

"That's as it should be. Zane shouldn't have been able to get his hands on this. There's a very highly placed leak somewhere."

"May I?"

He pushed the comp over. "Be my guest. I'll want copies of these. Someone set me up, and while I may never get even, I want to know the truth."

She nodded slowly, obviously distracted. "Sure. You can hide it with the weapons. I'll send Zane's kit with you. None of their bugs covers it directly. If they find your stash, it might add twenty years to your sentence."

Adam allowed a wry smile onto his face. "Man, you really have a hard-on for me. Even after you saw I didn't do it."

Price stared at him, her eyes cold. "I've hated you for a decade. I've dreamt of what I'd do to you if I could get away with it. That doesn't go away in ten minutes."

She reached out and tapped her comp. "As far as I know, this might be faked. Even if it isn't, we're not going to hug this out any time soon."

"Finally, something about you that I can understand. So, Agent Price, what other files are on that thing?"

"I'll tell you after I finish going over your record. You might want to read along and tell me if someone changed anything important. If *I'd* framed you, I wouldn't leave your personnel file untouched."

He read as she scrolled down his service record. It had been a while, but everything seemed accurate.

She poked around on the chip and found reports on the Mars incident. Those were a bit messier. Not precisely inaccurate, but muddy. His superiors had stuck up for him and his people. That was good to know.

The RIS people had lied their asses off. Their report was completely different, and there weren't a lot of survivors to clear things up.

They'd redacted the agents' names, of course. The report noted that the RIS had seized all the helmet video for "security reasons." An action his superiors strongly protested, though they'd lost that battle.

There were hints that the government would bring him and his men up on charges outside the Army chain of command, but that hadn't happened. Everything had just gone away.

The last entry was when he'd resigned his commission. His superiors were pretty blunt that even though they'd believed him, his career was over. There'd been no reason to stay.

"That looks about right," he said. "No obvious omissions or additions."

She shook her head. "How could my superiors have missed something like this? It's so damned heavy-handed. They confiscated the helmet videos. Clearly, that should've led to an internal investigation."

After a moment, she took a deep breath and stared at him. "Unless there was some kind of cover-up inside the RIS. Maybe that's what Zane was looking into. It would explain why he didn't tell our manager. This sounds completely off the books."

Adam pursed his lips. "If someone got wind of it, they'd have ample reason to shut him up."

He looked around. "I assume you swept your room for bugs. If they know who you are—and I assume someone in the RIS would—then they might have eyes and ears on us right now."

* * *

THAT HUNG in the air for a moment, and Rachel upgraded her opinion of the man. A little. That was solid thinking.

"I swept for bugs when I checked in," she said. "I have monitors to tell me if anyone gets into the room, something like the wire you use to tell you if someone accessed your weapons cache, but high tech. Good work, by the way."

He grunted sourly. "Obviously not, if you spotted it."

"Call it good for a gifted amateur. I also scan the room for bugs whenever I come back in. That's just good tradecraft. We're not being monitored."

She looked at the other files. They had encryption, but she recognized the format. RIS dossiers and mission files. Not surprising since RIS personnel were involved.

Her comp was able to open them easily enough. Anyone else would've had a much harder time.

The first file on the list was about one of the RIS men assigned to the Mars raid. So were the next two. They came from her organization's paramilitary group. All were ex-Army with experience in units like Hale's.

That made sense. She'd be out of her depth in a firefight. She could shoot, but not like trained warriors.

But why'd they go off on unarmed office workers? They had to be more discerning than that. They were former pros. A slaughter was completely outside their training.

Interestingly, none of them was with the RIS now. Two had moved on, and one was dead. A suicide, or so the record said.

There were attached notes in what looked like Zane's writing style. He'd confirmed the details of the suicide, but seemed to think the man might've had help.

He'd also followed up on the other two. It seemed they'd left government service entirely. They now worked for the Janus Corporation.

Well, wasn't *that* interesting?

Did it explain why Zane had come to Jove Station? Was the RIS involvement why he hadn't told her anything? Did he distrust her? Or was he protecting her?

She looked at the other files and found Paul Jacoby, her first line manager. He ran dozens of operatives spread all across the solar system. And he'd managed the people on the Mars raid, back in the day.

"Are you going to keep me in the dark?" Hale asked.

She shook her head and looked up. "Sorry. I'm still trying to process all this. There are dossiers for the three RIS agents assigned to the raid with you. Zane was obviously looking into the whole situation.

"He came out here because two of the shooters now work for Janus. The other one blew his brains out a few weeks after the Mars attack. Maybe he had a guilty conscience. Or maybe someone worried he might."

"You are one paranoid chick."

Rachel smiled. "Chick. That's old-fashioned and sexist. Congratulations on the twofer. Zane also has a file on our boss. He assigned these three yahoos to your team ten years ago, so Zane suspects he's dirty."

Hale raised his hands in a questioning gesture. "So, what do you do now? Call someone? Have him arrested?"

"You need this thing called proof for that. All we have is enough circumstantial evidence to suspect him. We have no way of knowing if he's as high as it goes. Or if he's an unwitting dupe following orders.

"Frankly, with all of the survivors heading out here, I think there's more to the story. Let me keep looking."

She brought up the next file. It was a still from one of the helmet cams on Mars. Zane had highlighted and enhanced one of the civilian shooters.

It wasn't much, because enhancement relied on the details the camera recorded, but some sharpening was possible. It came at the expense of adding a little guesswork to the image, but sometimes that was okay.

In this case, it looked as though Zane had an ID to go with the face. She remembered the shooter from the first pass. Hale had killed him, so there didn't seem to be much need to identify him. Surely, someone had done that after the attack.

The tag marked him as Oscar Crabtree. She closed the image and found a dossier on the man. He wasn't Martian. He came from Pallas. A water miner by trade.

He had a somewhat colorful mix of run-ins with authority figures, but nothing that explained why he was on Mars shooting at the Army. The worst offense in his record was an assault in a bar with a broken bottle. Over a woman, no doubt.

Zane referenced another file. She searched the list and found it.

This one was eye-opening. Mister Crabtree was a suspected affiliate of a Disruptor cell in the belt. Based on this designation, he'd been under observation for months before the attack.

That was standard practice. If you found one, there'd be more. The RIS wanted to identify any known compatriots in the hope of compromising other cells. Or even someone in the layer of oversight above them. Whoever they were.

How had he gotten from the belt to Mars? And why? This really made no sense. The Disruptors attacked corporate and government facilities. They assassinated high officials. They actually *approved* of other groups resisting the Republic. They should've seen the Free Mars movement as comrades in arms.

Yet at least one of them had been there to attack the inevitable armed response after the bombing. One where rogue RIS agents murdered dozens of innocent people. How could they have known the action wing was going to bomb the dome?

If that's what had actually taken place.

The Republic blamed the attack on the Martian resistance, but the supposed attackers had all died in the blast. What if the Disruptors were behind it? And, by implication, someone in the RIS?

That scared the hell out of her.

"I think I see what Zane was doing out here," she said. "One of the shooters on Mars was a known Disruptor affiliate the RIS had under surveillance before the raid.

"His file has no information about how he got to Mars. Or that he ever did. The agents watching him dropped the ball, and the post-attack forensics don't mention him at all."

Hale frowned. "How is that even possible? They had that building locked up tight and the man's blood was everywhere. I saw to that. I didn't shoot anyone up bad enough for facial recognition to fail."

"I'm only coming up with one answer that seems to fit the facts," she said slowly. "Someone in the RIS is working with the Disruptors. Maybe someone in the Janus Corporation, since your brother came out here so quietly."

She looked him dead in the eye. "He found the proof to exonerate you and uncover the real bad guys."

Hale nodded slowly. "And now they have him. They've had him for months. Is he still alive?"

Rachel considered lying, but shook her head. "That's hard to imagine. Maybe they'd keep him alive for a few weeks to be sure he didn't tell anyone else. They'd have broken him long before now."

Hale looked as though someone had punched him in the gut. "So, he finally stood up for me and I let him die. That's just about par for the course," he said bitterly.

"Is that your answer for everything? Self-pity? Pick yourself up, soldier. He was my partner. He left me in the dark, too. If I'd have been here, they might never have made a move. This is on me as much as it is you.

"Are you going to let them keep you in that pit of misery, or are you going to get to the bottom of this? We're in this together. Do we make them bleed or go home?"

His lips thinned and his nostrils flared. "We make them bleed."

She smiled coldly. "I hoped you'd see it my way. We need to go over all these files and start planning. Whoever tried to kill you is eventually going to figure out that I'm here, so we need to punch back fast.

"Let's order some food and dig in. I happen to have a bottle of good Earth whisky. Better than the one you have stashed, by the way. Let's drink to our new partnership."

Rachel had no idea how she was going to get past the negative feelings she had for this man, but if her partner—and the evidence—said he was innocent, it fell to her to make the effort. No matter how hard it was going to be.

9

Adam watched the spy lady work while he sipped his whisky. It was good. Damned good. He shuddered to think of how much it must have cost even before the expense of shipping it out here.

"How the hell can a government employee afford this stuff?" he asked.

She glanced over from her comp. "I lifted it from a bastard I met on the trip out. I consider it fair payment for him groping me. The thing at customs was just icing."

"That was you? Man, you're vicious. You find anything else?"

"That last chip you opened had a lot of files covering Janus Corporation officers and staff. All stuff pilfered from the RIS databases. I can't imagine how Zane got his hands on it. I suppose I'll never know now."

That soured his mood right up. He imagined it would take a while before he stopped blaming himself. If ever. He'd discovered over the years that he was good at blaming himself. He should've been Catholic, as the bad old joke went.

"What I want to know is why you're still alive," she continued. "That trip down to Jupiter should've killed you."

"I'm just that good," he said with more smugness than he should've allowed himself.

"That's bullshit."

That set him back a step. "You don't know me. I have skill at that kind of thing."

She sighed. "It shouldn't matter how good you are. A bomb packed in behind one of the thrusters would've killed you right away. Hell, why only sabotage two thrusters? Why not all six? The emergency transponder wouldn't have let anyone know.

"They had any number of ways to make your trip inevitably fatal. Why go halfway? Why even give you a fighting chance?"

It did seem odd when phrased that way. "I don't know. Maybe they didn't have time. Maybe they're sadistic. Or incompetent."

"Anyone that could capture someone like Zane without leaving a pile of inconvenient bodies isn't incompetent. They had a reason for leaving you potentially alive. Probably something important. We just need to figure it out."

He rose to his feet. "You'll need to figure that out on your own. I have to find Jason before he starts tearing up the station. He knows I came here and that I thought you had something to do with the sabotage."

"That's fine," she said. "I'm good at data mining. These files will keep me occupied for a while."

Looking more than a bit hesitant, she stood and extended her hand. "I misjudged you, Hale. I'm sorry for that."

He shook it slowly. "It takes someone big to get past something like Mars. I appreciate it."

The corner of her mouth rose a little. "I never said I was past it. That's going to take a long time. I'll put my negative feelings to good use, and you have my apology in advance for the inevitable backsliding."

"No one can ask more than that. Thankfully, I'm a loveable guy."

"No more booze. You're drunk."

He grinned and headed for the door. "See? It's working already. I'm headed back to the launch bay, but I'll be at the club later. After a close call like this, people will want to see me face-to-face. That's how we roll. Come by. That'll give you some exposure."

"As in dress scantily? I don't need that kind of exposure."

"Jason wouldn't mind. No, I mean with the divers. If someone got to my ship, one of them might have seen it."

"Or done it. Does one of them have a grudge?"

"It's possible," he admitted. "If so, then you'll really need to get past their guard to ask the right questions. I look forward to seeing a professional at work, because they won't make it easy."

He let himself out. No one seemed to pay any attention as he left the hotel, but he doubted he'd know if a spy was following him.

Adam arrived in the launch bay just as Jason was finishing up. His friend was even grimier than normal. He'd almost completely disassembled the ship.

"Dude!" Adam said, eyeing the various parts of his ship scattered around the bay. "Can you even put this thing back together again? I have cash that says you end up with extra bolts when you're done."

Jason put on his affronted face. "I know where every bolt and plate goes. Trust me, everything will be triple inspected before I'm done. Extra bolts," he added in a disgusted tone. "You're an asshole."

"That's what they tell me. You find anything?"

The slender man wiped his hands on a handy rag that looked like it might have made them even dirtier. "Maybe. It's hard to be sure. I'm so paranoid right now that minor flaws look suspicious. Nothing that would crash the ship, though. Everything that was going to break already did."

He threw the rag down. "How was the woman? Was she behind this? What's in the bag?"

The bag held his brother's spy kit. Price had tucked it into a shopping bag to conceal it from casual observation.

Adam considered how much to tell his friend. There was no guarantee this bay wasn't bugged. He needed to get some tips on finding the damned things.

"Just some stuff I picked up. She doesn't seem the type to do this. Not enough mechanical knowhow."

"Pity," Jason said. "Now we have to think about other divers.

Some of them are asses, but I can't even see Double Dick doing this kind of thing."

"Me neither. Look, you've been at this nonstop. Let's call it a day and get something to eat. The others will keep me up all night, if I let them, so I'll need my strength."

The nausea the doctor had warned him about had arrived, but it wasn't too bad. At least, not yet.

Jason clapped him on the shoulder. "Let's do it. I hear the diner has a special on Mexican food today. I've been craving tacos."

"Those yahoos have never even looked up Mexico on the net," Adam said reprovingly. "Remember when they tried Indian food? I almost combusted later that night."

"You said you liked to live dangerously."

"Man. Two close calls with death in one day. The gods hate me."

* * *

RACHEL READ every single document before she started putting together her notes. By the time she was done, it was late and she was cross-eyed.

Zane had uncovered quite the potential conspiracy. The attack on Mars wasn't the only oddity her partner had found, though it was the most bloody.

There'd been a few notable intelligence failures since the massacre. Disruptor attacks that the RIS should've discovered before it was too late.

One was the assassination of a high-ranking Republican official in the Department of the Navy. They managed to smuggle a bomb onto his shuttle.

It turned out the people responsible were on the watch list and somehow managed to slip away from their minders. They vanished after the attack.

There were similar events after that, too. Different RIS managers were responsible for the operations, but they all reported to the same woman. Including Rachel's own manager.

Alice Evans, an upper manager with the RIS for three decades.

She had plenty of successes under her belt to balance things out, but the major lapses with known Disruptors seemed to all lead back to her.

Zane had her full record on the chip. Nothing screamed that she was on the take, but the woman's brother was a senior vice president with Janus Corporation. He ran the FTL construction program.

More coincidences. Enough to draw Zane's attention. Enough to make him afraid to inform anyone in the chain of command about what he suspected.

Since something had happened to him almost as soon as he'd arrived, he'd been right to worry.

Why had the same people ignored her arrival? The ID she was using was a RIS cover with her real name. It wasn't even fake. Just misleading.

If someone in the RIS was watching, they should've seen her once the passenger list from *Calypso* arrived. Either they wanted her to look around or, more likely, they couldn't afford to kill every RIS agent that wandered onto the station.

She'd conducted regular checks for tails and bugs without noticing anyone. Perhaps she'd slid in under their radar.

Until a month and a half ago, she'd been in Chicago. Her current instructions were to unofficially look for Zane and then move on. Maybe they wanted her to do exactly that. Without knowing who all the players were, it was hard to tell.

One thing she knew for certain, if she poked her nose too hard into their business, someone would try to shut her up.

She didn't have enough data to be sure she was even on the right track. All she knew at this point was that Zane had checked in and someone at the hotel had lied. Someone highly placed.

There'd be a record of that somewhere.

Her patch into the guest services system was still active, but that didn't mean they were unaware of her penetration. Paranoia was the RIS way. She needed to be careful.

A little basic snooping made her moderately certain they hadn't detected the tap. There were no monitors or logs watching her little channel. Or maybe the person doing the countersurveillance was a lot better at this than she was.

She accessed the logs for Zane's room. After he supposedly missed his check-in, there was a single use of a management key. Then room service again. Twice in the same day.

That probably meant someone had come for his belongings. They hadn't searched well enough to find his kit. Then they'd cleaned the room.

The management card linked to Vasily Aslanov, the senior night manager. Yet he'd accessed the room in the early afternoon.

Rachel wanted to look at his company mail, but the business system was separate from the guest services side. She'd need physical access to his comp.

That was frustrating, but not fatal. She'd consider her options tomorrow. Right now, she had to get going.

The divers probably weren't involved in Zane's disappearance, but that didn't mean one of them hadn't tried to kill Hale. Still, she had to be sure.

Rachel locked her comp and stashed the chips away in her kit. If someone tried to get into her system, they'd think they'd succeeded, right up until the comp crashed hard.

She had a copy of all the files for Hale. It was the price for his assistance. She'd pay it and damn the consequences. If she trusted anyone back on Earth, she'd send them a copy, too, but she didn't. Not now.

Once she had everything put away, she headed for the Great Red Spot. She took a meandering path, wary of tails. No one seemed the least bit interested in her.

The outer club looked much the same as the last time she'd visited. The inner one—the one frequented by the divers—was packed and wild. Much more so than yesterday.

The man of the hour was the center of attention. She supposed that was only natural. He'd cheated death.

Rather than approach him, she decided to circle the bar and see if anyone had what seemed like an unhealthy interest in either of them.

After twenty minutes, she'd decided that everyone looked

genuinely pleased with the exception of one man in a booth at the back. He wasted no effort in hiding his disgruntlement. Or the glares he shot at Hale.

"Don't pay him any mind," a man said as he stepped up to the bar. "That's Double Dick. He doesn't like anyone."

She turned her attention to the man. It was Hale's partner, Jason Chang. She'd watched him bounce between Hale and a stacked blonde at a table near the dance floor.

"He looks like the kind of guy who'd sabotage a ship," she ventured.

Chang held out his hand. "Jason Chang. He's just pissed because he set a new record for depth and Adam is getting all the attention. He'll get over it."

"Rachel Price. I'm a friend of Adam's brother."

"So he said. I wish he'd stopped in to see Adam. Those two need to settle their bad blood. Family is more important than whatever came between them."

"I agree. Well, it seems as though your friend has his hands full. Why don't you give me the lowdown on what I'm getting into with the diving community?"

He picked up the drinks he'd ordered. "Come join us and I will."

Rather than going over to Hale, he led her to the table with the blonde.

The other woman smiled at Rachel. "Hi! I'm Cindy Stevens. You must be the mysterious woman in Adam's life. I'm with Jason."

Rachel shook the woman's hand. "It's not like that. I'm just out here trying to find any information about his brother."

Cindy nodded. "Ah, I get it. Security said he'd come onto the station. If you don't mind my asking, just how close are you and… I'm sorry. I don't know his name."

"Zane. We were dating pretty seriously," she lied. "He was about to pop the question, if you know what I mean. I'm worried sick about him."

The other woman's expression turned sad. "That's terrible! I hope you find him. Maybe he took a ship somewhere else and the data got lost somehow. He might be on his way out to Saturn or Uranus."

"Then he'd better keep going," Rachel growled. "He should've sent me a message."

Movement at the door attracted her notice. Two men had just come in. The same two security guys who'd interrogated her. Only this time they weren't in uniform. They headed right for Hale.

Uh oh. This could mean trouble.

10

Adam kept a cheerful expression on his face, but he really wanted to head back to the shop. He could only take so many people congratulating him for surviving. The other divers were low-key about it, but the groupies were too damned clingy.

He saw Rachel Price when Jason brought her over to the table where Cindy was waiting. Had his friend just seduced the spy? Or was it the other way around?

The three of them fell into talking like old friends while Adam started untangling himself from the people around him. He'd almost made it when two men interjected themselves into the conversation.

"Mister Hale," the taller of them said. "You might not remember me, but I'm Sergeant Gavin Starnes from security. This is my partner, Mason Saint James."

That prompted Adam's memory. "Sure. You came over to the shop a few times after I moved in to make sure I was up to code. Is there a problem?"

"Maybe. We were investigating something in the area around your shop earlier today and saw a woman at your door. I'm pretty familiar with the regulars in the neighborhood, but I don't know her.

"Her ID said she was Rachel Price. She came up in the database as a recent arrival. She said she was looking for you. Is that right?"

Adam inclined his head toward the table where Price sat. "Is that her?"

The security man looked over and nodded. "That's her. So, my radar was off. I was sure she was up to no good."

"I know about her. Better safe than sorry, though. I appreciate you boys looking out for me. This has been one of those days."

"So I heard. You ever thought of taking up a less dangerous sport? Like javelin catching?"

Adam grinned. "Good one. Maybe I'll take it easy for a while. Thanks again for looking out for me. Can I get you boys a beer?"

The older man started to shake his head, but his younger partner cut in. "That sounds great. Thanks."

Starnes gave the other man the stink eye, but didn't dispute his call. The two of them wandered over to the bar. Adam took advantage of the momentary lull and headed for Jason's table.

He almost made it before Double Dick stopped him.

The old man's glare smoldered, and he stuck his jaw out. "You think you're all hot shit because you got lucky."

Adam really didn't want to fight with the man, but he couldn't help himself. "Yes and no. I got lucky, but I'm not hot shit. Well, okay, maybe I am, now that you mention it."

"Asshole. Tonight was supposed to be my night and you screwed it up. You screwed with the king and he almost ate you. I hope he finishes the job."

Without waiting for a response, Double Dick stomped off toward the exit.

Adam finished walking over to Jason's table, putting the bitter old bastard out of his mind.

"I see the three of you have met," he said as he sat down. He raised a hand toward the bartender and saw the busy man note his request for a beer.

Cindy smiled at him. "You've been holding out. Why didn't you tell us someone was here looking for your brother? Are you going to help her find him?"

He gave Cindy an annoyed look. "Like I told Miss Price, I can't find someone who isn't here."

Jason rose to his feet and held his hand out to Cindy. "Let's go dance."

Now it was her turn to look annoyed, though she covered it well. Jason's girl loved to gossip. Adam shot his friend a smile.

Once they were gone, Adam leaned closer to Price and spoke just loud enough for her to hear him over the music. "You have any luck?"

"I traded one mystery for another. It turns out Zane thought my boss's boss was involved in a number of incidents concerning the Disruptors. The twist comes when you look at the woman's family.

"Her brother is a big man out here. Randy Evans. He's in charge of FTL for Janus. Do you know anything about that?"

"I know what everyone knows. A number of corporations expanding the colony worlds buy the ships to grow the interstellar economy. Hell, there's a waiting list that stretches out over a decade, I hear. A few rich bastards even picked ships up to use as yachts. Janus also provides drives for the Republican Navy.

"If you mean the technical end, they keep that totally secret. The drives come out as a black box. No one really knows what's on the inside. And they're booby-trapped. If someone opens one, boom."

"That's a little extreme, isn't it?"

"I suppose that depends. No one knows exactly how the FTL drives work. Sure, they're Alcubierre drives that use some kind of exotic matter to generate negative energy and warp space, but the details are closely guarded. I don't even know where they put them together."

She frowned. "How can you not know? They have to come from somewhere."

"Janus has facilities all over the Jupiter system. One of them has the secret drive works, but damned if anyone knows for sure where it is. Whoever works on them does so without mixing with the rest of us. They're totally segregated."

She seemed to consider that. "People retire. They quit. Janus has built FTL ships for forty years. Someone knows where the drives come from."

He grabbed the beer a server set in front of him and took a drink. "Yet no one is talking. They must pay really well for people to keep their mouths shut, or they've automated the facility. If that were the case, only a handful of people would know the specifics. That makes it a lot easier to keep secrets."

Price took a slow sip of her wine. "Well, the man in charge of that program might be connected to what happened to Zane. I want to get into the hotel night manager's work mail tonight. He'll probably be on duty, and I'll need your help."

Adam shook his head. "I'm no spy. Covert ops are someone else's game."

"I just need a good distraction. I'm sure you can keep him occupied long enough for me to break into his office. Someone gave him instructions to clear out your brother's stuff. We need to know the next link in the chain."

Adam couldn't care less about his brother. At least that's what he told himself. But he did want to know who was behind the Mars massacre. They needed to pay.

"Alright. Count me in. What do you need me to do?"

* * *

RACHEL FOLLOWED Hale into the hotel with a well-concealed smile. This would definitely be a major distraction.

He was, to all appearances, drunk as a skunk. Worse, he was in the company of a number of what he called groupies, and those people were staggering for real.

The knot of people made several course corrections on the way to the front desk, but managed to dock without incident.

"I want a room," Adam slurred. "A big one. Where we can keep the party going."

The young woman behind the desk gave him a somewhat strained smile. Rachel doubted she wanted anything to do with a loud, drunken disaster.

"We're booked up," she said with a somewhat weak tone of regret. "Perhaps the Savoy has an opening."

"Bullshit!" Adam almost shouted. "I know you have something. Call the manager."

Rachel slid around the group and into an alcove near the door leading to the offices. When the time came, she wanted to have as little chance of discovery as possible.

As expected, the woman couldn't summon the night manager fast enough.

When the door opened and Aslanov came out, Rachel caught it before it closed. Moments later, she was in the restricted section of the hotel.

This late at night, there weren't a lot of staff on duty. The guests were mostly asleep, so the hotel only needed a skeleton crew.

Finding the man's office was simple enough. It was the one with the light on.

The room was compulsively neat. Every book on the shelf beside the desk arranged by size from small to large. The papers in the bins lined up so the edges were sharp. There wasn't a speck of dust in sight.

As she'd hoped, he hadn't locked his comp. Why should he? He was all alone.

She plugged a data chip into the system. It automatically uploaded a program designed by the tech wizards at the RIS.

The screen blanked and then cleared again. She could work in this new display area and not move a thing on the desktop her target had been using.

Rachel accessed Aslanov's mail. Tons of work-related drivel, but he seemed to keep everything. Perfect. She might be able to recover a deleted message, but that was never certain.

A search for Zane's name didn't turn anything up, but the suite number did. A message from a Janus Corporation address that bluntly instructed Aslanov to clear it out and make it seem as though no one had checked in.

The address wasn't very descriptive. A series of numbers and letters that seemed random. That didn't tell her who was orchestrating this from inside Janus, but it did tell her that someone was definitely dirty.

A noise in the hall made her snatch the chip out of the comp and scurry behind the door to listen more closely. It couldn't be Aslanov. Hale would still be causing a scene out front.

A man in work coveralls whistled tunelessly as he walked down the hall toward her. He had a ladder, which he set up under a light fixture. He was changing the bulbs.

That would make slipping out a lot more complex, but she wasn't done in the office yet. Perhaps he'd be gone by the time she finished.

The comp had reverted to the previous screen as soon as she'd yanked the chip, but the program was still at work. She needed to plant a receiver to access the restricted system.

Under the man's desk was perfect. No one would spot it there. A bug with video went on the inside of the bookshelf where it was out of the way but gave her a good angle of the room.

Once she finished, she checked on the man in the hall. He seemed to be mostly done, so she might be able to slip out in a few minutes.

That plan flew out the proverbial window when he closed the fixture up and headed toward Aslanov's office. She ducked behind the open door again, hoping he'd keep going.

He walked into the office instead.

Thankfully, he only stayed long enough to filch some sweets out of a container on the desk. He smoothed them back down, so he'd obviously done this before and knew how to keep his petty theft a secret.

Once he was gone, Rachel started breathing again. He'd gone on to the next fixture, so his back was to her. Time to go.

* * *

Adam gave the man a long stare over the tip of his nose. "I don't know what kind of game you're playing, but I'm getting pissed. I want a freaking room and I want it now. Isn't my money good enough for you?"

The manager's professional smile never wavered. "Of course it is, sir. I'm terribly sorry, but with the influx of people the diving games have brought onto the station, we simply have no rooms left.

"I'd be happy to give you a discount on a stay some other time, but I really have to agree with Veronica that the Savoy would be your best bet tonight."

A beefy man that had to be with hotel security had arrived and was standing patiently off to the side. Time was growing short. Price needed to speed things up.

"I think you're bullshitting me. Just give us a room and we'll all get on with our lives. Tell you what. Here's something for your trouble."

He proffered a completely inadequate bribe.

The man stared at the money and shook his head. "We don't need payments over and above the price of a stay here, sir. I'm afraid I've been as patient as I can. It's time for you and your friends to leave."

That was the security man's hint. He stepped forward and smiled.

Out of the corner of his eye, Adam saw the door leading to the manager's office open and Price slip out. She ducked into the alcove leaving no one the wiser.

Adam made a show of sneering at the security man. "Fine, we'll go. But you can expect a nasty review for this terrible service."

He didn't wait for the manager to answer before he turned on his heel and staggered toward the front door. His cobbled-together group of would-be partiers flowed along behind him, venting their outrage on his behalf.

Once they were outside, he shook his head. "Those bastards at the Savoy will do the same damned thing. Tell you what. Come back to the Spot tomorrow night and we'll bring the roof down."

That wasn't really satisfactory to them, but they only grumbled as they dispersed in search of a different party. Price stepped up beside him as soon as they'd dispersed.

"Are you really going to party with them tomorrow?"

"Hell no. I have better things to do. Like sleep. Did you find anything?"

She nodded. "I found a message from someone in Janus telling him to clean out Zane's belongings. Whoever it was had them delivered to a storage facility the hotel uses for lost and found items and misplaced luggage.

"We could go after them, I suppose, but it hardly seems worth the effort. I have his kit. The rest of it is just clothes."

"So, what's your plan? Do you have a name?"

"No. Whoever it was covered their tracks. I'll need to get into their systems and figure out who it is. I need to anyway, if I'm going to find the renegade RIS agents. They're out here somewhere. Probably not on this station, since you'd recognize their faces."

He nodded. "I might be able to help you with that. I'm back on the job tomorrow, so I can probably come up with a reason to be in the headquarters building. I'm not sure about sneaking you in, though."

Price smiled. "I have a plan."

"Why does that fill me with dread?"

11

Rachel made her way back into the hotel and to her room without causing any undue stir. Out of habit, she checked the recorder she'd trained on the front door.

Interestingly, it had data.

The video showed that someone had come into her room shortly after she'd penetrated the offices below. One of the former RIS agents.

A chill ran down her spine as she watched him search her room thoroughly. He tried to access her comp, but had no luck. She'd check it to be sure before she trusted it.

She didn't have a bug in her bathroom, but she knew he'd searched it thoroughly based on the time he spent in there. Luckily, she'd taken her kit with her tonight.

Rachel watched him plant some bugs. She decided to let them stay. False intelligence would help her, if she planned it out well enough.

Obviously, she'd attracted enough attention to warrant a visit, but not enough to draw a kidnapping. Two such disappearances in a row would trigger someone at RIS headquarters to look into the station a lot more closely.

She hoped that kept her enemies from doing anything rash.

By now, they undoubtedly suspected why she was here. They couldn't know how much data she had or they'd have searched harder for Zane's kit. They had to believe she was just nosing around without the benefit of detailed intelligence.

Also, just because Janus owned and controlled Jove Station didn't mean everyone was in on the conspiracy. They couldn't make too many waves without attracting undue attention.

Well, if they thought they knew who she worked for, she should use that to her advantage. Rather than play a meek game, it was time to go big.

Rachel opened an application on her comp and started recording. She gave the date and time. "I've made initial contact with Adam Hale. Based on his commentary, he never met with his brother, but I'm not convinced that Agent Hale never arrived.

"I'll begin talking with hotel staff and people close to the brother. If that doesn't produce any leads, I'll contact station security in an official capacity, as we discussed.

"At this late date, I'm unsure if Agent Hale is still here. It's possible that he moved on to another location. If so, someone there might remember something."

She paused the recording for a moment and paced as though she were thinking. Then she sat back down and continued the report.

"I'm loath to contact our inside man at Janus, but if I can't find any definitive answers, I will. I'll be discreet.

"If I come up blank in the next few days, I'll depart the station for the primary assignment. I can always come back. At this point, the odds of finding Agent Hale alive are slim. We may never know exactly what happened to him."

She gave the camera a serious look. "If I fail to report in as scheduled, there may be more to this situation than we believed. I'll leave my data in the agreed upon location for any follow-up teams. Once I move on, we can stand down for the time being. Price out."

Rachel encrypted the recording and sent it out through the station's communications suite to Earth. An expensive decoy, but worth the money.

The drop she'd used was one she and Zane had used in the past for keeping data off the official grid. No one at the home office would ever see it and ask awkward questions. Like, what mission was she on, exactly?

Hopefully, the confirmation of her "official" status would keep the bad guys from doing anything hasty. Her comments about Hale might keep him safe for a while longer. Though, now that someone had tried to kill him, that wasn't a sure bet.

After that, she checked the hotel systems. Her favorite night manager had added the agent to her suite's occupant list. The bastard could waltz in whenever he liked.

Aslanov was getting on her nerves.

She connected to the man's comp and looked through his mail. There it was. A message to let someone in to whatever room he wanted. It had come in just after she'd scanned for the room number. Dammit.

The sender was her new friend at Janus. She set up a relay to forward any new messages from that address to her com. That would let her know if they decided to move on her. She added a check for her room number and name, just to be safe.

Once she'd shut down her comp, she took a shower and got ready for bed. It was humiliating, knowing that they'd be watching her, but that almost assured they wouldn't suspect she was onto them.

No woman in her right mind let unknown men spy on her in the shower or bedroom. Let them think she had nothing else to hide.

She lay awake in the dark with her eyes closed. Tomorrow, she'd start making some countermoves against her new friends. She'd be up early to meet with Hale, but not for the planned operation at the headquarters building.

No, that was too dangerous now. She'd have to teach him what to do so he could compromise their systems himself.

No doubt he'd love that.

* * *

ADAM SLEPT FITFULLY. The adrenaline from the dive combined with his jitters over the spy shit to keep him tossing and turning. The promised nausea had arrived with a vengeance. Now if only the fatigue had helped him sleep.

The fact that someone was watching him didn't help.

He wondered if Price had planted bugs, too. Maybe there was a whole host of people watching him sleep.

Once sleep finally came, he woke groggily the next morning to the blaring of the alarm clock. He swatted it and staggered into the shower.

Twenty minutes later, clean and dressed, he drank a cup of coffee to wake up and headed for a cafe he occasionally used. Price was supposed to meet him there.

Since he usually ate at home, the odds of someone listening in here were slim.

She was already seated at a table, looking entirely too rested for his dour mood. She had a plate of scrambled eggs and waffles sitting in front of her.

He plopped himself into a chair and glared at her. "Why aren't you exhausted?"

"Practice," she said as she ate. "If you can't rest, you'll make mistakes. I've already scanned the place for bugs. We're clean. I've also been watching the patrons. No one stands out as a watcher."

He nodded and turned his attention to the young guy with the unfortunate tattoo of a mermaid on his arm taking the orders. "I'll have what she's having. And some coffee."

Adam eyed her milk. "How can you have that stuff in the morning? You need caffeine to wake up."

"Not if I want to avoid the jitters. I had a visitor last night just after our little operation. One of the renegade RIS agents is back on the station. He tossed my room and planted some bugs."

"You slept with them watching you? How can you do that?"

"Training. The fact they're watching me means we have to change our plans. I can't risk going into the headquarters building. You'll have to plant the hack for me."

Adam made a point of raising his eyebrows. "What makes you think I can do that? I'm no secret agent."

"You don't need to be. It's as simple as getting into a secured office and plugging a chip into someone's comp. Less than five seconds and it's uploaded and running."

"Uh huh. Then the alarm goes off and they haul me into security."

"Normal checks won't spot it. Even if something does trigger an alarm later, no one will associate it with you. Because, as you say, you're not into spy shit."

She slid her napkin over to him. Inside the fold was a data chip, which he slipped into his pocket.

His coffee arrived, and he took a big drink. "This is going to go all to hell. I don't know why I'm even helping you."

She gave him a cold smile. "Because someone killed a lot of innocent people on your watch and you want to see them pay. No matter what you tell yourself, you want to avenge your brother."

He sighed. "I'm going to regret this. I just know it."

* * *

WHEN THEY FINISHED EATING, Rachel had him walk up the block. She went the other direction. The cameras she'd planted before heading into the café would tell her if someone was trailing them.

The way this kind of thing worked, they'd probably have a couple of people following her. They'd trade places often. That way she'd be less likely to notice them.

Basic surveillance. They'd change hats and jackets, too. Anything to look different each time she checked her six.

And she *would* check. If she just blithely wandered around, the former RIS agent would become suspicious. He'd expect a certain level of caution from anyone on an op, and she had to give it to him.

Whereas they could send a single person after Hale. Perhaps two, just to be cautious. A normal person would never notice anyone following them.

Not that they needed to follow him. Hale was going to work.

They'd know exactly where he was. That probably meant he'd be unwatched until he got off again.

Once she was sure Hale had had plenty of time, she made a show of checking her com. The video recording showed him passing her cameras without any obvious tails.

She'd already stopped a few times to look into shops and crossed the street once, looking back the way she'd come. All standard countersurveillance moves.

There was at least one guy back there. She'd dubbed him Mister Mustache. He stopped when she did and loitered if she slowed down.

He wasn't RIS trained. No real agent would ever do something so obvious. They'd keep on as though they had nothing to do with her and let someone else take over. This guy was purely amateur.

She made a big circle, walked past the cameras, and turned toward the port. She might as well ask a few public questions. That would match up with her fake report and keep them satisfied she was looking the wrong way.

Once she'd passed the cameras, she checked her com and found Mister Mustache in her recording. It also had the guy who'd broken into her room tailing both of them.

Interesting. Why send a pro *and* an amateur? That made no sense.

The ex-RIS agent seemed willing to let the other man lead the way. That suited her fine. Until she knew more, she didn't want to trigger an overt response. Not after she'd gone to all the trouble of putting off their guard.

The station had a lot of traffic—particularly with the games taking place—so she doubted she'd find anything interesting, but you didn't hit it lucky by sitting on your butt.

Which was true about other things as well. Maybe she could use Mister Mustache to her benefit.

She ducked into a shop entrance and waited. When he hesitantly came into sight a minute later—no doubt checking to make sure she hadn't slipped out the back—she stepped into his personal space.

"You've been following me for a while. Don't you know that's kind of unnerving for a woman? Who are you and what do you want?"

"This is some kind of misunderstanding," he stammered. "I was just minding my own business."

"By being right behind me every time I checked over the last six blocks, including when I made a U-turn? I don't think so. I can call station security, if you'd like. I'm sure they'd love to ask you a few pointed questions."

"Ah… there's no need for anything like that." He slumped a little. "I *was* following you, but I swear it wasn't anything sinister."

She allowed her expression to show her skepticism. "So exactly what is it, then?"

He reached toward his jacket, and she grabbed his arm. "Slowly."

"I'm just getting my wallet."

Which was exactly what he produced. He extracted a card. It was a press pass from one of the larger news organizations in the system. It identified the man as Malcom Enright.

She frowned. "Why is a reporter following me around?"

"I've been watching you," he said. "You've been hanging out with Adam Hale, one of the bigger local storm divers. Don't deny it. I've seen the two of you together several times now. I'm working up a profile on you before I interview him for a system-wide broadcast.

"The fact he has a new girlfriend will make it to the top of the sports feed. Your face is going to be all over the system by this time tomorrow. Let's go have a cup of coffee, and you can give me an exclusive that puts you in the best light before everyone starts digging into you."

She felt the color drain from her face. The last thing she needed as a spy was to have her image potentially seen by billions of people. This was a disaster!

12

Adam sauntered into the Janus Corporation headquarters building as if he owned it. That didn't stop him from being hassled by the security guys behind the desk, though.

He couldn't blame them with the Disruptors lurking in the shadows. He hardly ever came here, so most of them had never met him.

The smaller of the two scanned his company ID and let him pass. His partner frowned as though there was something wrong and he was trying to figure it out.

Maybe that was on purpose. Get people to act guilty and then follow up.

Adam gave them a smile and headed deeper into the building. Most of the execs insisted on being down at Earth gravity, but the construction boss was on station standard.

That was probably because she spent almost as little time in the building as Adam did. Except for the early shift paperwork. Not that they used real paper anymore, thank God.

Kira Houston had been in her position as the manager of the construction crews since before Adam had hired on. Unlike most of the stuffed shirts in the upper levels of the company, Adam respected her.

She went out with the teams most days and got her hands dirty. She'd hired on as one of them twenty years ago and knew their jobs intimately.

He made his way to her office and rapped his knuckles on the door.

She looked up from her comp and smiled. "I was wondering if I'd see you today. Come on in and have some of this swill I call coffee."

Adam dropped into the chair in front of her desk. "Your coffee is better than mine. Of course, at your exalted salary, you can afford to have the good stuff imported."

"If by 'the good stuff' you mean imported from Ceres, sure." She rose from her desk and made them both a cup of her admittedly decent coffee. She knew how he liked it.

She handed a mug to him and perched herself on the edge of her desk. "I hear you had a mechanical failure yesterday. I'm glad to see you made it back up. You know that crazy shit will get you killed, right?"

"It was a close call," he admitted. "I think it might have been sabotage."

She straightened abruptly. "Seriously? Have you called station security?"

"Not yet. I don't want to kick something like that off when I'm not sure."

Kira set her mug down on the desk. "You should call them. Get the investigation started. They'll have a lot of potential suspects to screen. You're not the most lovable guy."

He grinned. "I knew I could come to you for a pick-me-up. Seriously, though, it could just be a mechanical failure. Jason Chang is looking over everything. If it was tinkered with, he'll know."

After a sip of hot coffee, he continued. "I hear Dick Dickerson made a new record on depth."

She nodded. "That's what I hear, too. Almost thirty bars deeper than the previous record. That may not sound like much, but every new milestone means we can build better probes to understand the big guy. It might get him a gold medal."

"I guess I've never understood why Janus is so interested in the technology we're developing. They pay big money for it. What do they use it for?"

Kira shrugged. "I'm not really sure. Not my department. They drop a bunch of probes into the atmosphere and blather about their commitment to science. With what that costs, plus what they pay you crazy people, they must mean it."

She leaned forward. "How are you? If you need a few days off, you've got them coming. But not if you're going to pull some fool stunt and try to win those stupid games."

He shook his head. "My ship is toast and I'm not doing this for any kind of recognition. Let Dickerson sweep the damned things.

"I'm a little off balance, but I need to get back to work. That'll get me on the straight and narrow. I knew you'd be wondering, so that's why I dropped in. I appreciate you wanting to give me space, but I'm good."

"Well, if that changes, I expect you'll tell me. I still think you need to clue security in. If someone tried to kill you, they'll probably try again. Or they might attack someone else.

"You need to stop people like that before they get a chance to hurt other people. Besides, we kind of like you."

That brought a smile to his face. "Thanks."

He set his empty mug down by the coffee maker. "I'm taking the telemetry down to the dive coordinator. My ship took a couple of pretty heavy lightning strikes. Nothing worthy of a payout, I suspect, but they'll want the data."

She shook her head. "You're nuts. You need to quit while you're still alive."

"Maybe I will. After one more big dive."

"You're absolutely hopeless. Get out of my office and go do something useful. We're on a deadline with *Javelin*. I want to turn her over to FTL today, so your people need to hustle."

Adam shot her a salute. "You got it, boss lady. See you around."

He went to the nearest lift and down to the executive level. The security there was tighter and more observant. With the Disruptor threat, he couldn't blame them for wanding him again.

Leo Gentry, the man who took the data, was a vice president of something, but Adam wasn't sure what. He only did the dive stuff on the side and always seemed a bit surly. Like it was beneath him. It probably was.

The guard escorted Adam to the door and knocked. Gentry looked up. His expression soured just a bit. "Come in. Hale, isn't it? I hear you had some kind of issue yesterday."

Adam sat without asking, earning a scowl. "I took a couple of lightning strikes. It knocked out two of my thrusters and all my electronics. I barely made it back out."

The man sat up straighter. "Lightning? Let me see the data."

A little nonplussed at the hint of eagerness in the man's tone, Adam handed him a data chip.

He plugged it into his comp and frowned. "This is empty."

"Sorry, try this one." Adam handed him the telemetry chip and took Price's spy one back and tucked it away.

There was no indication of an alarm, so she must've known what she was talking about when it came to security.

Gentry studied the data on the screen for a few minutes and started nodding. "This is good. We haven't gotten any detailed records on the behavior of lightning and the strikes. We've lost a number of probes to stuff just like this, and the data will come in very handy."

He pulled a chip from his desk and put Adam's away in the drawer. "I'll talk with the port and have them waive the rescue charges and cover your medical treatment. That's standard when someone gets injured on the job. Since we're buying your data, I'll treat it that way."

That was uncommonly, and somewhat suspiciously, generous. "Thank you."

"It's our pleasure. Here's a record of the agreement." He handed Adam the new chip. "The payment will be in your account shortly. Janus thanks you for your assistance."

Recognizing the somewhat curt dismissal, Adam rose to his feet. "I'd best be getting to work, then."

The guard escorted him back to the elevator and sent him on his way. He checked his com while it rose.

The deposit was already in his account. It was significantly larger than he'd expected. More than he'd ever received at any one time, in fact. More than enough to fix the ship and give Jason and him a big payday.

This made no sense. What was really going on?

* * *

RACHEL STARED at the reporter in unfeigned horror. Having her image all over the system would ruin her career as a covert operative. She had to derail this guy before he even got started.

"You have this all wrong," she said with as much calm as she could muster. "I'm not his girlfriend. I'm here looking for his brother. He and I are supposed to be married and he's missing."

Enright frowned. "A brother? I didn't know about a brother."

"Zane Hale. He came out here a few months ago from Earth and never came back. Station security is aware of it.

"Honestly, before you make a big mistake and say Adam Hale has a new girlfriend, you'd best check. I'd hate to see you make a fool of yourself. You seem like a nice guy."

He didn't look convinced. "Seriously? Why are we just hearing about this?"

She shrugged. "I have no idea. Maybe they're keeping it low-key to investigate. All I know is that I need to find him. I don't want my face plastered all over the system saying I'm seeing someone else before my wedding.

"I just arrived yesterday. What kind of woman do you think I am? And how big will the lawsuit be when I sue you for screwing my life up?"

That made him back up a little and raise his hands. "Hey, now. Let's not get too hasty. I'll look into this, and if you're telling the truth, I'll keep you out of it. A missing brother is bigger news than a new girlfriend, anyway."

Not the best outcome, but better than nothing. "I don't want my name or picture used. I'm not a public figure and I'm not part of the story."

Of course, in outing him, she'd just thrown her partner under the proverbial bus. He'd be out, but at this point, having his picture in the public eye might be for the best. If he wasn't dead, someone might come forward. Even if he was, the RIS might figure something out.

The reporter nodded. "I'll keep you out of it, but I want you to give me the information on the brother. I'll have you as a confidential source and keep you in the deep background."

"Let's go find a place, and I'll give you an hour. I want to get to the port today and see if anyone saw him."

The man nodded. "I have a number of sources. I can get his picture out and see if anyone remembers him. I'll share everything with you in exchange for the exclusive. That means I'm the only reporter you give an interview to."

Rachel smiled. "I promise that I'll avoid every other reporter like the plague."

* * *

ADAM FELT a weight lift off his shoulders as he exited the headquarters building. It still didn't mean they wouldn't discover what he'd done, but it made him feel as though he'd gotten away with it.

He took the next shuttle out to *Javelin* and floated his way up to the habitation torus, the extended ring that allowed centrifugal force to keep the crew in a semblance of gravity once the ship was in motion.

His people were hours away from delivering *Javelin* to the FTL team. The hull was finished, the decks were in, and the regular drives were operational. At this point, all that remained was verifying the control systems.

The station crews were stocking the cargo area with backup equipment, spares, and food. All the things a crew in space would need. The FTL team only had to install the black box drive and complete the final workup. A few days would see the ship delivered to the customer.

That's how the construction process worked. Different crews would work on each stage of construction and then hand the ship off to the next group when they finished their part.

Adam and Jason had been on the finishing team for five years now. They'd get the ship done and test out the normal space systems prior to handover. Sort of like a preliminary shakedown cruise.

Jason was filling in for him. Not that his people needed much supervision. They were pros. They'd all worked on every aspect of ship construction other than the FTL systems.

His friend floated over and clapped a hand on Adam's shoulder. "I didn't expect to see you in today, bro. You were in the hospital. You should take it easy."

"I feel fine. Besides, I had to go turn in the telemetry data. They paid us for it and forgave the rescue and hospital fees."

Jason's eyes widened. "Seriously? I expected this little disaster to set us way back. This is great!"

"You have no idea." He held up his com so his friend could see the deposit amount.

Jason's eyes rounded. "Holy shit! That's almost fifty percent more than what Double Dick was bragging he got paid. And he was probably exaggerating."

"That's what I said. To myself. As I walked out with the money."

The little Asian man grinned. "We're gonna party like never before, bro. I can't wait to tell Cindy. She might make an exception for you now."

"Pass. How are we doing today?"

They got down into the details of the testing schedule. He already knew where they were by heart, but he had to stay on top of the specifics if they were going to wrap up on time.

As they went through it, his people came up singly and in small groups to make sure he knew they were thinking of him. It was heartfelt and a bit embarrassing, but he loved them all like brothers and sisters.

He decided that he *would* have a party tonight, but it would be with the construction crew.

Once they had everything covered, Adam gave Jason a steady

look. "Houston said we should report the sabotage to security. I think she's right. It might be connected to Zane's disappearance."

"Seriously? You never even saw the guy. Why would something that happened a few months ago lead to this?"

"I think it's tied into Mars."

His friend knew all about the incident. They'd gotten drunk too many times for the story to stay a secret.

"Wow. I can see we need to have another heart-to-heart."

"Make sure everyone knows I want to have a little get-together this evening. Just us. Just family."

Jason nodded. "Good call, bro."

Adam looked over his friend's shoulder and spotted Jack Drake from the FTL team coming up the corridor. It was time to start coordinating the test flight and handover. *Javelin* was about to become someone else's baby.

13

Rachel breathed a sigh of relief as soon as she'd ditched the reporter. What a disaster. If he put her face on some sports program, her career was over.

He'd seemingly agreed that Hale and Zane were the real stories. The hints she'd dropped that Hale's misadventure might be connected to his brother's disappearance sent the man's thoughts off in a useful direction. He'd made haste to start checking it out.

She grinned. Hale wouldn't thank her for the added publicity, but he'd brought it on himself. Let him deal with the consequences.

Rachel arrived at the security checkpoint and waited impatiently for them to give her a thorough look. Once they were satisfied that she wasn't armed or strapped with any kind of explosive, chemical, or biological device, they let her into the port offices.

Since she'd called ahead, a lower level management drone was waiting for her. He barely looked old enough to shave regularly.

He extended a hand. "Miss Price? Edward Langstrom, assistant to the vice president of port operations. We can talk in my office."

"Thank you for taking the time to see me." She gave him a warm smile and shook his hand gently. Soft and feminine were more likely to get useful results here.

The man led her to an elevator, and they took a lift down to about 0.8 G. His office was small, and he'd crammed it with knick-knacks. Small rocks seemingly from every single planet and moon humanity had visited.

She nodded appreciatively. "You have quite the collection. Did you gather them all yourself?"

He laughed and sat down behind the small but efficient-looking desk. "I wish. No, I bought them from a company that pays people to bring them back. I'm really proud of them."

Rachel took a moment to examine the collection more closely. She didn't give a damn about his hobby, but her interest would make him more likely to cooperate, even though she didn't expect to uncover anything.

"This is really cool. Do you have one from every planet and moon?"

"All of the rocky planets and most of the moons. See the little plaques certifying where they came from? Once I finish with the solar system, I'll start collecting from the colonies."

The containers were marked with the planet and the area they supposedly came from. It was probably some kind of scam, like when companies offered to name stars and extraterrestrial planets after people.

They probably all came from the belt. The cost to ship rock back from a place like Eris would be damned high, considering how far beyond Pluto it orbited. Why not lie and pocket the extra profit?

Still, not her problem.

She took the seat in front of his desk. "Again, thank you for taking the time to see me. Things are so crazy and I need to find out what happened to my fiancé, Zane Hale. He arrived here and then vanished. It's been months and security isn't doing everything they can. I'm sure of it."

The man's expression sobered. "I'm very sorry to hear about that. I took the liberty of checking the arrival and departure logs. He did pass through customs, but he didn't depart again. Whatever happened, it took place on the station proper."

That was about what she'd expected. "I'm worried that someone might have smuggled him back into the port and done something to him. Is there a way to be sure he didn't come through another way?"

Frankly, she was virtually certain he hadn't. If Janus, or some part of it, had kidnapped him, they had a number of other ways to get rid of him.

Langstrom frowned. "No one without the correct credentials can get into the port, even as a guest. We take security here exceptionally seriously. After the Disruptor attack, we instituted a completely new layer of checks and balances to be sure we kept the station safe.

"I know a lot of places say that kind of thing and then hire security people at the lowest wages and hope nothing bad happens, but that's not what we do.

"We pay top money for the best we can hire and then test them regularly with an opposition team paid to breach our defenses. They get big bonuses when they do and then we patch the holes. No one could have snuck in here."

He sounded confident, but then he would, wouldn't he?

This was only part of her cover, so it didn't matter if this angle failed. Still, she needed to play the role of worried lover convincingly.

"I'm sure security is *very* tight, but he got out of the station somehow. Can you do some kind of check to make sure he didn't come through again somehow?"

Langstrom mostly hid a sigh and gave in. "I have his data from his arrival inspection. I can run it past the monitors at all entrances. It'll take a few minutes."

"Thank you," she gushed. "Thank you so much!"

He worked at his comp for a few minutes and then leaned back. "The search is running. It won't take long to come back with a negative reading and then you'll know—"

Langstrom sat up abruptly and stared at the screen. "I don't believe it."

Shocked at the unexpected reaction, Rachel rose to her feet and stepped around the desk. She expected him to object, but he just stared at the image on the screen.

There, just entering the port through some maintenance hatch, was Zane. He wore what looked like a port utility uniform and had a badge that looked damned real.

Her "cover building" had just turned up an unexpected lead.

* * *

ADAM FINISHED his workday more restlessly than he'd expected. The events of the last day had left him feeling jumpy. Once they had completed the handover to the next shift, he and Jason headed for security.

Security headquarters on Jove Station wasn't much to look at. A plain but functional entrance led in to an equally bland lobby. One of the uniformed men at the desk waved them over.

Adam walked around two officers wrestling a shouting man in handcuffs and stopped in front of the desk. "I'm here to report an attempted murder."

That got the man's attention. His nametag said Davis. "Who tried to kill who?"

"I'm not sure who did it, but I'm the victim."

"Tell me what happened and I'll enter it into the system. A detective will call you back once that's done."

Adam explained the circumstances of the sabotage to the security officer.

The man entered the information and gave them a final questioning look. "Are you sure this was sabotage? Couldn't it have been equipment failure? Not to imply anything, but bad luck can kill you down there."

Jason shook his head. "No way. I found melted wires that bypassed the safety buffers. Someone put them there, so this was an intentional act."

Davis nodded. Whether that meant he believed them or was just acknowledging what the two of them had said, Adam had no idea.

"If you'll take a seat, one of the detectives will be right out."

Adam sat, and Jason dropped down beside him.

"Do you think they'll believe us?" his friend asked.

Adam shrugged. "Probably. They have to look, just to be sure."

The detective turned out to be a tall, slightly overweight woman with a pugnacious expression and bright-red hair that seemed disinclined to staying put.

She held out her hand. "Mister Hale. I'm Detective Amelia Quinn, homicide."

He admired her grip. "Detective. My associate Jason Chang."

Quinn shook Jason's hand as well. "If you'll come back to my office, I want to go over your statement in more detail."

She led them back into the maze of cubicles and then up an elevator to another floor. She stopped at a desk set in a small pond of similar desks.

Harried-looking men and women occupied about half of them, either taking statements or questioning people in handcuffs. The air smelled of unwashed bodies and burnt coffee. All in all, it seemed just about like one would expect from a security station.

Once they were sitting, she read his statement back and asked if it was correct.

He nodded. "That's right."

"First, let me say that I'm shocked you're still alive," she said bluntly. "Jupiter is nothing to dick around with. Have you considered taking up a safer hobby? Like bomb disposal?"

He allowed a wry smile onto his face. "Good one. Seriously, someone tried to kill me. We're not joking."

"Who hates you enough to want you dead? Another diver? A jilted lover?" She glanced at Jason. "A jealous partner?"

"Well, this turned ugly fast," Jason muttered. "I didn't try to kill him. He's my best friend."

"You'd be astonished how many best friends whack one another. And lovers, for that matter.

"Let me be frank, gentlemen. People kill for just a few reasons, once you boil it down: because they lost it with someone close to them, money, or to take out someone they're competing with in some way. While there are exceptions, they are few."

Adam nodded. "That makes sense. Well, I'm in competition with a number of people, but it's not a zero-sum game. I don't have to step on someone to do well. Neither do the other divers."

"I'm not sure that's true. What about the games? There are only so many places at the top. Even discounting that, I hear there's a big audience for the few of you crazy enough to dive. You make some bank on the videos and fame that generates. Even endorsement deals, am I right?"

He reluctantly admitted she was right. "That's not enough to kill over. The money all goes back into the ships."

"So, someone wouldn't benefit from extra cash to put into their ship? That's what we call motive here at security central. But that's not the only avenue. Is someone pissed at you for sleeping with their girlfriend? Or boyfriend? Your choice on that one."

He shook his head. "No. It's been a while and never someone else's squeeze. Or even someone that anyone I know is interested in."

She made some notes on her comp. "Have you pissed anyone off so bad they might want you dead?"

Adam sighed. "It's been a while and it was never public knowledge. I'm sure that isn't the reason."

Quinn raised an eyebrow. "The plot thickens."

"I used to be Republican military. I can't get into the classified parts of my work, but I was involved in the action on Mars ten years ago."

The detective frowned. "That was a Disruptor plot, wasn't it?"

"No. The Free Mars movement killed the governor and his staff."

Her expression cleared, and she nodded. "I remember a little now. A bunch of people were killed in the fighting. How were you involved? As a foot soldier?"

"I was in command of the team that secured their headquarters. Mistakes were made and people died."

Quinn sat back. "Well, that would surely make you a target. Why would they wait so long for revenge? Was your role common knowledge?"

He shook his head. "No. They don't release names for special operators. No one could easily find out it was me, much less where I went after I got out of the service."

"Maybe it took them a decade to make it happen." She leaned

forward. "Have you noticed anyone paying undue attention to you, Mister Hale? People spying on you or tracking your movements?"

This wasn't going the way he'd planned. Anything he said was going to make Price look like a suspect. Though, he supposed that was still possible. He really wasn't cut out for this spy shit.

"My brother supposedly came out to Jove Station looking for me. I never saw him, and it's been months. His fiancé arrived yesterday looking for him."

Quinn checked her comp. "I see the reports and the investigative notes. The woman is Rachel Price?"

He nodded.

She rubbed her chin. "It says here that your brother just vanished. Why didn't you come looking for him after we contacted you? It says here you were quote, uncooperative and surly, end quote."

Adam smiled sourly. "Zane and I weren't close. We haven't been for a long time. I didn't care that he'd vanished. I still don't."

She narrowed her eyes. "Yet it might be part of the background on the attack. What do you think of the woman?"

He shrugged. "She really cares for Zane. She wants to find him. That doesn't lead back to the sabotage. It had to be someone with knowledge of how our ships work to do it. I think that counts her out. Besides, I've spent a little time with her and she doesn't seem the type."

"That's something I'm more qualified to determine than you, Mister Hale. I think I have enough background information to start poking my nose where it belongs. I want to send a tech out to examine your ship. Today."

Jason nodded. "I have it torn apart. I was looking for other sabotage. I can take someone there right now, if you like."

"Let me call someone to meet you in the lobby."

She transferred her gaze to Adam. "Be careful, Mister Hale. If someone wants you dead, they'll try again. Vary your routine and be mindful of things around you. If something seems off, call security. I'd much rather expend effort on something that turns out not to be threatening than to have to cart off your body. Clear?"

This time his smile was fuller. "I'd rather avoid that, too. Thank you, Detective Quinn. If you need anything else, just call."

She escorted them back out to the lobby and left them there.

"Do you think they'll catch whoever did this?" Jason asked.

He shrugged. "I hope so. Looking over my shoulder for the next attempt would suck."

His com rang. It was the number Price had given him.

"Hale."

"We need to meet. I found a clue about your brother."

14

Rachel met Hale at a diner down the corridor from the one they'd used this morning. It was less of a pleasure to eat at. The coffee was vile, and the sandwich she ordered looked like someone had sat on it. Without pants.

She looked around carefully for the guy who'd been tailing her earlier, but he seemed to have found something else to do. She'd keep an eye out while meeting with Hale in case he returned.

Hale arrived a few minutes after she'd started eating and sat down across from her. "You really should run your meeting locations past me. This place sucks."

"Tell me about it." She dropped the sandwich and pushed her plate away.

"I visited the port this morning. It turns out Zane snuck in the same day he disappeared. They're not sure how he jiggered their security precautions, but I have some ideas.

"In any case, he went in, but never came out. The guy I talked to promised to get back to me, but I doubt that will happen. Frankly, I'm surprised he told me as much as he did. I think he was in shock."

Hale frowned. "Why would Zane be sneaking into the port? If he was investigating Janus, that makes no sense. Yes, they run the port, but it's not like anything there is connected to what he was looking for."

"He obviously felt differently."

"We know someone that works there," Hale said. "You met her last night. Cindy Stevens."

"What does she do?"

"Something administrative in the cargo department."

Rachael nodded. "We'll probably need to talk to her at some point. Zane obviously thought those ex-RIS spies had some connection to the port. We need to figure out what that was before security gets involved."

He shifted uncomfortably in his seat. "About that. My boss suggested that I go talk to security about the sabotage. When I spoke to the detective, she drilled in on the Mars incident. I didn't connect you with that, but she knows you're here looking for my brother. She's going to put two and two together."

She sighed. Just one more complication she didn't need.

"Don't worry about it. I think you probably made the right decision. Security needs to look into the sabotage. They have more resources than we do, and word is no doubt getting around. If there's any evidence, they'll find it. While they investigate that, we'll keep looking for Zane."

He waved away the surly-looking waiter and leaned back in his chair. "Exactly how do we do that?"

"I'll try to figure out exactly what Zane was looking for. He didn't say anything on the data chips, but he had a plan. He'd also have taken steps to make sure anyone following up would be able to figure out what he'd learned. Somewhere around here, he left a stash of information. We just need to find it."

Her com beeped. A glance told her it was the alarm she'd put on her room. Someone was there.

She brought up the feed and saw the ex-RIS spy who'd been following her earlier was back.

"I have to go take care of something."

"Problem?"

She shook her head. "Not really. My visitor is back. I want to trail him to his hideout, so I'll go watch the hotel."

"I could help with that."

"You ever had training to follow someone undetected? No? Then it's best you leave that to me. Work with Cindy to find out about Zane's visit to the port."

He rose to his feet. "What if you run into trouble?"

"I can handle myself."

He raised his hands. "No offense intended. Call me if you need backup."

"I will." She tossed down enough money to cover the horrible food and headed out.

Rather than take the most direct route to the hotel, she once again checked herself for tails. Nobody distinguished themselves, and she made it into the hotel without problem.

Would the intruder go out the front or use another entrance? The back way, or some variant of it, probably. That's how spies behaved. The fewer people that knew they'd been there, the better.

He'd take the stairs. Less chance that way that anyone would spot him. After all, who used the stairs when they could press a button and have themselves delivered to their destination?

Rachel hit the stairs and headed for her floor. The stairwell was just as deserted as she'd expected.

She was only a floor away from hers when her subconscious warned her something was wrong. She'd only just stopped when the door exiting the stairs flew open and the man she'd planned on following came rushing out at her.

With no time to go for her weapon, she lashed out at him.

He easily blocked her strike and bulled right into her, shoving her up onto the railing and most of the way over.

"Bye," he said as he gave her a final push. She went over the side.

* * *

ADAM KNEW Jason was going to be busy with security for a while, so he decided to go see Cindy by himself.

She answered the door with a seductive smile and then did a double take. "You're not who I was expecting."

He grinned. "Obviously not. May I come in?"

"Sure." She stepped back and smiled at him more naturally. "You're lucky I didn't answer the door naked."

"I'm not sure our idea of lucky is the same. Jason is showing off the ship to security, but I need your help with something."

"That might be a first. You've usually got a handle on everything. Drink?"

"Coffee, if you have any." He sat on the couch and watched her head into the open kitchen. Jason was a lucky man.

She dug around in a cabinet. "I'll make some fresh. What can I do for you?"

"I found out my brother was seen at the port. They're not going to tell me anything, so I'd like to see if you could help me figure out what he was doing there."

Cindy poured some water into the machine and raised an eyebrow at him. "I'm not in the port security department. Still, I might be able to ask a guy for a favor."

"I'm not sure exactly when Zane would've snuck in."

"He's in security. If they know someone penetrated the port, he'll know what I'm talking about."

She finished brewing the coffee and handed him a cup. "Sweetener? Cream?"

"Nah. This is perfect."

He sipped the steaming liquid. It *was* perfect. Not the locally grown crap, but something imported. Better than his boss's stuff from Ceres. Probably from Earth. Working in the port paid better than he'd thought.

She got on the com and dialed a number. "Hey, Jimmy. This is Cindy. How are you?"

She winked at Adam as she flirted with the unknown man for a short bit before getting down to business.

"I have a question," she said. "I'm hearing there was some guy that made it past security at the port. Is that true?"

The other guy said something, and she shook her head a little.

"No, I didn't hear much. I just thought someone as plugged in as you would know what was really going on."

She nodded as the other man told her something longer. "That's about what I heard. Do you know where he was headed or what happened to him?"

"Uh huh," she said a minute later. "No, that's all I wanted to know. Thank you so much. No, I can't tonight, but next week is good. I'll call and set up a time that works for both of us."

Cindy disconnected. "I feel bad about leading him on, but I'll take him out for coffee. They're all excited about your brother. He cloned someone's ID and waltzed right in."

Adam shook his head. "I thought that was impossible."

"Obviously not. They're all up in arms. He said your brother slipped into the cargo storage area, but they can't find any record he came back out. They're searching it right now."

He frowned. "That makes no sense. Why break into that? And what happened to him?"

She shrugged, an unconscious gesture that showcased her assets in a manner that would make anyone interested in the fairer sex take notice. "I have no idea. Maybe they'll find something. I thought you weren't interested in finding him."

"I'm not sure anymore. This mystery is getting weird."

"I'll say. How does your brother know how to clone supposedly unbreakable IDs?"

"There's no telling," he said casually. No need to mention who his brother worked for. "Still, thanks for getting that info for me. I appreciate it."

She smiled. "Anytime. Maybe you could join Jason and me tonight. We're hitting a new restaurant on the outer ring. I hear their vat-grown seafood is pretty good."

"I'll take a pass on that for now. Thanks, though. Tell Jason to tag me for the bill."

Cindy put her hands on her hips and narrowed her eyes. "You don't need to do that."

"Exactly. Thanks again."

He smiled at her and let himself out.

So, his brother had wanted to get at something in storage. That could mean any number of things. The most important thing was that customs didn't inspect anything in there, except for verifying there were no chemical, biological, or explosive readings.

He had no idea how he could follow up on that. The port wouldn't tell him anything or let him in. As far as Adam was concerned, that was a dead end. Price would have to do some spy shit to figure it out.

* * *

RACHEL MANAGED to grab the rail and hung on for dear life. She slammed against the side of the stairs, hanging over a drop of a dozen floors.

The man hit her hand as hard as he could, and she almost lost her grip.

She pulled her concealed pistol and shot him three times in quick succession. The loud blasts rolled up and down the stairs in the closed environment. They also set her ears to ringing.

The man staggered back and collapsed. He dug feebly at something in his jacket so she shot him twice more.

Then she had to set her pistol onto the landing and grab the rail with both hands. Her grip was slipping.

With more than a bit of difficulty, she pulled herself over the railing and recovered her weapon. A check of the man confirmed he was dead.

Well, this was going to be awkward to explain.

She waited for someone to burst in and all the shouting to start, but nothing happened. Could it be possible no one had heard the shots? That seemed unlikely.

Or was it because the night manager had taken steps to ensure the spy had some privacy to kill her?

She went through the man's pockets and took everything: wallet, gun, com, and keys. He also had a wickedly sharp knife that she kept.

He carried a number of bugs similar to those in Hale's workshop. These must've been the ones he'd planted in her room. He wouldn't have wanted to leave them for security to find during the investigation into her death or disappearance.

So, what would he have done with her body? Leave it for security to find? That might lead to some awkward questions.

A check of the hall found a large cart suitable for dumping linens into. It was about half full. She wrapped the dead man's body in several sheets to keep from getting blood all over her and heaved him in. Once she had him settled, she piled more sheets on top of him.

She used a towel to wipe up the blood in the stairwell as best she could and then went in search of a supply closet. Some cleaning chemicals made the rest of the red stain come up nicely.

Rachel considered her handiwork and decided no one would notice it now. Not unless they brought security right to this spot to do testing.

After one final check to be sure neither she nor the dead man had dropped anything, she pushed the cart down the hallway. There would be a staff elevator somewhere.

After two wrong turns, she finally found it. She made a detour to her room for her things. After confirming that the bugs were indeed gone, Rachel gathered her belongings. Those went into the cart with the dead man.

She saw a number of guests as she rolled the cart away from her room, but no one from the hotel staff. The guests might have heard the noise of her integrally suppressed pistol and disregarded it as something normal.

The staff wouldn't have made that mistake, so she was probably correct in assuming the night manager had directed them to steer clear of the attack zone.

The elevator then took her right up to the lightest gravity level. Signs gave her the option of heading for the laundry or the loading dock. Since she needed a ride, she picked the dock.

There was a small van backed up to the dock that made her wonder. A check of the man's keys confirmed it was his.

It only took her a minute to disable the built-in tracking device the manufacturer had installed in the van. A closer search found a more sophisticated unit that she also rendered inert.

She opened the rear doors and slid the cart inside. It fit perfectly, and the lack of windows meant no one would see anything that aroused their suspicions.

The navigation unit had an address highlighted. A waste disposal subunit for the station. That would work.

Driving without a station license was the least of her worries, but she kept her speed to a safe level and positively dawdled all the way to the disposal plant.

As an automated facility, it was thankfully empty of people. She backed up to the dock and unloaded her grim cargo. The unit used plasma from the fusion plants to incinerate waste that couldn't be recycled, so it made short work of her problem.

For now, she'd hang on to the van. She might need it. It was a good place to stash her things until she found a better place to camp. Now that they were trying to kill her, she needed to stay out of sight.

She took the van to another part of the station, found one just like it, and swapped the ID plates. Now the authorities wouldn't be able to track her with automated traffic scanning when someone reported the van missing. She swapped the plates again a short distance away. That should muddy the waters, if they reported it at all.

Someone had obviously decided she was enough of a liability to get rid of. How would they react when their man vanished? Now, where could she hide?

As she ran the options through her mind, one stood out. She smiled. It was perfect, even if only good for a short while. No one would look for her there.

Besides, it was karmic justice.

15

Adam had almost made it home when his com signaled.

"Hale," he said as he brought it to his ear.

"Meet me in residential section G, level 7, unit 745," Price said.

"Sure. I have some more info on—"

"Save it," she said, cutting him off. "Tell me in person."

After she abruptly disconnected, he shook his head. Spies. Who could understand them?

Getting into the residential section was simple enough. It was supposedly secure, but he managed to walk in behind a teen talking on her com without any trouble.

He took the elevator down to level seven and looked around. A discreet sign pointed him in the right direction.

The door to the unit opened when he signaled. Price gestured for him to come in and glanced out into the hall, probably to make sure someone wasn't following him.

The quarters were neat to a fault. Obsessively so. And somewhat masculine, so probably a man's home.

"Whose place is this?" he asked.

"Vasily Aslanov's," she said as she activated the door lock.

"He's the night manager at the hotel and a pain in my ass, so I'm going to ask him some awkward questions when he gets home. I'm assuming he's at work right now, helping to cover up my murder."

He raised an eyebrow. "You're pretty spry for a dead woman."

"It didn't take. At least not for me. One of the ex-spies won't be troubling us again, though."

"Seriously? You killed someone? That's not good."

"I didn't have much choice in the matter. It looks as though I'll have to go into hiding. Someone obviously thinks I'm a pain in the ass, too."

He smiled. "So, this guy is on the take? Have you tossed the place yet?"

"I've looked around in some of the obvious spots, but I wanted that backup you offered before digging in. I can't watch the door and search effectively at the same time."

"Well, before you get started, Cindy came through. Zane went into the cargo storage area and never came out. At least not that anyone admitted to her. What could he want in a place like that?"

"Equipment, maybe. The RIS occasionally ships mission equipment. He might have brought something more serious than his kit and needed access to it. Either that or someone was storing something of interest to him.

"In any case, we'll need to try to find out what that was. I suspect sneaking in right now won't be possible. Not after the breach they've just discovered."

He wandered into the kitchen and opened the fridge. No beer. "So, we let it go?"

"Don't touch things," she said as she came in behind him and wiped the handle down. "We'll try to find out the details from the people that took him. Or we figure out where he stashed his ongoing report."

"It's a big station. He could've hidden it anywhere. Or nowhere. They might have caught him before he had a chance to leave notes. Hell, it might be electronic. We're never going to find it."

"Don't be so pessimistic. He'll have left it in a place I can find it. I just have to figure out where that is. Now stop looking for booze and watch the door."

He took up a position near the door and occasionally looked through the vid plate beside it out into the hall. It was late evening, so there was a lot of traffic and a lot of false alarms.

And one positive one.

The manager he'd bullshitted last night walked up to the door and started fishing in his pocket.

"Heads up!" Adam said as he ducked behind the door. "We have company."

"Don't let him see your face or hear your voice," she said as she hurried into the room and stepped out of direct sight.

The man walked in, looking straight ahead as he walked toward the kitchen. Adam pushed the door closed, threw himself on the guy, and clamped a hand over his mouth as he took him down.

The guy was wiry, but the contest of wills was short. Adam planted the man face down on the floor.

Rachel slipped a heavily folded cloth around the man's eyes and tied it tight. Then she held a device up to her mouth. "Scream and you die. Nod if you understand."

The voice coming from the device sounded nothing like her. It was flat and obviously comp generated. If Adam hadn't been looking, he wouldn't have known if it was a man or a woman.

The manager's head jerked spasmodically. "What do you want?"

"We're going to tie you to a chair. You won't see our faces or hear our real voices. Cooperate and we won't need to kill you."

At her nod, Adam jerked the man to his feet and hustled him into the kitchen. One of the hard-backed chairs would work for this.

He held the man in place while she used plastic ties to secure him. Then she strapped his ankles to the chair legs. The man might still get up, but he wouldn't be resisting very effectively.

"Well, Mister Aslanov, you've been a very naughty boy," Price said. "You let someone into our associate's room. Now we can't find her anywhere. Why don't you tell me all about that?"

"I don't know what you're talking about," the man said in a terrified voice. "What woman?"

Rachel sighed theatrically. "You want to make this hard? We can do that, I suppose. It's your blood and tears."

Adam spoke softly in her ear. "I'm not going to torture him and neither are you."

The look she gave him either meant she thought he was a wimp or an idiot. He wasn't sure which.

She pulled the device away from her mouth and spoke softly in his ear. "I'm not going to hurt him. Permanently, anyway. Go make some noise searching the kitchen drawers. Use a hand towel on the handles."

"My associate is looking for a rolling pin," she said through the device. "Do you bake, Vasily? You might not look at fluffy pies the same way once we finish with you."

Adam found a rolling pin and banged it on the counter. Aslanov twitched so hard he almost fell over.

At Adam's gesture, she handed the device to him, and he held it up to his mouth. "Where should I start? His knees?"

His voice sounded totally badass. Like one of the villains from the latest thrillers from Earth.

"Please," the man said. "Don't hurt me."

"Then start talking. We know about your contact at Janus and we know he told you to let the man into the room. Who is your boss and where has he taken our associate?"

Adam could almost see the lies racing through the man's head. He leaned close and whispered. "We've caught you with your hand in the cookie jar. Don't lie or I'll hurt you."

"Okay! They paid me to let the guy in. I don't know what he did with the woman. He had me clear the staff from that area of the building, so I think he kidnapped her. I swear I don't know where she is."

"Tell us about the man," Rachel said once she'd taken the voice distortion device back from Adam. "Who is he and who does he work for?"

"I don't know who he is. He never uses a name. And neither does the person that hired me. It's all done by mail."

"Has this man ever worked with you before? The one that kidnapped the woman?"

"Yes." Aslanov licked his lips. "He did the same thing with a man a few months ago. Just exactly the same. He searched his room one day and kidnapped him that night."

"You're certain that he took the man from the hotel?"

Aslanov nodded jerkily. "Yes. He had me purge the records from the system, but the guest was in the room.

"That was a pain in the ass. Security came around asking questions. I had to tell them the guest never checked in, but I don't think they believed me. They kept coming around."

"Where did the kidnapper take your guest? Why did he want him?"

"I don't know!"

Adam took the voice device and put his hand on the man's quaking shoulder. "You're not being very helpful. I wonder if your story will change after I whack your knee."

He slapped the man's knee with no warning. His hand wasn't a rolling pin, but the shock of the unexpected impact made the man think it was for a moment. Aslanov yelped and then started shivering even more strongly.

Rachel shook her head and retrieved the device. "Now, now. I'm sure Mister Aslanov can make it up to us. He must know something about the Janus mail address. People don't just get involved in a criminal enterprise without a very good reason."

"I never met the person," Aslanov said. "They contacted me via mail and offered me a lot of money to assist their man. I didn't know it was going to involve a kidnapping. Once I helped them, I had no choice but to keep doing it. They said they'd make me disappear if I didn't."

Adam pulled Rachel a little bit away. "I don't think he knows anything."

"Sadly, I'm afraid you're right."

She stepped over to Aslanov. "You're in luck today, Vasily. I believe you. We're going to finish searching your apartment and then we'll leave.

"You have a choice to make. You can either keep your mouth shut and no one will be the wiser, or you can tell the Janus contact and they'll think you're a liability. Unless you want to go wherever our associate went, I recommend you think long and hard about talking."

* * *

Rachel finished tossing the man's apartment but came up empty. Other than his eclectic porn collection, she found nothing untoward.

She erased his security logs and cut him mostly loose. By the time he freed himself, she and Hale would be long gone.

They made their way clear of the residential block at an easy pace, just two people in the crowd. No one would remember them.

"What now?" Hale asked. "We're back to square one."

"Not exactly," she said. "We know that your brother got into the port and then back out some way that didn't show up on their scanners. He didn't vanish there."

"Do you think Aslanov will keep his mouth shut?"

She shrugged. "He will, if he's smart. They'll kill him if he becomes a loose end. Hell, they might come and have a chat with him themselves. I left some bugs in case they do."

He gave her a look that said he wasn't happy. "You'd let them kill him?"

"I have no sympathy for him. He helped someone try to kill me. Odds are he did the same for your brother."

Hale digested that in silence for a while. "What will you do now? They'll be looking for you."

"I'll have to find a place to lay low. That won't be hard. This station has all kinds of spots that no one visits very often. I stole the ex-RIS agent's van, disabled the tracking units, and the disguised ID. In a pinch, that'll do."

"That's not really what I meant, though it's a good point. I mean in your investigation?"

They walked into a commercial area near the residential block. She kept them off the main passages as they headed back in the general direction of Hale's shop.

Security might still be able to find them in the cameras if someone thought it necessary to look for her here. She couldn't help that.

"I have the program you put into Janus's comp system. I'll try to find out where that address goes. Once I have a name, I can follow the trail to the person calling the shots. It'll be the guy I mentioned earlier, though. Randy Evans. The VP in charge of the FTL program."

Hale nodded slowly. "Right. Why would someone from Janus be hiring ex-RIS spies to kidnap and kill people?"

She smiled. "Because he has a secret. Something worth killing over. And something connected to your mission on Mars."

"That makes no sense. How could that be related?"

"Damned if I know. Once we figure it out, we'll be a long way toward finding your brother."

They walked a few blocks in silence. Hale finally spoke. "Do you think he's still alive?"

"No. They were going to kill me and burn my body, so I'm afraid that's where Zane ended up. This isn't a rescue mission anymore. Now it's payback."

He shook his head slowly. "I don't know if I care enough to want revenge. Not about Zane. Maybe over what they did on Mars."

Rachel stopped and pulled him up short. "You're being an ass. Your brother came here with all that information about what happened on Mars. He cared enough about you to risk his life. And to lose it. That deserves your full attention."

"Maybe. Probably. I don't know." He rubbed his eyes. "I've hated him for ten years. That doesn't just go away. I need to think about this."

"Then I suggest you do. I'll call once I have anything, so go back to your place. If anyone comes around, you never saw me after breakfast. Just keep your head down and focus on what security is doing with the sabotage.

"Someone obviously wants to silence you, too. Just not as openly. I'll solve my mystery, you solve yours. When one of us catches a break, we'll get back together."

"I suppose," he said. "I can call the number you used this morning?"

She nodded. "It's a throwaway. No one will be able to trace me. I'll see that you get a new com tomorrow. We'll keep changing them to keep the bad guys in the dark.

"Look, I know you don't like Zane, but he was a good person. He didn't betray you. He gave everything for you. The least you can do is respect him in the end."

Without waiting for Hale's response, she ducked into the crowd and headed off. She'd make a trip down to the maintenance levels. They were always good for little hidey-holes.

She hoped Hale came around. His help might make the difference between success and failure. Or even death.

If she could reevaluate him, he owed the same to his brother. She should've said that. Ah, well. Sometimes the perfect words came after the moment had already passed. She'd save them for later.

For now, she needed to find a secure place to work and eventually get some sleep.

16

A dam had barely gotten to the new ship his construction team was working on when Kira Houston called him back to the station. Security was looking for him.

Jason hadn't been out this morning, so he'd assumed the security techs had him at the launch bay. Maybe they'd found something else.

Detective Quinn was waiting for him when he stepped off the shuttle from the construction slip. "Mister Hale. Sorry for calling you back, but I need to ask you a few follow-up questions."

"Sure. Here or at the bay?"

"Here's fine, but we'll be heading for the bay before I let you go. Have you seen Rachel Price since we spoke yesterday?"

He decided he wouldn't mention last night. That would open all kinds of problematic lines of inquiry. "I did meet her at a diner shortly after we spoke. Why?"

"She's vanished," the detective said bluntly. "I went to see her at her hotel, and they told me she checked out abruptly yesterday. Did you tell her you'd spoken to us?"

He nodded. "I did, but she didn't seem concerned. She said she'd found out something at the port. Apparently, my brother had put in an appearance there before he disappeared. Not the public part. The secure storage area."

Quinn nodded. "So I heard. How did she find out?"

"She asked nicely at the administrative offices. All above board."

"Why would that cause her to disappear?"

"I'm not the detective. You tell me."

The woman smiled without much humor. "I get that a lot. The ID she boarded the station with is a fake, though it's a very good one. She's not who she claims to be."

"Then who is she?"

The detective shrugged. "I don't know yet. If she contacts you, call us."

"Sure. Any idea why my brother was sneaking into port storage?"

This time the woman's shrug was more elaborate. "Port security is in charge of that, and they don't feel like sharing. If I find out anything about your brother, I'll pass it on. The fact he was able to slip in there is kind of scary, though.

"What did your brother do for a living? All they'd tell me is that he worked for the government in a sensitive position."

Adam mimicked her shrug. "He never told me much. I figure it had a security clearance of some kind."

"I figured as much," Quinn said. "We'll get to the bottom of this eventually. Come on. I'll walk you to the launch bay."

"Did your people find anything?" Adam asked.

"The short answer is yes, but I can't give you the long answer. It's technical. I'll let the techs and your guy tell you in detail. Boiled down, somebody messed with your flight controls, too. Something subtle and not altogether successful, I gather."

She raised an eyebrow. "You really upset someone. Are you sure one of your diver friends doesn't want you dead?"

"Someone obviously does. I just hope your guys can narrow down the list of people."

They took an elevator down to the docks and walked into his shop. There were several security techs looking over the dive ship's controls with Jason answering questions.

One of the techs looked up as they entered. "Mister Hale, I'm Lieutenant Vitter from the security lab. I've been examining your ship, and I think we've found something. I'd tell you to look at it, but I'm not sure you'd know what you were seeing."

Hale shook the man's hand. "I'll settle for a layman's explanation, thanks."

The man gestured at the partially disassembled gear. "Someone reprogrammed the firmware to lock the controls if you hit a certain pressure threshold. You'd have dropped like a stone."

That sent a chill up Adam's spine. "What depth?"

"Ten bars."

He hadn't gone that low this time, but it had been close. If he'd been doing anything other than looking for lightning, he would've exceeded that limit.

"Any clue who might have done it?" he asked.

"Whoever it was, they had to plug into the port here," the man said. "We're checking for DNA and other evidence now. One thing I can say for sure, whoever did this knew the code in the hardware backwards and forwards."

"When was the last time the firmware was updated?" Quinn asked Jason.

The Asian man shrugged. "Not since we bought the ship. There's been no need to update it and risk any bugs. Adam's gone below ten bars before so this has to be a relatively new addition."

"I have something," the other tech said. "Some skin cells on a rough edge near the port. Even a little blood. The hacker must've scraped his arm. Since this hatch is normally closed and Mister Chang said they haven't needed to upgrade the firmware, I'm pretty sure it has to have come from the intruder."

The tech gathered a sample and put it into a portable device. A few moments later, it beeped. "I have a sequence," he said. "Running it through our database. I have a hit."

He looked up at them and frowned. "It's Mister Chang."

"That's impossible," Jason said. "I told you, I haven't been in there."

"That does make this awkward," Quinn said. "Mister Chang, I need you to come back to the station and answer a few more questions."

Adam put out a hand. "This is bull. He's my friend. He didn't do this."

The detective shrugged. "I go where the evidence leads me, Mister Hale. Perhaps there's an innocent explanation. If so, we'll find it."

"And if there isn't?"

She smiled grimly. "Then I'll arrest Mister Chang for attempted murder."

* * *

RACHEL HAD FOUND a deserted inspection station and crashed there that night. She woke with a crick in her neck. The dilapidated chair was a lot less comfortable than her hotel bed, but it beat a furnace.

She'd set her data mining bots to searching the Janus network carefully for any information on the mail address linked to the hotel and for access to the various protected subsystems. They'd keep poking around until they either found a way in or believed they'd been detected. In the latter case, they'd go dormant.

She'd also checked to see why her alert program at the hotel hadn't warned her about the impending attack. The answer was simple enough. The man who'd tried to kill her had sent his message from a different address and hadn't used her room number.

It was probably the account used by the dead man. She'd set up an alert for the new address, though she doubted the assassin had shared it with anyone.

The substation had minimal bathroom facilities, but they were more than she'd had in some field situations. She took care of business and opened a self-heating breakfast pack from the supplies she'd picked up last night.

It was crap, but better than what she'd eaten at the diner with Hale.

She brought up her comp as she ate and checked on the status of the bots. They'd located the address inside Janus that had sent all of the instructions to Vasily Aslanov. Whoever had used it had left nothing to recover.

There might be something in the system backups, but she didn't have access to those. At least not yet.

She tagged the address with a watcher to let her know the next time someone accessed it and to record what they did.

The bot looking at the personnel files had managed to penetrate the security firewalls. No surprise. It was the best the RIS could devise, constantly updated to meet an ever evolving game of protection versus penetration.

Rachel brought up the data she had on the newly deceased ex-RIS agent and did a facial recognition search for him using his ID image. It wasn't the easiest way to identify someone, but she knew he hadn't changed his appearance. There was no guarantee he hadn't used a false name, though. She would have.

To be thorough, she started one for the last remaining living agent as well.

It took a while, but she finally got a hit. He'd been using the name Ulysses Abrams. Shock of shocks, he worked in the FTL department. He was a special assistant to Senior Vice President Randy Evans.

She narrowed the search for the second man and tagged him almost immediately. He was living as Everett Gaston, also a special assistant to the almost certainly dirty Evans.

Finally, a break. She knew who to look for. Evans would be inaccessible behind his security, but the second spy would be leading the search for her. She could return the favor and maybe take him alive. The questions he could answer might make everything clear.

The first thing she needed to do was alert the Inspector General's office at RIS headquarters. Now that she had reasonable suspicion that Alice Evans was dirty, she needed to get the ball rolling.

That's when she ran into the first real sign that Janus was searching hard for her. The transmission was under an assumed name, but it didn't complete. It went into some kind of holding status.

The bland notice assured her that the communications techs were aware of the issue and working diligently to correct it.

Uh huh.

Since they hadn't targeted the name she'd used specifically, it had to be some kind of scanning program. If the message was from a known business or person and seemed innocuous, they'd probably let it through. Eventually. Anything hinky would never leave the station.

Since she'd encrypted her message, it would stay in this state until they found out her cover name hadn't sent it. At that point, they'd work on tracing it back to her.

By the time they did, she'd have moved on, but they'd still know for sure that she was alive before much longer. As if they weren't operating under that assumption already.

An attempt to delete the message was unsuccessful, also no surprise. If she could get access, she might be able to hack the com systems and see what she could do from there.

Well, she'd best pack up and go looking for a new hole to hide in. She'd picked up clothes and makeup to disguise herself last night when she'd gotten her supplies. It was time to use them. The bad guys would almost certainly tap into security cameras and try to locate her that way.

It was a brute force method that would take time to execute. It also required resources they might not be able to bring to bear without tipping their hand. Still, she couldn't take chances.

She called Hale on the throwaway com before she packed the last of her gear. He answered on the first ring.

"We need to talk," she said.

"I'll meet you at—"

"Stop. They might be either monitoring this com or saving all signals for later searching. Give me an hour. I'll tell you when you can ditch your tails, if you have any."

"How will I find you then?"

"You'll see."

The line was silent for a moment. "I'm game."

"See you in an hour."

Rachel killed the com. Literally. She crushed it under her heel and pocketed the identifying chips. They'd know she'd used it once they found the hideout, but they wouldn't be able to divine the number or her call history.

Locating Hale wouldn't be a problem, since she'd given him his throwaway com. It had a tracking device that only she could trigger. She'd get out of here and locate him. And, if she were really lucky, she'd find his tails before they found her.

17

A dam fumed about the delay, but he really couldn't blame Price for being careful. Some dangerous people wanted her dead, and security would probably hold her still for them to take a shot. He'd wander around the area near his shop while he waited.

He was almost certain at this point that they were dealing with two sets of enemies. One adversary seemed to have no problems killing people and making the bodies disappear. The other had gone to great lengths to make the sabotage look like an accident.

If anything, the latter was too subtle. An explosive device would've eliminated him as sure as a bullet to the head, and Jupiter would've eaten his bones. No one would've been the wiser.

Admittedly, explosives were hard to get here, but not impossible. Not if you knew the right people and the amount was small. It would've taken almost nothing to blow a panel off the side of the dive ship. Then he'd be dead.

It was as though they wanted him to have a fighting chance. Even before he'd known he needed to watch his six. It made no sense.

Adam was inclined to think he was facing a disgruntled diver. One with some kind of twisted need to give him a chance to escape death. To beat the odds.

The local community wasn't that big, and he knew the other competitors in the games only by reputation. So, he'd focus on the ones closest to him first.

The hardcore divers numbered less than two dozen teams. Call it sixty people, tops. It had to come from them. No one else knew enough about the dive ships and the conditions down there to be so subtle.

That's what Detective Quinn had thought, and he now suspected she was right. Her list of motives probably fit the bill, though he'd bet on jealousy.

Double Dick now stood at the top of his list. The man knew how to nurse a grudge until it died of old age and then mount it to admire later.

No one else stood out to him. If it weren't Double Dick, he'd be at a loss how to figure this out. Especially with Jason in custody.

He had no doubt that Detective Quinn would detain his friend. The evidence was too straightforward. DNA where none should be.

That made him wonder how someone had gotten hold of Jason's skin cells and blood. Surely, that had to be a clue.

He didn't know if Quinn would follow up on that, but he sure as hell would. People left dead skin cells all over the place, but not in that kind of quantity. And blood was a totally different beast.

Someone had managed to nick his friend without it seeming odd. That wouldn't be easy.

His com chimed. He pulled it out of his pocket and frowned. It wasn't showing a call.

The chiming continued from his pocket.

Nonplussed, he reached in and found a second com. One that hadn't been there earlier.

He answered the call. "That's a neat trick. You've figured out how to teleport matter."

Price's voice had a hint of a smile to it. "That's me, top-drawer scientist. But really, I'm more of a magician. I slipped it into your pocket a few minutes ago."

"You're good. I never felt a thing. You might have a future as a high-class pickpocket."

"Your tails never saw me, either. You have at least two, by the way. One from security and the other probably works for the bad guys. You think you can ditch them?"

He smiled. "That's my magic trick. I'm not sure how you found me, but can you do it again?"

"As long as you hang on to one of the coms, sure."

"You bugged them?"

"I used a tracker. The kind the bad guys will have a lot of difficulty finding before we meet and you dump them. How long will it take you?"

Adam altered course, headed for the Janus docks. "Give me half an hour."

"See you then."

He pocketed the com and sped up. Once he made it through the security checkpoint, he ducked into one of the suiting rooms. It held all kinds of big extravehicular suits. They needed bulk to resist the intense radiation pouring out of Jupiter.

He opened one up. Then he triggered the lock on the other side of the room to cycle. While it went through the process, he climbed into the suit and buttoned up. He slid the shaded visor down over his face. No one would be able to see him without opening the suit up.

Five minutes later, a man stepped into the room. He checked the lock controls. It would show the last time it had opened.

The man cursed and ran back out of the room.

Now he'd be trying to figure out where Adam had gotten off to. That was just fine.

Adam waited fifteen minutes longer to be certain no one else came in. That turned out to be a good call. Just before he was about to open the suit, another man came into the room. It was the younger security guy he'd met at the club. Mason Saint James.

The man checked the lock controls, shook his head, and smiled. He left at a much more sedate pace.

The next five minutes trickled by at a glacial pace. Adam wasn't sure he was safe, but he couldn't wait forever.

A group of workers came in just as Adam finished exiting the suit. They knew him and spent a few minutes congratulating him on his survival.

He made nice, but slipped out as soon as he could. There was no sign of either tail as he exited the security area. Since Price could track him, he picked a random level on the elevator and headed off.

* * *

RACHEL STEPPED UP BESIDE HALE. "Give me both of the throwaway coms."

He handed them over, and she stripped out the chips from inside both of them before tossing them into a trash bin. She handed him a fresh one.

"This has my new number in the contacts list. I'll use it for the rest of the day."

He shook his head. "This is getting crazy. Someone planted DNA to frame Jason Chang. Security hauled him in."

She frowned and pulled him into a random eatery. She took a booth at the back of the room with a good view of the door and access to the kitchen.

Once the server took their order, she leaned over and spoke softly. "That doesn't make any sense. Why would they waste so much effort on a frame job?"

"I think there must be two sets of bad guys."

"Wait. What?"

"Hear me out," Hale said slowly. "The sabotage is too subtle. They framed Jason and made killing me harder than it had to be. Your guy would've just shot me down and burned my body."

She leaned back and considered what he was saying. It made a twisted kind of sense, she supposed.

"If that's true, it makes our jobs a lot harder. That means the motive for killing you isn't your brother or the Mars incident."

"That's not certain," he said. "All it means for sure is that two different groups of people are making moves. For all we know, their motive is the same."

Rachel shook her head. "I don't believe in coincidences. How would someone else have found you way out here? Either we're dealing with the same people or the reasons for what they're doing have to be different.

"I think you're interpreting this the wrong way. At the very least, you're missing something. If they planted evidence, it wouldn't have been before the dive that almost killed you. There was no need if you died. This sounds like a cover-up after the fact to me."

"How did they even know I'd call security? I was ready to chalk this up to equipment failure until Jason found the sabotage."

He snapped his fingers. "I need to tell Detective Quinn that. Why would Jason do something to implicate himself? He's the one that decided to find the root cause of the failures."

"It does sound convoluted," she admitted. "Even spies aren't that crazy.

"Speaking of spies, I followed up on the program you uploaded into the Janus comps and found that the two ex-RIS agents now work for Randy Evans in the FTL department. That's a smoking gun."

He smiled. "So, now you call in the cavalry to arrest them?"

"I wish. They have the com system tied up. No messages off the station without someone looking at them. They'll find the report I tried to file and know I'm still alive. They'll move Heaven and Earth to track me down now. We'll have to stay separated or I'm afraid they'll kill you just to play it safe."

His smile turned shark-like. "I'm a lot harder to kill than I look. Besides, you took out one of their heavy hitters. They'll be much more interested in you."

"Thanks for that ray of sunshine. I'm going to work on setting a trap of my own to get someone to talk to me. You focus on your enemy in the shadows. When I find something, I'll call you.

"I stashed more coms with your guns. They're labeled by date. Pull the chips and destroy them when they expire."

"Yes, Mother. I'll also work with Cindy to get as much data as I can from the port. She has some access there. Unless you figure out how Zane slipped back out, I doubt you'll get past the increased security. Especially since they're looking for you.

"I mentioned that, didn't I? Quinn went looking for you at the hotel, and they said you checked out. That has her very interested."

Rachel snorted. "Then she doesn't really believe that your friend was involved. He and I are not connected. She's just leaning on him because she can't leave a stone unturned."

The server returned with their food. It was surprisingly good. Much better than the crap she'd had for breakfast.

They ate in silence, and she used the time to consider their situation from every angle she could think of.

The more she thought about it, the more his theory of two villains made sense. Solving one set of problems might be difficult with the second team meddling. She had to focus on the threat to her mission.

"Have you considered turning over the evidence you have to security?" Hale asked. "I'd say blowing your cover is the least of your worries right now."

That was a good point. "How much do you trust Quinn? This is a pretty unbelievable story."

He shrugged. "She seemed like a straightforward sort. The bad guys already know you suspect them. Getting the information out might give them more of a headache than it causes you."

"I'm not going in," she said. "That's a death sentence. But I'll think about what you're saying. If I think this will work, I'll have you give her a call and set up a meeting. I'm not putting classified information on an open com system."

"I have to go back and talk to her anyway. If you like, I can give her this com. They already know I went off the grid, so I can tell them we met. She'll be mad, but I'll bet she gets over it pretty quick."

Rachel considered her options and decided it was probably the best course of action. "Fine. But I won't talk long enough for her to trace me."

"That's no skin off my nose. Meanwhile, I'll start pushing on the people I know. One of the divers has to be involved in the sabotage. The frame-up was too technical to be an outsider. Especially if it was done on the fly."

She stood. "We've been here long enough. Keep me in the loop. I'll call you on the next com tomorrow morning. I suggest you take some time off from work to get your mystery taken care of. Besides, I might end up needing your help."

He nodded and stood, tossing some cash on the table. "My boss suggested I take time off, so that's not a problem. Good luck."

She headed out through the kitchen. A few people gave her looks, but she walked as though she owned the place and no one stopped her.

The rear exit led into a service corridor. She picked a direction and started walking. There was no one in sight, so they'd lost all his tails. That probably pissed them off.

Once she'd cleared the area, she'd take the stolen van to a public spot with lots of potential exits and wait for the detective to call. She'd have to be very careful, or they'd catch her. And that meant death.

18

As expected, Adam's reception at security was chilly. Detective Quinn confronted him as soon as the uniformed officer escorted him to her desk. "What the hell kind of game are you playing, Hale?"

He sat down across from her. "I suppose I could ask what you mean, but that seems silly. I ditched your tail. And the other guy following me."

Quinn opened her mouth to respond hotly but shut it again. When she'd visibly counted to ten, she continued. "What other guy?"

"Part of that isn't my story to tell, but he's associated with the people that probably killed my brother."

Her skepticism visibly doubled. "How did you deduce that, Detective Hale? What makes you think your situation has anything to do with your brother?"

"Honestly? I'm not sure that it does. I think there are two different groups at play. Ones with different goals. I misled you earlier."

"I'm shocked. That never happens in my line of work." She leaned forward abruptly. "Stop yanking my chain, Mister Hale. Stop playing at this like a cozy mystery. This is your life at stake."

"Actually, I'm beginning to think there's a lot more on the table."

He looked around to be sure no one was listening in. "My brother worked for the Republican Intelligence Service and so does Rachel Price."

Quinn tapped her fingers on the desk. "You seriously expect me to believe that they're spies? Come on, Mister Hale. You've got to tell me what you're on so I can share it with my friends."

"You laugh, but it's true. I've known my brother all my life, and I worked with him in a professional capacity while I was in the Army. He really was in the RIS back then. As far as I know, he still is."

"And Miss Price? You've worked with her, too?"

He shook his head. "No, but she was his partner."

"How do you know that? Because she told you? Just how gullible are you, Mister Hale? Did you know I used to be a princess of Mars before I moved out here? I have a tiara and everything."

"I believe her. I suspect you will too, once you talk to her. I met with her after I ditched my tails."

She shook her head. "Let's say I buy into this fairytale. Who abducted your brother, and why aren't they connected with your attempted murder?"

"I'll leave part one to Price. She wants to talk with you about that. The reason she's not at the hotel is that someone tried to kill her. She's on the run."

Quinn stared at him without saying anything.

"I know this sounds even more contrived than before, but she has irrefutable proof that she is connected to my brother. Videos from my helmet cam on Mars. Unredacted military and RIS files. All locked under a code that my brother and I shared when we were kids. That can't be faked."

She sighed. "Let me tell you how I'd do it. I'd give you a chip with the files locked down and tell you to try old passwords. I'd have it set up to unlock on a certain try, no matter what you typed. Voila, it must've had something to do with your past."

"There were multiple chips and they all opened to the same password."

"Fine, the later chips just opened on the first try." She threw up her hands. "That only proves that you're easy to con."

"I've met the ex-RIS agents that took my brother before," he said hotly. "They were on the Mars mission as embedded RIS operatives. I remember it as if it happened yesterday. It was real."

"Have you actually seen these supposed ex-RIS agents here on the station? You have only her word on the matter, don't you?"

They stared at each other for a long moment before she slowly shook her head. "Fine. Say it's all true. Why does that mean there are two groups?"

"Because group one tries to kill people in public places. This attack on me was too subtle. They left too much to chance. A small charge would've ended me. Even with the Disruptor paranoia, they could've gotten enough. Or the firmware set to a depth anyone would get to.

"Speaking of which, if you think Jason is guilty, why are you getting all bent out of shape about Price? If she's behind this, Jason isn't your guy. And vice versa."

He held up a hand when she started to speak. "I think his DNA was planted after security came into the picture. Specifically to frame Jason so the real people wouldn't be found."

"This takes the cake," Quinn said. "Seriously. It's the most outrageous story I've ever heard, and that takes some doing. Have you considered a career in writing adventure fiction? The David Wood estate is always looking for new ghost writers."

He dug the throwaway com from his pocket and slid it across the desk to her. "Call Price for yourself. She won't send classified material over an unsecure channel, but she wants to prove this to you. You have no reason to hold her yet, so why not hear her out?"

"I should have my head examined," Quinn muttered as she took the com. "I'll do this because I want to meet this woman, but don't think for a minute that I'm buying this crazy story.

"And if she and I meet, I want you to come along. Then you can hear how a real detective takes someone's tall tale apart."

He smiled. "This is going to be fun to watch."

"Keep saying that, right up until I charge you with being an accessory to something."

Quinn activated the com. She must've found Price's number. After a moment, she spoke. "Miss Price? Detective Amelia Quinn, station security. I just spoke with Adam Hale. If you'd like to meet, I have a few questions for you."

After a moment, the woman nodded. "I know the place. We'll see you there shortly. I'll be the one annoyed at all the bullshit this case is generating."

The detective disconnected the call and slid the com back over to Adam. "I'm not happy about these games, Mister Hale. This had better be worth my time."

"I think you'll agree it wasn't a waste once you see what she has."

"You'd better be right." Her tone promised he'd regret it if he wasn't.

Price had better be damned convincing.

* * *

RACHEL HAD CHOSEN a small park with a lot of potential exits for the meeting. They could adjourn somewhere less public once she'd convinced the detective she wasn't insane. The bench was surprisingly comfortable.

The larger area had the benefit of allowing Rachel to be sure there weren't any extra people moving in to take her into custody. A few hanging out nearby as backup was prudent, so she'd let that pass. She expected no less of the supposedly canny security detective.

On the minus side, it meant there was no way to be absolutely sure that one of the bad guys wasn't going to find her.

She couldn't watch every angle, but she'd placed cameras in all the major access corridors leading to the park. If the ex-spy showed up, her comp would warn her.

That did nothing to protect her from other people working for the man, so she'd just have to be vigilant. Since Hale was coming along for the visit, he could help. He was ex-military. He should be able to spot an ambush before it closed on them.

Her comp tagged Hale and an unknown woman coming down one of the corridors half an hour later. It also spotted the two security patrolman that she'd spoken to at Hale's place, trailing along in civilian clothes. They'd be Detective Quinn's backup in case things went sour. All fine and good.

The detective walked across the open space, put her hands on her hips, and scowled down at Rachel.

"I don't appreciate having my time wasted, Miss Price."

"Then have a seat and I'll make it worth your while. Hale, do us the favor of keeping an eye out for any unwanted visitors. Not the two security patrolmen lounging near the café across the way. I know about them."

"I told her you'd spot them," he said smugly. He stood behind the bench and started scanning the people in the park.

Rachel ignored him and turned her full attention to Detective Quinn. "I'm sure you found my story a little hard to believe."

"That's a significant understatement. So, let me get this straight. You're a RIS agent. A spy."

"I am. I'm sure you've run my ID and something looked off."

"You mean that it's a fake? Yeah, I saw that. You must've paid a good sum for something of that quality."

Rachel smiled at the security detective. "It's not a fake. It's a cover ID I use for travel. It has my real name because I'm not supposed to be on an active case yet. Still, it never hurts to make sure that someone can't trace it back to my real ID number.

"But because it's an official ID, it has a means of verification built in. One that your system will recognize, if I give you the correct code."

Quinn raised an eyebrow. "Seriously? You honestly expect me to buy into that? Fine. Give me your code."

"Bring my ID up on the system and tab into the traffic citations listing."

Rachel waited for the detective to get her com out and do so. "Now type in your own badge number."

"There's no place to do that here."

"Do it anyway."

Quinn's eyes widened. "It opened a data entry box. What the hell?"

"All Republican security systems have this hidden authentication built in, but only active and retired RIS agents know about it. Type in this code."

She recited a long series of numbers and letters that the detective dutifully entered. When the woman's eyes widened even further, Price knew she'd gotten the official verification that Rachel was an active RIS agent and instructions to assist her as much as possible. It also had a number the woman could com for verification.

Quinn's eyes narrowed as she turned her full attention on Rachel. "You have my undivided attention. I can't see any way you could've buggered our security systems, but even if you did, that means you're not a normal citizen. So, for the moment, I'll give you more time to convince me."

Rachel launched into her story. "Adam Hale's brother is my partner. He came here to investigate something that I think involves both the Janus Corporation and the RIS. It goes back at least to the attack on Mars.

"I believe the man behind the curtain here is Randy Evans, a vice president with Janus. His sister is my boss's boss. I strongly suspect that she played a hand in assigning the agents to the Mars mission."

The detective nodded. "Let's say that's true. Why should I believe the Janus Corporation—for whom I work—is involved in something like that? What would they hope to gain?"

"I'm not sure," Rachel admitted. "I've managed to connect the dots, but I have no idea what their ground game is. Honestly, I doubt the entirety of Janus is involved. That plot is a little too baroque for my taste.

"All I can tell you is that the ex-RIS agents that were on Mars are here, too. Let me show you the video from Adam Hale's helmet cam."

The detective watched the video dispassionately. "Well, that could've gone better. I assume you're telling me that the shooters were the ex-RIS agents in question."

Rachel nodded. "Here are their dossiers." She showed Quinn their files. Then she brought up the Janus personnel files.

"They certainly look like the same individuals," Quinn admitted. "Mister Hale said that one of them made an attempt on your life. Which one?"

She pointed out the dead man. "This one. He attacked me at the hotel, but I escaped. I've seen the other one tailing Mister Hale. Both of them purportedly work for Randy Evans."

A blatant lie in the case of the dead man, but confessing even a self-defense killing to the security detective was further than she was willing to go. Much less telling the woman she'd incinerated the body.

Quinn looked her in the eye. "Why didn't you call us then? Have you seen your attacker since the incident at the hotel?"

"At the time, Mister Hale hadn't vouched for you. I can't be sure who is working with this cabal. And no, I haven't seen the man since the attack."

And no one would ever see him again, she added mentally.

Quinn considered her for a moment with an expression of professional doubt. Rachel made no move to fill the silence. She knew all about interrogation techniques.

"What are you hoping I can do for you, Miss Price?" Quinn asked after a moment.

"Honestly? Stay out of my way. Investigating this is hard enough. Doing it while security suspects me of trying to murder Hale is impossible. I doubt the attempt on his life was connected. It feels different. By the way, they're trying to frame Jason Chang."

The detective shrugged. "Maybe. Perhaps even probably. I still have to prove someone else is a viable suspect before we can shift our attention."

"We have company," Hale said softly. "Don't look up, but the man who was following me is over to your left. He just arrived. Past the patrolmen, over by the artificial trees."

Rachel spotted the man out of the corner of her eye. He looked as though he were reading a handheld and drinking coffee. He had dark glasses and a hat on. She wondered how he'd gotten past her hidden cameras. Ah well, she couldn't cover every access route.

Just then, her com went off. She casually glanced at it and spotted the living ex-RIS agent coming down the corridor. He wasn't alone.

She smiled at Quinn so their watcher wouldn't know anything was amiss. "They're coming. We need to get the hell out of here."

19

A dam listened to Price with a growing sense of detachment. Combat—or the possibility of it—always put him in that frame of mind. Cold and ready. Too bad he didn't have a gun.

Quinn stood when Price did, but she resisted leaving the bench. "Even if people are coming, they're not going to try anything in public. I have men watching us and can call more quickly."

Price shook her head. "They wouldn't be coming in force if they were worried about security. I'm not willing to take that kind of chance. We go."

The detective raised her com to her lips. "Quinn to Backup One. Move in and beware of potential hostiles. Lock down the park."

There was no response to her command.

"They're jamming us," Adam said. "Move to the corridor beside the deli. I know a place we can relocate to."

Price took advantage of Quinn gesturing for her patrolmen to come over and slid a sleek pistol out of her jacket. She covertly slipped it to Adam, and he hid it behind his leg just in time to avoid any awkward questions from the security detective.

The man he'd spotted as part of the ambush was watching them closely and speaking casually into his com.

It was as though a switch flipped inside him. He felt his military training snap into place as though he'd never left the service.

"They know we're onto them," he said. "They'll shift forces to block our retreat. Get moving."

The man on the com stepped behind the trees as soon as they started moving. Detective Quinn saw that and made the correct call.

"Gun!" she shouted, drawing her pistol and assuming a two-handed shooting stance.

The two patrolmen spun and drew their own concealed weapons.

The man behind the tree fired at them, but they hit him first. The shooter staggered back and fell.

Everyone in the park started screaming and running in every direction. In moments, the scene had devolved into total chaos.

Adam turned his head and spotted two men running into the park from the corridor beside the deli. They had weapons out and didn't look like security. When they raised their guns, he knew for sure.

He opened fire on them. At this range, he was shocked when one of them actually fell. The other hit the ground and continued shooting.

Price opened fire with another weapon, but not at the man in front of Adam. A glance told him half a dozen other hostiles were coming in behind the security men.

They wisely retreated, firing at the new threat.

Without waiting to see if anyone was behind her, Price ran toward the deli. She fired at the prone man while on the move.

Adam tugged on Quinn's arm, and she fell over. Not from the yank, but from a bullet wound to her chest. He scooped her up and hauled ass after Price. He hoped the patrolmen were taking the chance to run like hell.

Price must've hit the man on the ground because he stopped shooting. She crouched beside him and covered Adam's retreat.

The men chasing them continued firing, and Adam heard a round snap past his head as he ran. He made it to the corridor.

"Where are we going?" Price asked as they mixed in with the terrorized crowd fleeing the shooting.

"If we can lose them for just a few minutes, we'll get away. How's Quinn?"

"Bad," Price said. "We need to get her help fast or she'll bleed out. The patrolmen have the others held back, but they won't last long. They'll have to retreat or die. Go."

He sprinted into the crowd, using his bulk to force an opening where he could, but not knocking anyone down. The last thing he wanted on his conscience was a mass trampling.

The hospital was too far away to make any difference for Quinn, but he knew a guy one deck up that might be able to help.

By some miracle, they made it to the stairs and up without anyone shooting at them. He ran down a series of turns in the corridor and into an ethnic Chinese apothecary. Jason's cousin ran it.

Not that Adam expected herbs and poultices to help the gravely injured security detective. Thankfully, Paul Wong was ex-Republican Navy and an emergency medical tech.

Wong was quick on the uptake and motioned for them to follow him into the back. "Holy shit, Hale. Did you shoot someone?"

"Not her. She's a security detective caught in the crossfire. We can't run for our lives and save her. I need you to do your magic."

"Call emergency services," the smaller man told Price as he grabbed a bag of gear and started ripping things open. "Get someone here now or she's not going to make it. You know I'll have to tell them what happened."

"I wouldn't expect any different," Adam said. "Do what you can while we try to keep anyone else from dying."

Price set the shop com down beside Chang with the line open to emergency services. Then she tugged Adam away from the table where the other man was struggling to keep the detective alive.

"We need to get out of here. They'll be monitoring the emergency response lines."

He shook his head. "They'll kill them both before anyone gets here."

"Not if we find them first. It's time to spring our own ambush."

She examined him critically and grabbed a jacket off a hook on the wall. "Put this on."

"It's way too small." He nevertheless took it from her and slid it on. As expected, his arms protruded a good four inches, and there was no chance he could fasten it.

"Doesn't matter," she said. "You're covered in blood. Security would snap you up in five minutes."

He scanned the street as they left the shop. "I can't believe they came gunning for us like that. It's completely insane. The Republic will investigate something like this, no matter how they try to cover it up. They're going to find the Janus link. That's suicide for them. They have to know it."

"Or they know something we don't. I'm tired of being on defense. Let's go take one of them prisoner."

He felt himself smiling. "Now we're talking."

* * *

RACHEL HAD Hale take them back toward the park. They'd only been on the run for a few minutes, but the others would find them quickly. They had no choice because security would be all over the area very shortly, in spite of whatever they'd done to jam the coms.

The enemy had to strike now or give up, and they'd made this a huge public spectacle. They might as well take advantage of the moment. She'd do everything she could to help them come to that conclusion.

Once they were safely clear of the apothecary, she found a closed shop. It only took a moment to force the lock. That might set off a silent alarm, but with security spread thin, they'd be a while responding.

"Set up across the street," she told him.

Rachel ran to the back of the shop and opened the com she'd picked up off the dead man she'd paused beside. It wasn't the only thing she'd filched. Waste not, want not.

She selected the last incoming call and called it back. When a man answered, she set the com on the floor.

"We should be safe here for a while. The owner won't be coming in with all the ruckus. You can go wash up in the back. I'll keep an eye out front."

With that hanging in the air, she slipped silently back out of the shop and over to where Hale was waiting. There was no one else in the store with them, so he must've scared off the owner.

"I signaled them on the dead guy's com. They'll be along as soon as they trace it. When they go in, we take one of them. Hopefully, we'll get the big man himself. He'll probably let the hired guns rush in first."

"We take one of them *if* the opportunity presents itself," he argued softly. "We might make this happen against two people, if they're so focused on getting us that they make a mistake. If they stay in groups, we abort."

Rachel grimaced. "Fine, but if I make the call to move, you back me. Once we have our target, we slip out the back way and get lost."

He checked his weapon. "I'm low on ammo, so we can't afford a firefight. In any case, these guys can't stay in one place too long or security will catch them, no matter how buggered the com systems are. They'll move in fast, so we have to be ready to go as soon as they get here."

She handed him her spare magazine. "I can get by with the pistol I stole from the guy I took the com off of. And I have an ace up my sleeve."

They hunkered down and waited. It didn't take long for the bad guys to spring their ambush. Unfortunately, it was from the rear of the shop across the way.

The windows to the target shop blew out in an unexpected blast, showering the corridor with glass. Someone had tossed in something explosive. Then the shooting started. What they were aiming at was anyone's guess.

"I hope the owner had insurance," she said.

"It looks like you were a little too convincing," Hale said with a smirk. "They breached the back entrance and came in hard."

Rachel sighed. "They'll come out front to make sure we're not hauling ass down the corridor. With all the people running around, they won't be sure. Get ready to pounce if someone stays back to cover the shop."

The attackers came out of the trashed shop in force, sending everyone running even faster. They spotted something interesting to the right and headed off as a group. She didn't see the ex-spy.

He came out last, talking rapidly on his com while two men covered him.

"Let's move back from the window and out the rear of the shop before they spot us," Hale said softly.

"Wait for it," she said without taking her eyes off the prize. "Let's see if one of his guards moves far enough away."

"That wasn't the plan."

She smiled. "And here I thought danger was your middle name. Be ready to back my play."

"Damned spies," he muttered. "Next you'll want a martini."

"Shaken. Not stirred."

When the ex-spy pocketed his com, he gestured for his men to go after the others. They trotted off at speed while he followed a bit more sedately.

"Here we go," she said.

Rachel opened the door as silently as possible. She came out low and fast, curving around to come up on the man's rear.

Instead of her pistol, she had a shocker out. It would deliver an incapacitating jolt of electricity to the target, either knocking him out or rendering his resistance pathetic.

The man must've sensed her at the last moment. He turned abruptly and fired a shot where her chest would've been if she were standing. It was loud and missed her by inches.

She jammed the shocker into his crotch and let him have it. He screamed like a little girl and collapsed.

That got the attention of the man's closest minions, but Hale was ready. He lit them up before they managed to turn around. Both went down hard.

Rachel swapped the shocker for her pistol and snagged the man's com. She'd yank the battery as soon as she could.

Hale snagged the man and tossed him over his shoulder while she backed up with her weapon out. The larger force had turned around as soon as the shooting started and was on its way back. Time to make a speedy exit.

She fired at the enemy to force them to seek cover while they slipped into their hidey-hole. She locked the door and they retreated to the back of the shop. An exit there led into a service corridor.

Hale raced to the right and she followed closely, taking a moment to disable the captured com. A service elevator got them to a different level and away from immediate discovery.

Of course, the few people they saw gave them strange looks because of the unconscious man.

"He can't hold his liquor," Hale said with a laugh.

That wouldn't keep security from hearing about it once the news of the attack in the park came out. She only hoped that one of the security men had escaped and told their colleagues that she and Hale had been defending themselves.

The corridors started getting seedier, and the people they ran past stopped paying them any attention. That was much more to her liking.

Hale took some stairs of questionable stability up to the lightest gravity she'd felt on the station. He opened an old hatch with writing so faded she couldn't even make out the language.

The lights came on when he pressed the switch, but they took their time. Only half of the ceiling panels worked. A few flickered distractingly.

They were inside the stripped remains of a control room. One large window looked out into a darkened area that felt huge. The glass was long gone. Only a few shards covered in grime remained.

The interior of the room had the skeletons of a few consoles and chairs that some kind soul had cut open to see what kind of stuffing they had.

She picked the one that seemed sturdiest. "Put him there."

As soon as Hale dumped the unconscious man, she started stripping their prisoner.

"Um… what are you doing?" Hale asked.

She grinned at him. "You wouldn't be complaining if this was a hot lady. This kind of guy probably has all kinds of interesting things stashed on his person. I intend to find them all before he can use them to escape."

"Do you have hidden things?"

"You'll never know."

Rachel dumped the man's clothes on the floor and gave him a close search before using ties to bind his wrists behind the back of the chair and his ankles behind the shaft under the seat.

He didn't have anything on his body or in his hair, but a good look at his clothes got a wallet, two other guns, a concealed knife, and a lock pick sewn into a seam.

She laid them out on one of the stripped consoles. "He'll be coming around soon. What is this place, and how likely are we to be disturbed?"

"It's an old cargo facility. The station grew around it and it's now completely enclosed. It hasn't been used in decades. Druggies occasionally come here, but I'll wedge the door shut. Security won't bother us. Not for a long while, anyway. What's the plan with our prisoner?"

The man was starting to twitch. He'd wake up soon enough. "I'm going to get answers to our questions. After what this guy and his people did, are you going to quibble about my methods?"

Hale shook his head. "No. What are you going to do with him when you have our answers?"

She smiled coldly. "That depends on how cooperative he is. Can you find out if Quinn and the patrolmen made it?"

"I'll make a call."

The prisoner moaned. "I'll wait with our friend while you do. Use the throwaway and disconnect the power when you're done. Keep it short."

Rachel squatted in front of the man and smiled when his eyes fluttered open. "Good morning, sunshine! I hear you were looking for me. The good news is you found me. The bad news is that I'm not tied up naked for you to terrorize. Awkward, huh?

"I'll give you a minute to finish waking up, but you need to be thinking about how you're going to make me happy, because that's the only way you're surviving this question-and-answer session. Got it?"

He spat at her and missed. "Screw you."

She grinned. "This is going to be fun. Let's see how much of your anti-interrogation training you remember. There'll be a quiz when we're done."

20

Adam tried to call from the abandoned cargo control room, but the com reception was crappy. He pulled Price away from her fun long enough to tell her he was leaving for a bit. She didn't seem happy, but she rarely did.

He unblocked the door and made his way back to the more populated areas. This was the kind of place where you wanted your back against a wall at all times. He found an alcove with a view before he tried his com again.

"Hello?"

"Cindy, this is Adam. I need your help."

"Holy crap! You're all over the news! Security is looking for you and your friend. Something about shooting a detective."

That wasn't promising. The patrolmen should've been able to clarify things, if they'd survived. Or if their superiors had believed them.

"Don't believe everything you see on the news. I need you to call someone for me and ask a few questions."

"I can get in big trouble just for talking to you."

"Look at it this way. I doubt they'll be holding onto Jason for anything now."

That provoked a short silence and a laugh. "I suppose not. Who do you want me to call, and what's the question?"

"I need you to com Jason's cousin, Paul Wong. I'll give you the number. I want to make sure the detective survived."

"I don't need to call anyone about that. She's in the hospital in stable condition."

He relaxed a little. Medical care was exceedingly good nowadays. If they got ahold of you while you were still breathing, they'd probably be able to save your life. Quinn had a good chance.

"What about the patrolmen at the park?"

"I don't know. There was a big shootout, as I'm sure you already know. Someone killed several people. I hope it wasn't you. Oh, there was some kind of secondary shooting event a little later and an explosion. Did you start a war?"

"That's not a bad description, just not in the way you think. Thanks, Cindy."

"Wait. I found out something else about your brother. The guy from port security called me back with something interesting.

"It seems your brother hacked their system to get his badge authorized, which freaked them out, but he also arranged for shipping some cargo out of storage without the usual checks. That *really* has them running around in a panic."

"Interesting. Do you know where it went?"

"No, but I'm sure security is all over it. It could have anything in it."

"Thanks, Cindy. I owe you another one."

Adam disconnected the call and looked up the non-emergency number for security. He'd have to move before he made this call. No matter how short he kept it, they'd get some kind of lead, and he didn't want them searching this area too closely.

He bought some clothes of questionable origin and dumped the ones he'd been wearing. He also lost the jacket. It was so small that people were giving him odd stares.

Once he looked relatively normal, he took the back way a quarter of the way around the station. After he was in a safe spot, he called security.

"Security desk. Officer Riley. How may I direct your call?"

"This is Adam Hale. I need to speak to the detective investigating the shootings. If you try to pawn me off while you trace the call, I'll disconnect."

The man hesitated for a few seconds. "I'm putting you through. Stay on the line."

Moments later, another man spoke. "Detective Sergeant Pride. Is this Adam Hale?"

"Yes. I wanted you to know we had nothing to do with that attack. And we didn't shoot Detective Quinn."

"We know that much. Someone took a video of the attack and you carrying Quinn to safety. The patrolmen told us the attackers were after you. Tell me where you are so we can get you into protective custody."

That was a relief. He was in enough trouble for the things he was going to do. "They blocked your secure coms and are connected with Janus. You'd better triple the guard on Quinn. I don't know who is in their pocket.

"That's why we can't come in. These guys will kill anyone to get at us. Jason Chang isn't part of this."

Adam disconnected the call. The battery went into a bin and the com in another. He stashed the chips in his pocket.

He made it back to their hiding place without any problems. Things looked about like they had when he'd left. Honestly, that surprised him. He'd expected a lot more blood. There were barely any bruises.

"Did he start talking?"

She shook her head. "No. Not yet, but I'm a patient woman. How's Quinn?"

"Alive. Ditto the patrolmen. For once, security knows we didn't start this ruckus. Some citizen recorded most of the fight on his com and turned it over." He looked at their prisoner. "Smile. You're probably all over the network."

"That doesn't make one bit of difference," the man said. "The people I work for will squash the investigation, and you're still going to die. Just like your brother."

Adam closed the distance between them in two quick steps and smashed his fist into the asshole's face. His nose broke with a satisfying crunch. That made the bastard yelp.

"I suggest you don't push me," Adam said in a low, grim voice. "I was there when you butchered all those people on Mars. Don't. Push. Me."

The man's smug expression was gone, replaced by more than a hint of fear. He wisely kept his mouth shut, so Adam released him and backed up.

"I also got some interesting information from my contact," Adam said to Price. "Step into my office."

The two of them backed far enough away that the prisoner couldn't hear them. She shook her head. "I thought I was the violent one."

"You're the scary one. *I'm* the violent one. Cindy told me her contact in port security called back. Zane hacked their system, as you suspected. He also arranged to ship a crate out of storage without a customs check. I'm betting it had something interesting in it. Maybe even him, since he didn't show up leaving the place."

Price pursed her lips. "Well, that certainly does open some interesting possibilities."

"Unfortunately, it didn't stop them from picking him up," Adam said softly. "And killing him."

"We don't know that for sure. That idiot wanted to yank your chain. It's still possible Zane is alive and in their custody."

"But how likely?"

She shrugged. "Not very, but I'm not giving up hope. We need to get this guy talking. I have some drugs that might help, but I have them stashed at my hideout. Can you keep an eye on this asshole without tossing him out the window?"

"It's been years since I defenestrated someone."

That got a laugh out of her. "You are full of surprises, Hale. I didn't think you knew words that big. It might take me a while to sneak around, so don't get worried if I'm not back soon."

He looked over at the prisoner. "Be careful. These people are desperate now."

"I'll bring back something to eat. You have any preferences?"

"Surprise me."

She left without any further ado.

He sat on the edge of one of the ruined consoles and watched the prisoner. This was going to be a long few hours.

* * *

RACHEL FOLLOWED Hale's example and picked up some clothes to change her appearance. She'd need to change her hair color and style before too long.

She bought dark glasses to break up the lines of her face in case they'd started looking for her via automated facial recognition. She picked up some for Hale, too.

Even sticking to the smaller corridors, she still had to dodge two security patrols. They were heavily armed and armored. The attack in the park had really shaken the station.

She took her time and made sure no one saw her go into the maintenance passages. It was all for nothing, though. Someone had taken everything. Even the hidden kit.

The thieves had destroyed anything they hadn't taken. And someone had defecated in the middle of the room.

Classy.

The kit wouldn't have meant anything to common scavengers, but the fact she'd hidden it made it valuable. She needed a new plan.

There was Zane's kit, but it was in Hale's shop. Security would have his place under observation. Janus probably had someone keeping an eye on it, too.

That was going to make getting in a lot more challenging.

Her earlier search had told her the place had several entrances, but none of them would be safe now. At least none of the regular ones.

The industrial area was multi-level. That meant it had places with up to three stories on the same deck. The shop only had one story. That left a gap, if she could get there unseen.

Several nearby businesses had the potential to allow her access. She just had to scope them out without someone spotting her.

Rachel managed to get on the correct level without arousing any undue suspicion. Once there, she eyed the building from up the street. No one stood out as watching it, but they might be using cameras. She would.

The pedestrian street was too wide to jump across, no matter what the movies led the public to believe.

The building directly against Hale's place connected to the roof of the entire level, so there was no gap to exploit. The one on the other side of the service alley was two stories. The gap between them was wider than she liked. Possible, but only if she could get up to full speed. And there'd be a hard landing.

It also made getting back out problematical.

Well, she'd have to figure that out when the time came. She needed Zane's kit, or the bastard would never talk.

The next challenge was getting up to the two-story building's roof without someone seeing her. The place was some kind of manufactory, and it was open. The employees would raise an alarm if they caught her inside. Especially since she'd need to sneak in the back way to avoid any awkward cameras out front.

Oh well. If it was easy, anyone could do it.

The rear of the building offered her a possible way out of her predicament. The second story had an emergency escape ladder with roof access. The bottom rung was ten feet in the air, but some kind soul had parked a delivery van nearby.

Rachel looked around and then climbed onto the roof of the vehicle. She had to make a running start from the front, but caught the ladder on the second try.

After a few moments swinging wildly by one hand, she managed to get herself oriented and climbed up to the second floor.

Just in time for the driver of the delivery van and another man to come out of the building.

She flattened herself as closely against the window as she could, only to find herself staring at the back of someone's head. The woman was working on her comp, so Rachel hoped she wouldn't turn around. If she did, things would get awkward fast.

The two men seemingly talked forever before the driver left and the employee went inside.

Rachel climbed to the roof. It didn't have to protect against the weather, so it was made of the same metal as the building. The builder had added a thin coating for grip, but it was still slicker than she liked.

She walked to the side of the building and eyed the distance. It looked even wider than she'd expected. Her heart started racing.

Well, no use putting things off.

Rachel backed up as far as she could, took a series of deep breaths, and raced across the roof as if her life depended on it. It might.

She managed to plant her foot against the lip and flew across the gap. As soon as she left the building, she knew she wasn't going to make it, but still managed to lock her fingers onto Hale's roof.

Her body slammed into the wall, knocking the air out of her lungs and almost causing her to fall. It was like doing a belly flop into an empty pool. Nothing felt broken, but she'd be feeling this for a while.

She gritted her teeth and pulled herself up, rolling onto the roof and staring at the ceiling. Her entire body ached. She'd pulled muscles she'd never suspected she had.

Once she could move again, she rose and staggered to the roof hatch. It was unlocked, surprisingly. She'd have expected Hale to be a little more security conscious.

She opened it gingerly, ready to stop if it squealed. It didn't. Someone had oiled it well. This must be how the Janus people had gotten in to plant their bugs.

The drop was onto the open floor. Landing made new parts of her hurt. She crouched down and listened. If someone were here, her best defense was her ears.

"Don't move," a man said from behind her. "Hands up where I can see them."

21

———

"This doesn't have to end poorly for you," the ex-spy told Adam.

It had been a while since Price had left, and he'd been expecting the man to bargain. The bastard had more patience then Adam had expected.

"Why would I possibly believe you?" Adam asked. "You killed my brother. I gotta tell you, there's no coming back from that. He might've been an asshole, but he was my asshole."

"Still, it would be rude of me not to let you make your pitch. Gaston, isn't it? Not the same name as when I met you, but I get it. That was another life. So, go ahead. Tell me how I can get out of this alive."

The man smiled wryly, which looked odd when combined with his smashed nose and bloody face. "I suppose I can't blame you for taking my offer with a grain of salt. It's quite simple, really. My organization can't afford to have you causing trouble. We can pay you a lot of money and send you off to anywhere else in the system. Otherwise, we have to kill you."

"You still haven't explained how I know I'll live. You'll forgive me if I'm not the trusting type."

"Do you have a choice? A special Janus team will take over the investigation into the terrorist attack, and they'll see you whisked away, if you're not killed resisting arrest. Poof. No more Adam Hale.

"If you release me, I'll personally guarantee your lives. Don't be like your brother and force my hand."

Gaston leaned forward as far as his bonds allowed. "Whether you know it or not, you've actually been quite helpful to my organization. I am making you a real offer."

"I see a few problems. One, I don't trust that your boss will honor your bargain. And two, you slaughtered a bunch of civilians on Mars and blamed it on me and my people."

Adam stood and smiled coldly. "Not to mention I hear your people killed some new folks today. That pisses me off. An ambush in a park? Really? There were kids there.

"Tell me, did you make that same kind of offer to the third man on Mars? The one that supposedly killed himself."

He stepped over and put a hand on the prisoner's shoulder.

"Let me run a scenario by you. He didn't like whatever plans you had going and you killed him to be sure he kept his mouth shut. Then you staged it to look like a suicide. What's to say I won't have the same thing happen to me?"

Perspiration beaded the man's forehead. "You don't know the kind of people I work for. You'd be much better off taking the deal. That way you could at least be sure your other friends don't suffer for your intransigence."

"That's the wrong thing to say."

He grabbed the man—chair and all—and dragged him over to the smashed window. The huge chamber beyond was dark, but Adam could just make out something on the floor below them. A catwalk hung suspended beyond the control room.

"How far down do you think the floor is?" Adam tipped the man out face first. "Looks like at least thirty yards. Maybe more. A man could break a lot of important things in a fall from this high, even in low gravity."

"I'm not going to tell you anything," Gaston said hoarsely.

"I'm not asking you to. I know enough to kill you without any qualms at all. I already know your boss's name. Randy Evans. He'll tell me what I want to know. Execs just aren't that good at resisting this kind of thing. No RIS training. That'll be a lot easier."

He tipped the man out.

"Wait! Wait! I'll talk!"

"You mean you'll stall," Adam corrected. "You'll tell me something so I'll spare your life. That's no fun. Besides, Zane left some data chips—which is how I got your name—so I know some of this already. Like how you used the Disruptors. More than enough to know when I'm being bullshitted."

"Janus is connected to the Disruptors. They brought them in on the Mars job."

Adam laughed. "You expect me to believe that Janus is working with those crazies? A major corporation that they bombed? Try again."

"Who do you think finances those nutballs? The explosion here was just to make Janus look innocent. It wasn't even the Disruptors.

"Do you know what Janus is? The god with two faces. The god of beginnings, transitions, and endings, among other things. It's a fitting name for them, let me tell you. Is that enough to whet your appetite? Enough to get you to pull me back in so we can talk like gentlemen?"

The door behind Adam crashed open, and he caught sight of men with weapons. They didn't look like security.

He let go of the spy, grabbed his pistol, and crouched low. The man fell through the smashed window with a scream.

The intruders were already shooting. Several shots went over Adam's head even as he returned fire.

The first man through the door took a round in the throat. He staggered back and blocked the rest of his team before he went down. The second man dove for cover.

That gave Adam just a few seconds to act. There were probably too many people for him to handle, so he needed an exit strategy. One that didn't involve falling to his death.

He pocketed the pistol, jumped up into the windowsill, and threw himself toward the catwalk.

And missed.

* * *

RACHEL DID as the man ordered and raised her hands. He'd gotten the drop on her. Reaching for her weapon would almost certainly get her shot.

"Price?"

She turned her head enough to make out her captor. It was Hale's friend, Jason Chang. He only had a large wrench to menace her with.

Well, this was embarrassing.

Rachel lowered her hands and turned to face him. "In the future, might I suggest you avoid attempting to detain an intruder unless you're really armed? An actual burglar might have shot you."

The man shrugged. "I didn't expect to find anyone in here. Security cut me loose and insisted I let them search the shop. You just missed them."

"I can live without meeting them. Hale's safe, but I need to get some gear to ask a bad man some important questions."

Chang raised an eyebrow. "I can't imagine what you'll find here to help you with that, but be my guest."

She led him to the place Hale stashed his weapons. Hopefully, he'd managed to hide Zane's kit there before everything blew up.

"I'm pretty sure that a rusted-out air circulator isn't the answer to your prayers," Chang said with a lopsided smile.

"Shows what you know." Rachel opened the machine up. Hale's private stash of papers and cash were still there.

"Dude! Look at that. I had no idea Adam put stuff in there. That's pretty clever."

"No, clever is putting a second hidden stash under the first."

She moved the obvious stuff to the side and opened the hidden panel. The weapons were still there, and so was Zane's kit. Perfect.

Chang's eyes bugged out. "Holy crap! Those are military-grade weapons! Security would freak!"

"Then I suggest you forget you saw them. Could you go get a large pack from Hale's closet? I saw one there when I bugged the place earlier."

His eyes narrowed. "So, the story about Adam's brother being a

RIS agent was true. Don't blame Adam. He was *really* drunk. You aren't his brother's fiancé. You work for them, too."

"Keep it under your hat, but yes. Hale knows. That's a big part of why that attack in the park happened."

"Are those the same people that framed me? I'm going with you."

Rachel let him go without agreeing. His skills might be useful, but he could also be a hindrance. She needed to consider this carefully.

Once he returned, she packed the large bag with handguns and ammunition. There were a few carbines with folding stocks. They barely fit, and the ammo for them made the pack almost too heavy to lift.

That's what decided the issue in Chang's favor. She wasn't going to throw her back out trying to carry the damned thing.

"Here."

He eyed her doubtfully. "If security catches me with all that stuff, they'll never let me out."

"Not if you're helping me. Hale doesn't know this, but I'm officially authorizing him to assist me on behalf of the Republic. You, too. These weapons are part of our mission gear. Security can scream all they like."

"And if we lose?"

"Then being locked up for the rest of our lives really isn't a fate we need to concern ourselves with. We'll be dead."

She put the machine back the way it had been and faced Chang. "You'll need to leave first. The people watching this place will swarm as soon as they see me."

"Then don't let them see you."

"I'm a spy, not a ghost."

He grinned. "You mean I know something you don't? There's access to the building next door. We can head out that way and no one will see us."

"I didn't see anything like that. How do you know about it?"

"I'm an engineer. I take things apart to see how they work. Adam's sewage system wasn't very good when he bought this place. The access turned up while I was fixing it. The building next to this one shares the tunnel. Come on."

She put a hand on his chest. "Wait. This place has bugs. Tell me where we're going."

"To the back of the shop, adjacent to Adam's rooms."

"Go around the other side, then. That's clear of bugs."

He led her through a maze of equipment and to the back of the shop. She'd been here before, but hadn't paid as much attention as she should have. She'd been looking for a stash at the time.

Now she gave the various tables and disassembled parts a good look as they went by. There was a lot of junk. "It looks like you could build a second ship from all this stuff."

He tossed a grin over his shoulder. "Just about. Most of it isn't easily repairable, but we have all the systems represented here. We use them for parts."

Chang led her to a cranny at the back of the shop. It had a table on top of a rubberized non-slip mat. He rolled the empty table clear and folded the mat back. A recessed floor panel sat beneath it.

"Why hide it?" she asked.

"I didn't, really. I needed a table to do some delicate work. I figured I could move it if I needed in there again."

He grabbed the recessed handle and opened the panel up. The dark area under the floor looked to be about four feet deep and was far grimier than the room where they were keeping the prisoner.

"That's disgusting," she said. "Have you considered cleaning it out?"

Chang shrugged. "Why bother? It'll just get nasty again. Let me grab us some coveralls."

"Grab some lights, too."

She used her com to cast a dim light into the hole while he set the bag on the table and went back into the shop to rummage around. The opening led to a low tunnel with pipes running along the walls. It would be a tight fit for Chang with the pack. Good thing he was small for a guy.

He came back with some coveralls that were only clean when compared to the tunnel they were about to go into.

Rachel sighed and slid one over her clothes. She was about to drop into the opening when something made a noise out in the main shop area.

She put a finger over her lips to warn Chang and then slipped out enough to see the rest of the building. She heard the unmistakable sound of someone moving around.

"We have company," she told Chang softly. "We need to hide how we got out of this building. Take the pack and get going. I'll be right behind you. Lights out."

He lowered himself into the pit with surprising grace.

Rachel rolled the non-slip mat and slipped it under a bench. She moved the rolling table as close to the open panel as possible. It was wide enough to slip over the access, though getting the thing to move with the panel almost closed was going to be fun.

She had just enough space to reach out through the slightly open access panel and move the table a few inches at a time. It wasn't nearly as quiet as she'd have preferred.

The sound of someone coming into the general area made her heart thud, but she kept inching the table along until it completely hid the panel.

A pair of black boots came into the alcove. The pants didn't look like security issue, so she'd be willing to bet it was Janus.

"Alpha Three, I thought I heard something in the back of the shop, but it's empty. My sector is clear."

He was undoubtedly reporting in over a com with an earpiece. Time to get moving before he discovered just how wrong he was.

She settled the panel into place. The dark was almost as impressive as the stench. She flicked her light on and breathed in through her mouth. It even tasted bad down here.

Chang had moved a dozen feet up the tunnel. She gestured for him to keep going and followed along. She hoped they got clear before the bad guys figured things out.

22

Adam barely had time to realize how screwed he was before he slammed into something a lot more forgiving than he deserved. Saying it broke his fall was perhaps a little too generous, but it beat slamming into the deck. Combined with the low gravity, he rolled off without any serious injuries.

The light from the ruined control room was just bright enough to see that Gaston hadn't been so lucky. He'd fallen into the gap between the pile of what was obviously some kind of old packing material and the bulkhead. It was unfortunately bare and unpadded. He'd also landed on his head.

It was still better than the bastard had deserved.

Someone started shooting from the shattered window, sending puffs of decayed junk into the air. Adam turned and ran into the darkness, which in the low-gravity conditions was more of a lope. Luckily, he'd worked in similar conditions before.

The attackers' lights weren't good enough to cover any distance at all, so they were quickly shooting into the dark.

He found a slumped pile of boxes and stopped behind it. They'd be after him in a moment, unless he slowed them down.

The light behind them silhouetted his attackers nicely. It was time to teach them something about tactical doctrine.

The pistol that Price had given him was almost empty, but he had the spare magazine. Making them keep their heads down was worth a few shots.

He could see three men looking for him. Taking out one of them would reduce their force by fifty percent, counting the man he'd dropped when they'd broken in. That would make them very leery of chasing him too closely.

Adam estimated the distance. Pistols were more accurate at longer ranges than most people believed possible, if the shooter knew the characteristics of the weapon and had time to aim.

He'd hit targets the size of a man's head at over two hundred yards in normal gravity. He wouldn't have to compensate as much here, though he'd have to do a lot of estimating in his head. The biggest problem was that he didn't know his borrowed weapon that well.

Once he thought he had the range, he aimed at the man to the far right. The middle of the torso would do. If he guessed wrong on the trajectory, he still might hit him.

He carefully squeezed off a shot and watched the bullet hit the man in the groin. Ouch.

Without waiting, he raised his point of aim and snapped off a shot at the next man. He was still turning to look at his companion when the bullet took him in the chest.

The last attacker dove back out of sight before Adam could shoot at him. Too bad. A clean sweep would've been really helpful.

There was some sporadic shooting from the control room, but nothing aimed. After Adam's eyes were as adjusted to the darkness as they were going to get, he headed deeper into the cargo bay. There were a number of hatches against the closest wall, but none of them opened.

Large vacuum doors dominated the end of the bay opposite the control room. The station had built up around the bay, so they shouldn't actually lead to space, but he wasn't going to take that kind of fool risk.

The catwalk he'd jumped for earlier led to a walkway around the bay on a second level. If he wanted out of this place, he needed to get up there.

He risked the light from his com, shielding it with his body. A rusted ladder led up. He didn't trust it, but he really didn't have much of a choice.

Two rungs broke off as he climbed. One in his hand and another under his foot. The noise of the latter rung hitting the deck was incredibly loud to his ears. He had visions of the gangway he'd jumped for earlier breaking away from the ceiling under his weight. That would've sucked.

Once he reached the dubious safety of the upper level, Adam headed for the area near the airlock. There was a hatch set in the interior wall. It resisted him, but there was a little movement. Enough to suggest that they hadn't welded it shut.

Adam used the rung as a makeshift pry bar. It snapped almost at once, but the hatch opened enough for him to get his fingers inside the lip.

He really had to be careful now. If he lost his grip while planting a foot on the wall, he might propel himself into the railing. It could very well give way and send him falling into the bay for a second time. Gaston's twisted body proved that was a bad idea.

There were more lights shining out from the ruined control room. Enemy reinforcements had arrived, and they were looking for him. It was doubtful they could see this end of the bay, but it was time to get going.

Three solid heaves got the hatch to open with an ear-rending squeal. The darkened corridor on the other side smelled as though no one had used it in a long while. Still, it had to lead somewhere better than here.

Adam pulled the hatch closed and forced the locking handle over with the remains of the rung. Unless they'd brought a cutting torch, that should keep them off his six long enough for him to escape.

The corridor led to some abandoned offices and another hatch. Someone had locked it on the inside, so that explained why the area was empty.

He unlocked the hatch with a fair amount of brute force and opened it. The corridor on the other side had the look of one that saw occasional traffic, and the air smelled better. Relatively speaking.

Adam pulled the hatch closed and headed off. Ten minutes later, he was safely in the occupied area of the station.

He bought a throwaway com and called the last number he had for Price. It went straight to voicemail, so he told her to contact him at this number and not to go back to the control room. In as few sentences as possible, he explained the ambush and Gaston's fate.

Now he needed to get out of sight. He figured he could kill two birds with one stone and investigate the sabotage to his ship by having a heart-to-heart with Double Dick. If anyone in the diver community was involved, it was Double Dick.

The ornery bugger lived in a shop similar to Adam's, but in a lower-class neighborhood. That suited the reclusive man. He didn't want anyone dropping by, announced or not.

It took a while to find his shop. It was at the back of an alley, and this place had far too many of those.

No one answered when he pressed the buzzer, but pounding on the door was more effective. It swung open a little as soon as he hit it. It hadn't been fully latched.

That was never good.

"Double Dick!" Adam shouted when he opened the door. "It's Adam Hale. We need to talk."

When the man didn't answer, Adam edged inside. The lights were on, and the place was a dirty mess. He'd have thought someone had tossed the man's shop if he hadn't known Double Dick as well as he did.

Being careful not to step on anything questionable, Adam made his way back to Double Dick's living quarters. He stopped when the smell started getting worse. The scent of rotting meat was unmistakable.

Shit.

He wasn't surprised to see a body sprawled in the man's living room. It looked as though Double Dick wouldn't be answering any questions today. Or any other day.

* * *

RACHEL FOLLOWED Chang up into the neighboring building—ironically, the one she'd jumped to Hale's roof from—with her senses tuned to their highest pitch. If someone called security on them, they might never get out of the area alive.

The access panel here opened into a mechanical room. Thankfully, there was nothing blocking the damned thing.

"Now what?" she asked Chang softly.

"Now we get the hell out of here."

She grabbed his arm. "Wait! We can't let them see us."

He frowned. "You're thinking like a spy. Don't make this more complicated than it has to be. I know these people. We're fine."

The hair on the back of her neck stood up as he opened the door to the mechanical room as though he hadn't a care in the universe.

"Hey, Jason Chang here," he shouted. "Just working on the pipes."

A well-built woman stepped into view and scowled at them. "Don't tell me the damned things are leaking again."

"Not at the moment, and I intend to see they stay that way. Karen, meet Rachel. She's helping me out today."

The other woman examined Rachel's hand before she offered her own. Considering the hygienic state of the pit, that was smart.

"Karen Wilson, shop manager for Union Systems. How'd you end up working with this bum? Lose a bet?"

Rachel smiled. "Rachel Price. That about sums it up, yeah."

Chang shook his head with an expression of long-suffering. "What is it with you ladies? Anyway, something is blocking the access panel on my end, so we need to use your fine exit. The one in back will do."

"That'll cost you a beer."

"Done. Come by the Spot any time you like. I'll make it worth your while."

"I'd rather come by when Adam's there. No offense to you or that hot little number you're dating."

"You keep on trying," Chang said. "Maybe one day he'll open up to someone."

Wilson led them to the back door of her shop and saw them out.

Rachel was surprised the woman hadn't commented on the backpack Chang carried, but she wasn't going to complain.

A quick glance around didn't show any obvious observers, but someone had seen her entering Hale's shop. Or they'd come looking for Chang. There was no way to know. In either case, they'd been looking for someone. The two of them needed to get out of the area quickly.

"This way," Chang said. He headed down the alley.

Rachel pulled out her com while she watched behind them for trouble. Once it finished powering up, she called the emergency security number.

"Station security," a man said. "Please state your location and the nature of your emergency."

"I just saw several men with guns break into Adam Hale's shop. Please send someone quickly. I think they're going to shoot someone." Just to be sure they had it, she rattled off the address to the shop.

She disconnected when the man tried to get more information out of her. Hale's name would sound the alarm fast enough, and they'd take any report of armed burglars seriously. Particularly after the gunfight in the park.

Rachel was about to yank the battery when she saw she had a message. She'd better listen to that before she dumped the com. Otherwise, she'd never get it.

Hale's recorded warning was worrying, but he'd escaped the attack. It was too bad about the prisoner, but the information Hale had extracted was useful, if confusing. Since she'd already called security, it was best not to call him back until she had a new com.

She made note of his number and stripped the chips and battery from the com.

"Hale ran into some trouble, but he's fine," she told Chang as she dumped the device into a drain. "We need to get some fresh coms before we get too far from civilization."

"I know a place."

That turned out to be a corner store in what seemed to be an ethnic Chinese quarter of the station. The storekeeper gave her the eye, but sold Chang half a dozen coms.

Once he'd handed them over to her, Chang led her deeper into the area and into a restaurant.

"We don't have time for lunch," she told him.

"You want a place to hide? My grandmother is the person to see. Now, shut up and let me do the talking."

He exchanged words in Chinese with one of the servers, and the woman led them into the back. A large man with intricate tattoos on his forearms frowned at them from in front of a closed door.

The server said something, and the man nodded before rapping on the door. A woman's voice answered before he opened it and gestured the three of them inside.

A frail woman of advanced age eyed them from behind a desk stacked high with file folders. The server bowed and said something to her. The older woman sighed and made a shooing gesture with her hand.

Chang started to speak after the guard closed the door behind the server, but the woman held up a hand.

"Please stop, Jason," she said in perfect English. "Your Chinese is execrable. Don't torture me with your latest attempt at proper pronunciation. What do you want?"

"We need your help, Grandmother."

"Obviously. Details, boy. Who is your friend?"

Rachel put her hand on Chang's arm. "Perhaps it would be better if I explain the situation. Madam, my name is Rachel Price, and I work for the Republican Intelligence Service."

The woman raised an eyebrow but said nothing. The guard stepped back and pulled a weapon from under his jacket. The older woman must've tripped a hidden alarm because, moments later, a number of other armed men burst through the door the server had just used.

Chang sighed. "I told you to let me do the talking."

23

A dam stepped into Double Dick's living quarters with care. If he left any identifying traces, security would assume that he'd done this. He was sure this wasn't a natural death. The timing was far too coincidental.

Double Dick lay sprawled beside his coffee table. Not that he'd been refined enough to use it for that. A forest of mostly empty beer bottles covered it. All except for one bare corner with an electronic pad.

Using the corner of his shirt, Adam picked it up, turned it on, and read the current document.

I know you'll figure out I tried to kill Hale and I'm not going to prison. Screw all of you.

It sounded like Double Dick, but there was no way the selfish bastard would kill himself. Or that he was subtle enough to try to frame Jason.

Not that Adam thought Double Dick was innocent. Someone had modified the firmware on Adam's ship and figured out how to sabotage it. That fit the dead man perfectly. He was an accomplice. Adam just didn't know why.

Whoever was really calling the shots had killed him to stop any investigation. Too bad Adam was stubborn.

He pocketed the pad and carefully examined the body. There were no obvious wounds, so Adam suspected poison or an overdose of something. That was also way out of character for Double Dick. He'd have made his end violent and messy.

Now he needed to find Double Dick's stash. It might have clues as to who was behind this.

Adam found a relatively simple hiding spot and dismissed it at once as too obvious. No, this was to stop a thief from looking any further. It had a decent amount of cash and some precious metals from the belt. Nothing to write home about and far less than Double Dick was probably worth.

He finally found a devilishly clever spot beside the toilet tank. The wall looked seamless, but a button on the underside of the sink caused it to slide up, revealing a safe. One secured with a fingerprint scanner.

Well, this was going to be disgusting. Double Dick was already starting to bloat.

Adam pulled the blanket off the bed, scattering food wrappers, and returned to the living room. A few sweeps of his foot cleared the obstacles on the floor, and he rolled the man's body onto the blanket.

That made it easy to drag Double Dick into the bathroom. It took all Adam's strength to cinch the blanket closed and lift the dead man far enough to press his finger on the reader. The safe clicked open.

He dragged the body back to the living room and put it back the way he'd found it. Better everything matched up when security finally found him.

Once Adam had tossed the blanket back on the bed, he used a towel of questionable cleanliness to open the safe door.

The large stacks of money made him sure he'd found the real stash. In fact, there was too much. This was far above what Double Dick would've earned from his day job and diving combined.

He shifted the money and found another data pad behind the stacks. There was also an improbable amount of precious minerals stacked there. Double Dick hadn't trusted banks. Or anyone else, as the small arsenal at the back of the safe came to light.

Adam pulled the pad out and brought it to life. It seemed to be an accounting of Double Dick's finances. Cash in and cash out. Initials beside the amounts were the only clue who the transactions related to.

Two rather large amounts in the credit column had C.S. beside them. The timing seemed right for both Adam's last dive and the firmware update.

If that were true, he wondered what all the other payments from C.S. had been about. They went back more than a year.

That was far from the only large sum in or out, so this was going to take more investigative knowhow than he had. Under other circumstances, he'd just call security.

Unfortunately, he couldn't do that while he was burgling the dead man's home.

Adam eyed the cash. It might have fingerprints on it. He hated the thought of robbing the dead, but he'd take any chance he could to figure out who was behind the attack on him. Besides, the man had tried to kill him.

He went back into the shop and found a suitable tool bag. He dumped its contents onto the closest bench. With all the other clutter, it didn't seem the least out of place.

Then he emptied the safe. For good measure, he took the contents of the other stash, too. To say the bag was heavy was an understatement.

Adam took one last trip around to wipe everything he might have touched and stuffed the towel into the bag. Then he headed out the way he'd come in.

His skin crawled as he walked away from the shop. It felt as though everyone were watching him. That was ridiculous, so he just walked on as though nothing were wrong.

Price hadn't called him back yet, so Adam hoped she wasn't in some kind of trouble. He'd call her again once he was out of sight. They needed to solve these mysteries fast.

* * *

THE GUARDS quickly found Rachel's weapon and disarmed her. They then roughly seated Chang and her in chairs set before the desk.

The old woman steepled her fingers and scowled at them. "You bring a spy into my business, Jason? I confess that while I consider you a fool, I did not foresee you being a traitor."

"This isn't what it looks like, Grandmother," he said in a subdued voice. "In fact, it has nothing to do with you or the organization. Please, just hear her out."

One of the guards opened the bag Chang had been carrying and lifted it enough to show the woman the contents. That made both her eyebrows rise.

"The sight of these weapons fills me with curiosity, so I will give the woman a brief opportunity to interest me before I have her killed." She shifted her attention to Rachel. "Make it quick."

"Might I ask your name?" Rachel asked.

"My grandson has many failings. Basic courtesy seems to be among them. You may call me Grandmother Wu."

"Janus Corporation is trying to kill us. They've already eliminated my partner, Adam Hale's brother. The shooting in the park today was them."

Wu grunted. "That is interesting, if true, but I fail to see how it is relevant to me."

"We came to buy shelter, Grandmother," Chang said.

"What insanity made you believe that I would want the money of someone who works for the government?"

Rachel smiled. "I'm sure you get more of that than you're willing to admit. Come now, madam. The RIS pays all kinds of people for information and support. I couldn't care less that you're heading a criminal enterprise. In fact, I like the advantage that offers. I'm a spy, not security."

The older woman's eyes narrowed. "There is some truth to what you say, but the shooting in the park troubles me." She shifted her gaze back to Chang. "Did you know security found some people burgling your shop? There was another gunfight there."

The young man grimaced and shook his head. "I'm not surprised.

They were searching the place as we left. She warned security they were armed."

"That was good, then. I do not approve of such violence. It's bad for business."

The old woman considered Rachel. "Jason is a good boy, if stupid when it comes to women. He wouldn't have brought you here if he really thought you meant me harm.

"So, Adam Hale's brother was a RIS agent. I would never have guessed. Tell me what happened to him."

Rachel shrugged. "I still don't know the details. People working for Janus took him months ago. It has something to do with the Disruptors."

That news elicited a scowl from Wu. "Those animals destroy everything they touch. The death they caused here is still fresh in my memory. A number of people I know died that day."

"Then perhaps it would interest you to know that Janus actually carried out the bombing to make it look like the Disruptors did it."

Wu froze. Then her expression turned thunderous. "You think me a fool? My patience is at an end."

"Adam Hale just called me with that news an hour ago," Rachel said calmly. "He'd been questioning a man who used to work for the RIS. The same man in charge of the people that shot up the park under the orders of someone at Janus."

Wu drummed her fingertips on the desk. "Adam Hale has been a good friend to my worthless grandson. I must hear what he says for myself."

"Then allow me to give you his number. He's on the run, too. We're trying to find a place to plan our next move in safety."

Wu dug into her desk and pulled out a com. No doubt one that wouldn't trace back to her. "Give me the number."

* * *

ADAM'S COM sounded just as soon as he'd left the area around Double Dick's shop. He didn't recognize the number, but only one person would be calling.

"I'm glad to hear back from you," he said. "I was starting to worry."

"It's not yet time to stop doing so, Mister Hale," an unknown woman said. "The woman and Jason Chang have come to me with a story that I want to hear you confirm."

He stopped and stared at the com. "I don't know you."

"Hale, just tell her what you told me in the message," Price said from somewhere nearby. "Before she shoots me."

"That's not the best way to win friends," he told the unnamed woman.

"I'm giving you the benefit of the doubt, Mister Hale. For your friend's sake, tell me what I want to know."

It wasn't as if he really had a choice.

"Fine, but if you hurt her, I'll hurt you back. Understand?"

"That is a given, Mister Hale. Proceed."

He put his thoughts in order and started. "I told her that the Janus people found me. The ex-RIS spy died in the attack, but he told me something new before he fell. Janus is somehow connected to the Disruptors. They set the explosives here to make it seem as though the group were behind the attack. It was some kind of camouflage."

The woman made a noncommittal sound. "That is difficult to accept at face value. And you believed him?"

"I was about to toss his ass out a window, so I'm thinking he was honest, for once. It kind of fits with the other information we've been able to dig up. Damned if I know why Janus would be involved, though. Is that what you wanted to hear?"

"It's enough to buy you time to explain this to me in more detail. They say you seek a place of safety. I will see to that in exchange for all the information you possess about this attack and Janus."

"I don't know you."

The woman chuckled. "Ah, but you do, I suspect, if only by reputation. I am Grandmother Wu."

That put this into a different perspective. Wu was the undisputed head of the criminal element here on the station. She was also Jason's actual grandmother.

"I suppose I do. Your word is good with me. What now?"

"I will hand this com to one of my associates, and he will direct you to a place of safety. I will accompany Jason and your friend there and you will tell me the complete story. If what you say is true, there is a cancer on this station and blood is called for."

He laughed without much humor. "Then I can assure you that you'll hear a lot more than you bargained for. These people are scum. I'll see you soon."

A man came on the line and gave him directions to a building in Chinatown. It was a safe enough area, not like the old vids from Earth, but closemouthed. If Grandmother Wu hid them, they'd stay undiscovered. Even from Janus.

He put the com away and started walking. Things were beginning to fall into place. It felt as though they'd almost discovered what had happened to Zane. If they could get their hands on Evans, they'd know for sure.

24

Grandmother Wu led the way through the back of the restaurant and out to the loading dock. A battered delivery truck stood waiting for them with its rear door already raised.

Inside, it wasn't set up for cargo, but for passengers. Someone had ripped the seats out of another vehicle and bolted them to the floor.

"Do buckle up," Wu said. "This truck doesn't have the smoothest ride."

"I take it you need to move people around without them being seen," Rachel said as she strapped herself in. She watched one of the guards tie their pack of weapons to the side rail. They'd put her pistol in with the rest. Trust only went so far, it seemed.

"Some that arrive on this station don't wish to be found again," the old woman said with a shrug. "In those cases, moving them to a place of safety while shielding them from prying eyes is worth a goodly sum.

"Tell me, Agent Price, if Janus is indeed working with the Disruptors, how do you intend to expose them? Why not call someone back on Earth?"

"If only it were that easy," Rachel said with a sigh. She explained how Janus was blocking direct communications with anyone else.

"Interesting," Wu said. She held out her hand and took the com that one of the guards handed her.

"I need you to send a message to your sister on Earth," she said after making a call. "Inquire about your nieces. Send it now while I wait."

A few moments later, her eyes narrowed. "I see. Call me when it goes through." She handed the com back to the guard.

"It seems you are correct about the 'technical difficulties' the station arrays are experiencing. Another point in your favor. So, they will not allow suspicious messages out until they deal with you. That could prove awkward if it takes long."

Rachel nodded. "I hope so. The only way to stop them is to get word to RIS headquarters. To the Inspector General, to be precise. I'm certain that someone in my chain of command is involved."

"Oh?"

"The man we're interested in at Janus has a sister in the RIS. She's my boss's boss and almost certainly dirty. I have to get to someone who can see that she doesn't make my report vanish as effectively as they made Zane Hale disappear."

The van came to a stop, and the back door slid up. They were inside a warehouse of some kind, Rachel decided as she climbed out.

Wu walked to a door in the wall. It opened into a home of some kind. The sudden transition from commercial space to residential was pretty jarring.

The old woman smiled. "The entrance to this home lies on the other side of the block from the warehouse. An unaffiliated associate that is not connected to my business or me supposedly owns it. As a spy, I believe you would call it a 'safe house.'"

She gestured toward the chairs in the living room. "Please sit. One of my guards will make refreshments. The tea is excellent, though we also have coffee for those without refined tastes."

"Tea sounds fine," Rachel said. "To answer your question, I'm hoping your organization has access to a suitable transmitter."

The old woman shook her head. "Sadly, we do not. There has

never been a need to have a covert system. Perhaps one of the ships visiting the port?"

Now it was Rachel's turn to shake her head. "Their transmitters aren't that powerful. The fastest way we could use them to get a message to Earth would be to send someone there with it."

"That can be done, of course, but help would likely come too late for you. We shall consider other possibilities."

Once the steaming tea arrived, Rachel pondered the alternatives while she sipped the admittedly excellent drink.

"Perhaps there is someone who can help us," she said after a few minutes. "I met a reporter. Surely, someone with a journalist's connections could get a message out. Or at least be ready to tell the story when the time comes."

The old woman nodded. "It can't hurt to try. Give her a com."

One of the guards handed Rachel a com, and she looked up the reporter's number on the network.

He answered after a few rings.

"Hello again, Mister Enright. This is Rachel Price."

A loud squeak told her the man had just sat up straight in his chair. "Holy cow. What the hell did you do, lady? Security is looking for you as a 'person of interest' in the park shooting. Then a bunch of guys shot it out with security at Adam Hale's shop."

"I'm willing to explain everything to you in exchange for a favor."

"That depends on what the favor is," the man said guardedly.

"I want you to get the details of this story to someone on Earth. Before you say that I could do it myself, a simple call will show you that communications are being held up just to keep me from doing that."

"That's a pretty serious charge," the man said. "I'm not that big on conspiracy theories."

She waited a moment for him to make up his mind, and continued when he didn't speak. "Why don't we meet and you can hear me out for yourself. All I ask is that you don't involve security."

The man sighed. "I could get into a lot of trouble for something like that."

"You could, but sometimes getting the hottest stories means taking risks. If security picks me up, you'll miss out on the most sensational scoop of your life."

After a very long pause, he spoke. "I'm probably going to regret this, but I'm in. Where will we meet?"

"Give me your com number and I'll call you in an hour with details. Expect that someone is watching you, so no double-crossing. I'll see you soon."

Rachel hung up and returned the com to the guard, who started taking it apart. This operation was eating up a lot of communications gear.

Wu nodded her appreciation. "That was well done. I can have someone pick him up and bring him here after they search him for listening and tracking devices. That will give you time to explain the situation to me."

"I'll start as soon as Hale gets here."

"I'm already here," Hale said as he walked in from the kitchen with a guard at his back. He gave Jason and her a long look. "I'm glad to see you two in one piece."

"It's been close a few times," Rachel admitted.

Wu pointed to a chair. "Now you can explain this situation to me in full detail, Agent Price. Leave nothing out."

* * *

ADAM SAT beside Jason while Price laid out the situation for Grandmother Wu. He leaned over and whispered into his friend's ear. "What is she going to do? Turn us in for the reward, if there is one?"

His friend shook his head. "She doesn't cooperate with security like that. If she doesn't think she can trust you, she'll make you disappear. But I wouldn't worry too much about that."

"She's a real piece of work. Why shouldn't I worry?"

"Because she'd have already gotten rid of Price if that was the way things were looking. Trust me, she's already interested in this. That isn't to say she won't find some other way to come out ahead with the inside information, though."

Jason shook his head and smiled ruefully. "Dude, your brother was a spy? That's so cool."

"My brother was an asshole. I'd rather not have anything to do with him. If someone hadn't tried to kill me, I'd have told Price to get lost.

"Speaking of trying to kill me, I figured out who sabotaged the ship. It was Double Dick."

His friend scowled. "That bastard. He'll wish he was dead once I get my hands on him."

"Funny thing. He was dead when I found him in his shop. Someone wanted to make it look like a suicide, but we both know that isn't Double Dick's speed."

"Shit," the smaller man said. "There's someone else involved. Couldn't you be just a tad less epic in offending everyone around you?"

Adam smiled. "I don't do half measures. I found his stash and his financials. He kept everything in cash and hard metals. He also used initials for the people or businesses he dealt with. I'm hoping Price can decipher it."

Jason shook his head. "Let my grandmother figure it out. She has people plugged into every sector of this station. If anyone can put a name to them, it's her."

"What about finding fingerprints? I'm betting whoever paid him didn't wear gloves. Accessing that kind of database is going to take…"

Adam shook his head. "Never mind. Of course your grandmother has people in security on her payroll. Fine, I'll run it by her."

Price was wrapping up her presentation. "So, we think Janus is using the Disruptors. That probably means there's something buried in all the chaos those asses are causing that benefits Janus.

"The problem is sorting it all out and nailing it down. Once the RIS knows that they need to be looking, I hope they can spot a pattern. To get that started, I need to get a message to them."

Wu nodded slowly. "That is a good beginning, but it will not help you personally. You must strike the head off the snake and then vanish. Hiding from security on this station will be difficult for longer than a few days. Impossible for as long as help would take to arrive. The only successful strategy to save your lives is to leave Jove Station.

"The outgoing ships will be heavily screened, and even if I arranged to smuggle you onto one of them, the crew would discover you before long and hold you for a shuttle from the station. This is a tricky puzzle. I shall need to consider it carefully."

Adam cleared his throat. "While you're doing that, I have some information to add. The people that sabotaged my ship are definitely different from the ones working for Janus. I made a trip to a fellow diver's place and found him dead. There was a suicide note, but he wasn't the kind of guy that would kill himself.

"I took some stuff from his place that the person behind it might have touched, and I got his financial records. Something in there might just close off the second mystery. Oh, and according to Jason's girlfriend, Zane smuggled a crate out of secure holding on the port. She has no idea where it went or what was in it, but I'm betting it led to them killing my brother."

Wu glared at her grandson. "I do not like that woman. Grow up, boy." Then she frowned at Adam. "I am not in the habit of doing favors for free. The work for Agent Price promises to pay quite well. How much will you pay for this work you desire?"

He grinned. "Ten percent. I figure Double Dick owes me at least that much. It's in the bag I brought."

The guard lifted the bag onto the coffee table with some effort. Everyone leaned forward with their eyes wide when the man opened it.

"Jesus!" Jason swore. "How much money is in there?"

"I didn't bother counting it," Adam said. "Way more than Double Dick should have. The pad on top has his financials, but he only used initials to identify the other party. I'm hoping the person or persons behind the sabotage handled the money and left fingerprints. I assume you have someone in security that could run them down."

The old woman nodded, her eyes alight. "Ten percent is quite acceptable. I will have someone scan the money to isolate fingerprints of interest while one of my people knowledgeable in such things deciphers the man's financial transactions. It may take some time, but this should provide useful information."

Wu smiled at Price. "I shall take your initial payment from this as well. Your organization may repay Mister Hale."

"Don't worry, Hale," Price said. "I'm good for it. Unless I die. Then you're screwed."

Price smiled at Wu. "Is that good enough for me to get my weapons back? Oh, Hale, I brought a selection from your private reserve."

He grinned. "Excellent. I was starting to feel underdressed."

The older woman snapped her fingers, and a guard brought the bag over to Price. "My man will see that the reporter is vetted. Once he is certain there are no watchers, he will strip the man of any recording devices and take him to another building I own. You can meet him there."

She turned her attention to Adam. "While Agent Price does that, I find myself curious about this storm diving. If you want to kill yourself, can't you find a simpler method?"

He sighed. It was going to be another of those conversations. Why did everyone think he was crazy?

25

Rachel considered possible approaches she could take with the reporter as Grandmother Wu's man drove her across the station. Enright knew something was going on because of the shootings. She needed to get him firmly on her side as quickly as possible. Then, he might be able to use his contacts to get a message out. Somehow.

The driver pulled in behind an ethnic Chinese grocery, but led Rachel to the other side of the alley. The business there seemed focused on some kind of manufacturing. With all the materials being harvested in the belt, it was often more cost-effective to have the raw ingredients shipped to other locations so they could create whatever they wanted locally.

None of the workers paid them the slightest mind as the man led her upstairs. Several offices there probably served the workers below. He selected one seemingly at random and ushered Rachel inside. This one seemed like a spare, as there were no personal belongings.

His com rang, and he spoke for a few moments. "The reporter is clean," he told her after he'd disconnected. "One of my associates will bring him here in just a few minutes. He won't know where he is, so don't mention anything about this place or Grandmother Wu."

She considered giving him a lecture on operational security, but decided that would probably be rude.

Rachel sat behind the desk and queued everything on her comp. She only knew the reporter had arrived when the guard cleared his throat.

Another man escorted Enright into the office. They'd put a bag over his head and tied his hands in front of him. That seemed like a little bit of overkill.

The two guards let themselves back out of the room and closed the door behind them.

She rose to her feet and removed the bag. "My apologies, but a girl can't be too careful. Let me cut you loose." She used a pocketknife to cut his bonds.

Enright rubbed his wrists. "I feel as though I'm in some kind of noir movie. You don't have any gold statues you're looking for, do you?"

Rachel didn't understand whatever he was referring to and decided to ignore it. "I realize this must seem overly dramatic, but some very powerful people are trying to kill not only myself, but Adam Hale. If you'll hold your questions, I'll tell you everything right now."

Using the comp as necessary, she laid out the events that had brought her to this place and provoked the hostile response from Janus. Then she told him her suspicions.

The reporter seemed unconvinced when she'd finished. That was probably natural. His field required more than a healthy bit of doubt when someone told him a story.

"This's pretty hard to swallow. Even if I believed any of it, my editor would laugh me out of the newsroom. Lady, all you have is supposition. Do you actually have any real evidence?"

"You can test some of my story yourself. Send a message and see if they delay it. Contact security and find out who they think is shooting up the station."

The man grunted. "They're being less than forthcoming. They have a few images that someone took of people they're very interested in. You and Hale are among them. If there's a theory beyond that, they're not sharing it."

She perked up. "They're looking for some of the shooters? Let's see who they are."

Rachel used her com to look for the alert and sent the images to her comp. They popped up on the screen. One of them was very recognizable.

"Here we go. Compare this man on the left with the record I showed you of the ex-RIS spies."

He leaned forward and examined them closely. "I'll admit they seem to be the same person, but that's not very much."

"I know. All I'm asking you to do is contact someone on Earth and give them the files. How can that hurt?"

He scowled but slowly nodded. "I might have a way to do that, but I'm going to have to run all this past my editor."

"You can't tell him I'm a RIS agent. That's classified. Just tell him I'm an investigator for the government."

"Honestly, if there hadn't been an attack at Hale's place, I might not even believe this much."

She smiled. "Then let me give you another hot lead you can check out. Port security is looking for Zane Hale. He slipped into secure storage and had a crate shipped out. No one knows what was in it or where it went, but they're all stirred up."

"I'd heard something had them excited. I'll see if I can confirm any of that story. Whatever is happening, it has Janus in an uproar bigger than when the Disruptors hit the station.

"The port is on total lockdown. No one in or out, except employees in groups. They've also locked down their headquarters and the docking bays under their control. And an area in the civilian bays that I hadn't thought they were in charge of."

She handed him a data chip and grabbed the bag. "Here's everything. I suggest you keep this close to your vest or you'll disappear. It also has my contact number. Use it sparingly. Now, close your eyes and they'll take you back out and release you."

Once he was gone, she considered her options. They needed to do something soon, or Janus would catch them. Somehow, they had to find out what Evans and his people were really up to. Fast.

* * *

ADAM LISTENED to Price lay out what she'd learned from the reporter. None of it was surprising.

"We might be able to hide for a while longer," he said slowly, "but that's just pissing on the forest fire. We need to get our hands on Evans. He can tell us everything about what Janus is doing. He knows what happened to Zane."

He shook his head and smiled wryly at Price. "I had a realization while you were out. You know how you thought Zane came here because of me? Well, he didn't. He was onto this conspiracy and it just happened to involve my history."

"That doesn't mean he wasn't trying to clear you."

"Then he'd have contacted me. I can see where you might think that, but you're his partner. You almost have to like him.

"It took me a long time to realize it, but all he really cares about is himself. I'm still going to make whoever killed him pay, but that's just a matter of principle."

Wu had sent Jason off to do something and now sat alone with the two of them. "Janus is well guarded. How will you slip past their guards and seize this man? Once you have him, what will you do to make him talk?"

Price patted her bag. "I have something that will get him chattering. We don't even need to get him out of the Janus building. We only need about half an hour alone with him."

"I might be able to get us in," Adam said. "I know some people and I have access."

Wu shook her head. "They will be wary of you. You must slip in unseen. Just as your brother did in the port."

"I have a program running in their comps," Price said. "I might be able to use it to generate false identification for us. I need to access it and see what it's penetrated."

"I can call a few people and get something rolling on my end, too," Adam said. "Even with valid codes, we still need to find a badge reader without live guards. My team can get me the information I need."

"Do you trust them so highly?" Wu asked. "Will they break the law and company rules for you?"

"I suppose we'll find out," he said with a grin. "Maybe once I tell them the real story. It shouldn't take me more than a couple of hours to get what we need. If you don't hear back from me, then assume they turned me in to Janus."

"Have Jason help," Wu ordered. "Two people telling the story will be more believable than one. Your associates know both of you well. It will help convince them."

* * *

Once Hale was gone, Grandmother Wu focused her attention on Rachel. "While they are occupied, there is something you can do for them.

"The fingerprints on the money Adam recovered are indeed a match for someone on the station, but the identity of the person will cause both Adam and Jason much pain. The C.S. in the transaction book is Cindy Stevens."

Rachel found her eyebrows rising. "As in Chang's girlfriend? You're sure?"

"There is no doubt."

"Why would she try to kill Jason's best friend and frame him for the crime?"

"I have no idea," Wu said. "I've never liked the woman, and now I know why. I could take care of the problem myself, but it seems more suited to your skills.

"Besides, if I were to have her taken, someone might tell Jason, and that would damage my family. No, I think you owe them both enough to solve this problem."

Rachel nodded. "They've gone out on a limb for me, so I'll deal with her. What do you think I should do with her when I'm finished asking some hard questions?"

The old woman's eyes glittered. "Personally, I think you should skin her alive and toss what remains out an airlock. However, I've been known to be vindictive.

"If you can get enough evidence to turn her over to security, I suppose that will be enough. Barely. Perhaps you could beat her until that pretty face bleeds first."

"I can go over to her place and ask if she turned up anything on that crate Zane stole. It will make a good excuse to start the conversation."

Rachel smiled coolly. "Based on what might happen, I think I'd best borrow a vehicle without a driver."

"An excellent thought. I will see that you have what you need."

Once Rachel had the van, she drove near the woman's apartment and looked for observers. She found a man in a larger van just up the street. She was pretty sure he was one of the group who'd shot at them in the park.

Well, she couldn't let him see her here or they'd all come calling. Her best course of action was to take him out. He might be able to answer a few questions in the process.

She parked behind the man's van and gathered Zane's kit and her shocker. Gunshots would draw all the wrong kinds of attention, so she'd prefer to keep this quiet.

Once she was sure that the man's attention had settled back on the apartment up the street, she climbed out through the rear door of her van and made her way quickly behind the vehicle in front of her. A quick moment with her picks served to unlock his rear door.

She hefted the shocker, opened the door, and climbed in.

That's when she discovered his was a more sophisticated surveillance van than she'd anticipated. The rear contained a console with a number of monitors. A woman wearing headphones was watching them.

Rather, she had been right up until Rachel had opened the door beside her.

The woman went for something at her waist, so Rachel poked her with the shocker. The woman did the electricity dance and slumped in her chair.

That got the attention of the driver, who was out of the seat and coming for Rachel by the time she turned her focus to him.

He was a bit taller than Jason Chang and quick. A knife glittered in his hand as he tried to stab her. His other hand held her arm, immobilizing the shocker. The sudden stress set her injured side to blazing.

Rachel positioned her leg behind him and used it as a fulcrum to slam his head into the console. He collapsed to the floor without any further fight.

The condition of his head told her he wouldn't be causing any more trouble. He also wouldn't be answering questions.

Rachel leaned over when her bruised muscles complained. They still hadn't gotten over slamming into the building.

Once the pain died down a little, she tied the woman up with some handy wire. Rachel would take this van back to Grandmother Wu, and they'd have someone else to interrogate.

First, though, she needed to finish the mission at hand.

After she'd disabled all the coms in the van, she climbed out and observed the people walking by. No one seemed to feel that anything interesting had happened. Perfect.

Rachel crossed the street with the shocker tucked into the back of her pants with her blouse covering it. Depending on what Cindy had to say, she might need it again very soon.

26

Adam met with his key people over the space of an hour. It was more than a bit heartwarming. Jason drove one of his grandmother's vans while Adam and their guests talked in the back.

Between them, they knew of several low-traffic ways into the headquarters building. It was always possible those entrances had guards now, but he and Price only had to find one chink in the armor. The men and women he spoke with would poke their noses into the possibilities and get back to him.

One interesting piece of information came up during the discussions. Part of the docks that most people considered public had a heavy guard posted. For the life of him, Adam couldn't come up with a reason for that.

So, being the nosey sort, he decided he'd check it out.

Jason parked nearby, and the two of them casually made their way to the area that was now under guard. Armed guards in Janus uniforms stood around the entrances to a large bay. One that they'd fully sealed.

They pulled back to where the guards wouldn't see or hear them.

"That makes no sense," Jason said. "What the hell is in there? Better yet, what's worth putting armed thugs around it?"

"I have no idea. That said, I'm wondering if we can find out."

"They're not going to be cooperative if you ask to have a tour."

"No, so I'll need to be sneakier than that. I need you to run to the store and pick me up a wrist com and a remote controlled toy truck."

A look of understanding came across his friend's face. "I think I see. Be right back."

Once Jason was gone, Adam moved over to one of the bays near the suspicious area. It was currently unoccupied, and the door was unlocked. He wondered if that was because no one needed it or because Janus wanted it empty.

The air circulation grid feeding these bays was too small to allow a human being inside, but he thought a toy would fit without any problems. He left everything alone and made his way back outside to wait for Jason.

His friend made it back about twenty minutes later. He handed Adam a large box with a remote controlled blue truck. "Sorry it took so long. I had to try a couple of places to find one with longer range."

"Good thinking," Adam said. "The bay next to the target is unoccupied. I have no idea if they patrol it, but it was clear a few minutes ago. I'll get this toy going while you keep watch up the front. Once we get the truck in place, we can control the thing from out here."

He opened the box and pulled out the small truck. It would easily fit through the vent. The bumper worked nicely for attaching the com, too. The video feed would be at about the right height to peer through the grates.

The com was a standard wrist unit, so the straps fit on the truck's bumper just fine. He set the com to silent and auto answer. That way he could just leave it in place and call back later without running the battery down.

Adam left Jason in the front of the bay and started removing the grate. He worked slowly to avoid making any unnecessary noise. Once it was open, he slid the truck inside and ran it forward a little to be sure it worked the way he wanted. Only then did he put the grate back in place.

"What are you doing in here?" a woman's voice asked from up front.

Adam crouched lower and moved up until he could see what was happening. A woman in a Janus security uniform was looking suspiciously at Jason from near the front door.

"I'm looking over the bay to see if I like it," Jason said. "Why? Is it yours? The door wasn't locked and it looks unused."

The woman put her hands on her hips, and her eyes narrowed. "This area is off-limits. You need to leave."

"Off-limits? What are you talking about?"

"Turn your skinny ass around and walk off before I arrest you."

"Seriously? This isn't a Janus facility. You can't arrest anyone."

Adam slid along the circumference of the bay until he was safely behind the woman. If Jason could distract her, Adam might be able to slip out unseen. He gave his friend a rolling gesture with his fingers to keep things going.

Jason turned and took a few steps into the bay. "Come on. This place has so much space just sitting here empty. I just want a rental quote. How much?"

The woman followed his friend, giving Adam just the break he'd been hoping for. On silent feet, he slipped out the door and walked casually away from the bay. He arrived back at their hiding space just in time to see two more Janus guards arrive.

Moments later, they ejected Jason. His friend brushed his clothes off and yelled back into the shop. "You don't have to be asses about it."

He sauntered away under the watchful gaze of the female guard.

Once he was gone, she spoke with the two men and then returned to the other bay. They remained where they were. Adam wouldn't be getting back into that bay anytime soon, so he hoped everything worked.

Jason slid up next to Adam. "Man, she was uptight."

"For someone who lures women in like flies, you're not very persuasive with the fairer sex."

"I got you out of there, didn't I?"

"Sure enough. Let's get this thing moving. I hope the signal is strong enough from out here."

Adam called the makeshift video camera with his com. The image was clear, though somewhat dark. Not surprising. This wasn't dedicated monitoring gear with all the bells and whistles.

He sent the truck slowly down the air vent toward the guarded bay. It took a few minutes—and a number of course corrections to stay away from the walls—before he saw the light growing brighter ahead.

Once he had the new vent in sight, it took a little effort to get the com looking out into the bay itself. What he saw surprised him.

There was a ship about ten times the size of his sitting in the middle of the bay. What set it apart from the run-of-the-mill boats one saw every day was that it had aerodynamic lines. It was designed for runs in atmosphere.

He examined the engines and hull as well as he could on the small com screen. It looked as though it had magnetic protection like a dive ship, but he couldn't understand why. That thing was a monster. The drag had to be terrific. Why make a pig instead of a swan?

What the hell did Janus even need with a dive ship anyway?

They'd modified the bay, too. There was a hatch directly under the ship. Someone wanted to be able to go in and out without anyone being aware of them at all.

Interesting. He wasn't sure what they were doing here, but it had to be important. Add in the secrecy, and this was probably connected to Janus's schemes. Now all he needed to do was figure out how.

* * *

RACHEL SLOWED down when she saw Cindy's door was slightly open. With the hall clear, she pulled her pistol and came in ready for trouble only to find an empty apartment. Everything was in place, but no one was there.

The only thing that stood out was a folded piece of paper on the coffee table. She picked it up and scanned it after closing and locking the door.

If you haven't figured it out by now, you soon will, so I'm going to save us all a lot of trouble.

I know you've found my associate, but you didn't call security. That means it's only a matter of time before you figure out who was pulling his strings. Since people have been asking about someone with my initials, you've found something I missed and are most of the way there. Congratulations.

I'm sure it would've been a lot more satisfying for you if you'd busted in here and asked me some pointed questions, but I have no intention of getting caught up in whatever it is you're involved with. Seriously, you people are psycho.

While it would be very convenient of me to leave a nice, clear confession letter for you, that kind of thing leads to arrests and stays in places with bad food and worse company. I'll pass.

Instead, I'll let you figure it out for yourselves while I move on to less hectic parts of the solar system.

What I will *leave you, since it has nothing to do with me, is a name. I figure I owed Adam at least that much, even though I've already given him a gambler's chance. Which he won, you'll note. Lady Luck was on his side.*

My contact with port security called back with the name and address the crate went to.

Of course, there was no one there by that name and the damned thing was long gone, so they're still freaking out. Maybe you'll find it first or make sense of the shipping data.

The crate went to Baumgartner and Merrick Import and Export on Delta level. D-157-Q4 to be precise. The building was empty, abandoned for at least a decade, and no business by that name has ever existed on the station.

We'll never meet again, so I feel safe enough wishing you all the best with your current difficulties. Frankly, if you survive the week, I'll be amazed.

Ta.

Rachel put the note into her jacket pocket. There was no confession, but they'd find out why she'd done what she'd done eventually. At least her involvement explained how they'd planted Jason's DNA. She'd probably collected his skin cells with those long nails of hers. Probably the blood, too.

She hadn't said a word about Jason or their relationship. That was going to hurt the man. She'd obviously used him for his access to the diver community.

Rachel made a pass through the apartment, looking for anything interesting, being careful to wipe her prints away behind her, but found nothing useful. The woman had taken the essentials and abandoned everything else.

Once Rachel was sure of that, she left the apartment. The woman in the Janus van was still unconscious, as expected. She climbed into the driver's seat and drove back to Grandmother Wu's safe house.

The guard in the warehouse was surprised at the prisoner and the dead body, but he didn't make a fuss. That told her a lot about Wu's business right there.

They got her inside the residence and tied the woman up to a handy chair. Rachel then sent the guard off to recover the dead man's ID, dispose of his body, disable any tracking on the Janus vehicle, and retrieve the van she'd left behind.

Having minions was good. Even if it was only temporary.

Wu came in just as Rachel was finishing. She frowned at the prisoner. "This is not the woman Jason is enamored with."

"No," Rachel said as she set her kit onto the table and opened it up. "She's gone, though she did leave a note. She heard something about people looking for C.S. and decided it was time to head for greener pastures."

"A wise decision," Wu said grimly. "My people have determined where the large sums of money came from. Gambling."

Rachel nodded as she measured an injection of her favorite interrogation drug. "Money is one of the big ones. Since she infiltrated the divers group, I assume she was manipulating things to bet on them. With the games taking place, I'm sure the wagers are pretty large."

"Indeed, though in a worse manner than you suspect. She sabotaged divers and bet on their deaths to profit."

That stilled Rachel's hands, and she stared at the older woman. "Seriously? That's sick. If I'd had any idea, I'd have killed her already. I don't suppose there's a chance she's still on the station."

"We shall see. If so, it's possible that I can arrange something. If not, I still may be able to insert one of my people as a passenger to see that a suitable accident befalls her on the way to her destination.

"If all else fails, I can pay another organization to deal with her at the other end. No one crosses my family and lives to brag about it. Even if my grandson is an idiot."

"We don't need to mention this to them right now," Rachel said. "They have more pressing matters to focus on."

Wu nodded. "I think that wise. Who is this?"

Rachel finished laying out her gear and stepped back from the table. "She works for Janus. She and her dead partner were monitoring the area around Cindy's apartment for visitors. Probably hoping Jason would turn up."

"What do you hope to learn from her?"

"Their current plans. What they hope to accomplish. What she knows about security around Evans. We need to strike soon and I want to have as much intelligence as we can get. Once Hale gets back with a way into headquarters, I'll get us in."

The older woman raised an eyebrow. "How will you accomplish this? A false ID?"

Rachel nodded. "I've had time to check my bots. I can swap out some key details in an ID and make it work.

"For example, I can't forge a new set of identification. There are chips that I can't clone so easily. However, I can change this woman's file to have my appearance and use it to get in with her access. The dead guard can stand in for Hale."

"If they have access to the areas you need."

"That's a concern," Rachel admitted, "but these people worked for Evans. I'm thinking this will work out.

"Back to Cindy. She left some information relevant to that missing crate. Could you see if your people can figure anything out about it?" She handed the woman the note.

Grandmother Wu read it slowly. "I will have my people make inquiries."

"I hope they can track it down," Rachel said. "It might give us another angle on what Zane was up to."

A guard came in and whispered into Wu's ear. She nodded and dismissed him.

"Jason and Adam are back. They seem excited."

"Good," Rachel said. "Maybe they found an easier way into the headquarters building."

The female prisoner moaned.

"Our guest is waking up. Excellent. Things are finally starting to break our way."

27

Adam watched Price question the woman she'd captured with more than a bit of interest. He'd never been present at an RIS interrogation before. He wasn't counting the one in the cargo area, since she hadn't finished it.

She took it a lot easier on the prisoner than he'd have expected. No harsh verbal commentary and she even told the woman that if she cooperated, they'd stash her until this was over.

"You think she means it?" Jason asked him quietly.

"Yeah. I'm not sure why, but I do. Did your grandmother get anything out of the equipment in the van?"

"Not that she's said. But something's up. She's behaving a little weird. There's something she hasn't told us."

"About this?"

His friend shrugged. "I'm not sure. Maybe she'll tell you if you ask nicely. I'll just get a stern look. It's like I'm four."

Adam grinned. "That's not too far off. I'll go see what I can find out while you keep an eye on the proceedings."

He slipped out of the residence and found Grandmother Wu talking to one of her guards in the warehouse.

She gestured for him to approach. "Has your friend broken the prisoner yet?"

"Not yet. The drugs are starting to take effect, though. I wanted to ask you about something else. Jason seems to think you're holding something back, and I'd like to know what it is."

The old woman gave him a steady look, but relented. A small hand movement sent the guard away.

"This is not something that will help you in your current situation, but you deserve to know. I ask that you be sparing in what you tell my grandson as it will pain him greatly."

That didn't sound promising.

He listened to her story about Cindy with a sick stomach. "That bitch. Christ."

Adam rubbed his face with his hand. "No, I don't think I'll tell him about this just yet, but he's going to find out she's gone soon enough. Did she get away?"

Wu nodded. "She departed on the most recent flight to Mars. It was gone before I could get a man aboard. I'll have someone on the Red Planet deal with her."

"What about the crate?"

"None of my people are familiar with such a company. Security has already sealed the building the port delivered it to, but my contacts tell me there is no sign of anyone there. Your brother must have moved it again. I'm afraid it's a dead end."

The door to the residence opened, and Jason came out with a com. "That reporter Rachel spoke with is calling, but she says she can't break off the questioning or it'll screw up the woman's responses. She said for you to deal with him."

Adam took the com and unmuted it. "Hale."

"Mister Hale, it's an honor to speak with you. Malcom Enright, Republican News Service. I was expecting Miss Price."

"She's tied up at the moment. Perhaps I can help you."

"I'd imagine you can. I sent the message she requested. I had one of our techs bury it in a video file of the attacks here and sent it to the home office on Earth. It took a while for the station to let it out, but they finally did.

"Once I received the receipt from Earth, I sent a follow-up with hints to look into the data more deeply. I'm hopeful that will be enough since I can't make any live calls."

Adam smiled. "I'm sure that's the best anyone could ask for."

"Any chance I can get an exclusive interview with you? People will want to hear your side of this once things really break."

"Things are coming to a head, so I'm afraid not. I promise to send you any updates so that you can keep on top of the story."

The man sighed. "I suppose that's the best I could hope for."

Adam was about to disconnect when he decided to ask the man a question. "Before we go, have you ever heard of a company named Baumgartner and Merrick Import and Export?"

"As in Leann Baumgartner and Jenny Merrick? They died before I was born. I had no idea they founded a company."

He frowned. "Who are they?"

"I'm surprised you haven't heard of them. They solo climbed the summit of Olympus Mons with only the gear they brought with them. It was just after Earth founded the first settlement on Mars. They were major extreme sports figures of their day."

Okay, that was odd. If his brother had used their names on purpose, it had to mean something.

"Thanks for that bit of trivia, Mister Enright. Look for a call from me in the next day or so. Trust me when I say that this is going to go big. I'm not sure how, just yet, but I'm confident we really don't know the entire story."

"Good luck, Mister Hale. If the opportunity presents itself, I want an exclusive one on one."

"Deal."

Adam disconnected and removed the chips from the com. "That was interesting. Apparently, Leann Baumgartner and Jenny Merrick were mountain climbers. They did Olympus Mons way back."

"Hang on," Jason said, pulling out a com of his own. "We have an Olympus Mons Boulevard. That's not the official name, of course, but people have been calling it that for as long as I've been here."

The other man searched on his com and grunted. "I don't know if it's connected, but there used to be an import and export business there. Its name was Summit Import and Export."

"That can't be a coincidence," Adam said. "We need to go see what's there now."

Wu shooed them back toward the residence. "I will have some of my people take a casual look around, in case security has also made the connection."

The two men went back in to find Price winding up her interrogation. They sat in silence until she finished and gave the woman another shot. This one put her out.

Price sat down beside them. She looked tired.

"She works in Janus's security department. She does covert monitoring of people they're interested in. You, for example. I'll bet she's seen you naked."

"Lots of pretty women have seen me naked," Adam said. "What about the setup around Evans?"

Price shrugged. "She knows a little, but I'm not sure it'll be enough when the time comes. She wasn't in the inner circle. She has no idea they're working with the Disruptors and no clue what their secret agenda is."

"You're confident she wasn't holding back?"

Price nodded. "The drugs are damned effective. She told me everything she knew."

"Then it's a good thing we hit pay dirt. We found out what Janus is hiding on the docks." Adam handed her his com and connected it to the observation device.

She watched it curiously for a minute. "So they have a ship. I bet they have lots of them."

"That's a dive ship. A damned big one. Why would they need to go into Jupiter's atmosphere at all? There's nothing there of interest to a big company."

Jason shook his head. "Obviously not true. They've been paying big money for dive technology and data for years. It has to be for this. The question is what they use it for."

"You could always ask those people," Price said.

Adam took the com and examined the picture. A team of men

and women were going over the ship. It looked as though they were preparing it for a dive.

The door to the warehouse opened, and Wu stepped in. "My people are at the building once occupied by Summit Import and Export. It is not yet under surveillance, so I had them take a discreet look. I believe they have found your missing crate."

* * *

RACHEL GAVE the area around the former import export building a good look before she risked going inside. If she'd wanted to set up a trap for herself, this was exactly the right kind of thing to get her attention. Everything looked clear.

Whoever owned the place had kept it in good repair. Perhaps they hoped to use it again someday.

Grandmother Wu's people had already disarmed the alarm and opened the locks, so getting inside was as simple as walking in.

If anything, the interior was in better shape than the exterior. It wasn't furnished, but the owner had taken care to clean it thoroughly. Perhaps they were actively trying to sell or rent it.

If so, no one had come inside in the last few months. If they had, they'd have noticed the rather large crate in the middle of the ground floor.

Hale walked around the tall container slowly. "This is it. The original shipping instructions Zane used are printed right here. What do you think is inside it?"

"Damned if I know," she said. "My guess is that whatever's inside belongs to Janus. That's why they're so eager to catch us."

"Shall we open it up and see if it shines a light onto the conspiracy?"

She nodded. "Don't you need a tool?"

"Nah. Modern crates are self-opening."

Hale lifted a cover on the side of the crate, and pressed the button inside. The top lifted a little, and all four sides folded down to rest on the floor.

A massive machine took up most of the interior, but part of the crate held a full set of mission gear. It had everything she'd lost and more.

Rachel grinned. "This is going to make breaking into Janus a lot easier. Any idea what that thing is?"

She looked over at Hale as she asked the question and froze. He stood there with his mouth open, clearly shocked.

"What is it?" she repeated.

"This is a whole lot of trouble. It's an FTL drive."

"Seriously?" She looked at it closely. "I thought these things were so top secret that they never let one out of their sight until it was installed."

Hale ran a hand along the side of the machine. "That's right. I've seen exactly two in my time with Janus, and this is the second of the pair. How the hell did it get into the port at all? They don't even bring them onto the ship until just before we deliver it to the new owner. They have a special crew just for that. These things are booby-trapped."

She stepped back. "Then don't touch it. I don't want to get blown to tiny little bits."

He shook his head. "It's only going to go off if we try to open it. What do you have there?"

"It looks like a selection of the gear we normally take on missions, only more of it," she said as she started opening boxes to glance inside. "We're spies, so lots of monitoring gear, some intrusion tools, and weapons. Lots more than that, but you get the idea."

"Will it help us get into the headquarters building?"

She nodded with a smile. "Oh, yes. I can duplicate the cards we have so that the pictures actually look like us. We need to get this moved to a secure location. I don't trust that security won't come calling."

He walked over and spoke with Wu's people. They nodded, and one of them made a call.

Hale came back over. "They're getting a cargo hauler. They'll see the crate back to the warehouse. How long does it take to fix up the ID?"

"I can do it right now." She took a camera from the gear and snapped his picture. Then she scanned the dead guard's ID.

"I'll keep his uniform, but put your head in place of his." She downloaded the image into Zane's comp and unpacked the ID printer. It scanned the original badge's chips and accepted Hale's updated image. Five minutes later, she handed him a completely valid Janus ID.

"I'll need to update the files linked to these badges on their systems before we try to use them. I was saving that for last. Here, take my picture."

He took several images. "Smile. Normal people actually want to look good on their ID photos."

"You've seen how well that works at the DMV. If I smile, I look like a serial killer."

"Are you?"

She snatched the camera from his hands. "Jerk. Find out where that cargo hauler is. We need to get things going."

He frowned. "Just the two of us? That's a bit light, don't you think?"

She started constructing her ID badge. "Not really. If they catch us, we're screwed whether we have two people or ten. This is a sneak, not a smash. Get your head out of military mode."

"True," he said with a smile. "You know what our unofficial motto was on the strike teams? 'When it absolutely, positively has to be destroyed overnight.' I'm more used to blowing things up and shooting people."

"Save it for when we find out what they're up to. I'm sure you'll get to break things then."

Rachel looked over the comp's contents while her badge was printing. If Zane had left any other mission data, it would be here.

Unfortunately, it didn't seem as though he'd written any notes. That was too bad. She knew he often waited until a mission was over to type up his report, but that made piecing things together a lot harder.

What she did find was a schedule of some kind. Dates and times matched with what looked like latitude and longitude. The dates were all in the past. None was more recent than Zane's arrival on the station.

"I found something, but I'm not sure what I'm looking at. Are these coordinates for somewhere on one of Jupiter's moons?"

Hale looked over her shoulder. "I don't think so. I've been to all the major moons and there's nothing at these locations. Look at the times and dates. The coordinates are bouncing all over the place with each one."

She put her newly created Janus ID badge in her pocket. "Let's not ignore the obvious. They have a ship that they're getting ready to use. Can it make it to the moons?"

"Sure, but it couldn't land. They aren't built for that. They drop into the atmosphere and then boost back out. Jupiter's atmosphere slowly thickens up until it transitions to a supercritical fluid. I've been in that before. You can't see shit and you can't go very fast. Getting back out is a bitch."

Rachel hit the button and started closing the crate. "What about the coordinates? Are they a specific part of Jupiter?"

He nodded. "An area nearer to the northern pole. Call it the top quarter. They're all around that part of the planet. And before you ask, there's nothing there."

Several more of Wu's men came in and started fitting a lift to the crate. Rachel stepped back and shook her head at Hale. "The evidence suggests otherwise. Maybe Evans can tell us about it."

Hale smiled grimly. "He'll tell us everything he knows. Let's make this happen."

That's when a small commotion at the door started. Wu's men drew their weapons as a man walked into the building. Malcom Enright. The reporter had his hands up, and his eyes were huge.

"No need to shoot," he said carefully. "I'm just here to see Miss Price and Mister Hale."

The guards weren't at all pleased with this turn of events, but Rachel wasn't going to let them shoot the man.

"He stays with us. We'll blindfold him before we go anywhere sensitive. Put those away and get this crate out of here."

She turned her attention to Enright. "How did you find us and how did you get in?"

He smiled blandly. "Being a reporter means you have to be a researcher, at least if you intend to be a good one. I put a few facts together and spotted an unlikely coincidence. It led me here, as I suspect it did for you.

"As for getting in, I merely walked down the street as though I was going elsewhere, my eyes glued to my com like everyone else. I turned in to the building before the men watching the street could stop me. Is that the missing crate from the port? What's in it?"

Rachel shook her head, took his com, and disassembled it. She patted him down for anything else interesting. He was clean.

She stepped back and scowled at him. "You're far too nosey for your own good. Yes, it's the crate. And no, I'm not telling you what's in it."

The man pouted. "Ah, well. One can only try. I suppose now is a bad time for an interview?"

28

Adam watched Price stall the reporter until Grandmother Wu's men had the crate loaded. She only answered peripheral questions about what they were doing. That was to help keep the idiot safe. Janus would kill Enright if he knew too much.

Once they were ready to go, she put a hood over Enright's head.

They rode back to Wu's in relative silence once she stopped answering his incessant questions.

Adam arranged with Wu to keep the reporter locked up until this was all over. Things were about to get hot and heavy.

Price took the hooded reporter into the residence. She'd remove their gear and any incriminating data. They'd need some of it shortly. The rest wasn't safe to let the man snoop around.

Grandmother Wu wasn't pleased at the complication, but let it go. "What is in the crate your brother hid?"

"An FTL drive and his spy gear."

Her eyes widened. "That is indeed an unexpected turn of events. I can see why Janus might have killed him for such a grand theft. I wonder how much such a device is worth."

"A pile of money, but good luck getting it off the station."

"You're giving it to me?"

He grinned. "What would I do with an FTL drive? You need a ship for it to be useful. I can build one, and even fly it around in normal space, but I have no idea how the damned thing works."

"I shall ponder the possibilities."

Price came out of the residence shaking her head. "That man is a pain in my ass. More curious than a cat and smarter than he looks. He'd have made a good intelligence analyst. Did your people ever get back to you with information on the unguarded entrances?"

"Jason was supposed to gather that," Adam said, looking around for his friend.

"I sent my grandson to look into a few things," Wu said. "Mainly to keep him busy. He left a list of the currently unmanned entrances with me."

The older woman handed Price a data chip, which the spy plugged into her comp.

After studying the screen for a moment, Price nodded. "Several of these will work. Which one is closest to the supply department?"

He looked over her shoulder at a complete set of plans for the Janus building. She must've gotten it while she was hacking their system.

"This one," he said, pointing. "How are we going to fool the guards at the executive level? They might know me or the people we're masquerading as."

Price smiled. "I have a plan for that. I just need you to get us where they store everything."

She turned to Grandmother Wu. "Did you find appropriate uniforms for us?"

"Indeed," the older woman said. "I got them from the factory that makes them. The owner is an old friend. They are over here."

Adam followed her to a table and found the packaged uniforms. He pulled his out and read the label. It was his size.

Price picked hers up and gestured for him to turn around. "I don't allow men who haven't made me dinner to see me naked."

He laughed and did as she instructed. Once he stripped down, he found the uniform fit better than the one hanging in his own closet.

Price told him he could turn back around, and he found her dressed in an identical suit. They both looked like regular security personnel. They even had holsters for their pistols.

"Stash extra weapons and ammo in a bag," she said. "I'll take another one with my gear."

He selected ones he thought would be most useful if they ran into serious trouble. He brought more than enough ammunition. He wasn't running out again.

She gathered a bunch of gear from the crate. He had no idea what, but he trusted she knew her business.

Once they were ready, he commandeered Wu's van. He'd park it close enough to Janus for a quick getaway.

Approaching the building made him tense, but no one gave them a second look. After all, there were so many security people around already that the two of them blended right in.

The entrance they'd selected was unguarded, but he didn't relax until Price used her hack to update their badge files and it actually opened for them.

Once they were inside, he led her toward a cargo elevator that Janus used to get basic supplies into storage. It didn't go to any critical areas, so it didn't require them to use their badges.

It slowly took them down to the supply area. He stepped out when the doors slid open and scanned for people. The level seemed deserted.

"Now what?" he asked.

"We head to where we really want to go." She sent the elevator back up and pulled a tool from her bag. She used it to open the elevator doors.

To his surprise, the shaft continued down for several more levels. Ones the elevator had no buttons for.

"That's tricky," he said with a smile.

"The elevator used to service the executive levels, too. Security must've removed the capability after the supposed Disruptor attack, but they didn't block the shaft. Sloppy."

Price swung out onto the ladder. "Let's go see Mister Evans. I have a few pointed questions to ask him."

* * *

Rachel climbed down to the lowest level in the shaft and set her pack on the floor. There was a depression below the elevator doors to allow the elevator car to settle fully.

She used her light to see what she was doing. With the doors above them closed, it was close to pitch black in there. Most elevator shafts were lit, but not this one.

"The other side of this door is the supply area for the executives," she said. "Odds are good that it's empty, but we need to be on our toes."

She opened her comp and brought up the plans. "From here, we can skirt the outermost corridors until we get near Evans's office. The woman I captured said he has guards of his own, but not that many."

"Makes sense," Hale said. "He's safely down on the executive level. Once he's ready to leave, he'll boost his coverage. Are there any back ways into his office?"

"There is, actually. The adjoining office is listed as a spare. Its washroom is directly beside his. While we can't go from one to the other, we can climb into the ceiling and drop down into his washroom. It's behind his desk, so we should be able to surprise him."

She dug out her shocker and stuffed it behind her belt at the small of her back. "We'll try to leave no traces. It's best if they don't find the body until we're gone. They'll think he died of natural causes."

"You're going to kill him?" Hale asked with a scowl.

"You didn't have any problems shooting his minions. He's much worse than they are and he wants you dead just as badly."

"Yeah, but he isn't a combatant unless he's actually trying to shoot me. Killing him in cold blood is—"

"An execution," she said firmly. "Consider him guilty of war crimes. Since he undoubtedly had something to do with the Mars attack, he's guilty of exactly that.

"Look, we can't afford to let him escape. I'll record the interrogation. You might not like this, but it's the best option. We can't smuggle him out."

"But we can. The same way we're going in."

She sighed. "Why do you have to be so *stubborn?*"

"We have this pesky thing called rules of engagement. Murdering the bastard in cold blood isn't covered, even for war crimes. If we can get him out, that's what we need to do."

Rachel rubbed her face. "I'll consider it, if the extraction looks feasible. But you have to carry him."

"Done. Let's open this thing up and go get him."

She opened the elevator doors. As expected, the storage rooms were devoid of people.

The rooms let out into corridors only used by those who served the powerful. Of which security was a part.

Hale slipped the strap of his bag over his shoulder. "This way, right?"

She nodded. "Go straight until you hit corridor B3 and then turn right. Evans's guards won't see us at all. We'll come up on the other office from the far side."

Rachel tensed a little when they passed real security personnel, but the others only nodded cordially and kept walking.

Hale led them around the designated corner and then kept going until she cleared her throat. This section was clear of people, but she needed to hurry. Someone might come along at any moment.

She set her bag on the floor and extracted a toolkit. She used it to take the cover off the electronic lock and bypassed it. The door slid open, revealing a darkened office.

Rachel put the cover back on the lock, grabbed her bag, and headed inside. She closed the door behind Hale and snapped the lights on. It was deserted, just as advertised. It didn't even have furniture. Excellent.

Once she had her kit back together, she manually locked the entrance and stepped into the washroom. It was nice. The counter looked like real stone, and it was roomy. Imported marble had to be really expensive.

The tiles in the ceiling were the kind that pushed up. Perfect.

"I'll lead the way," she said. "They trained me to be quiet, and I don't want you falling through the roof at an inopportune moment. Once I take him down, I'll call you over."

"I'm not that clumsy," Hale objected. "They trained me to be quiet when I needed to be."

"Uh huh. That was ten years ago and quiet relative to shooting someone. Trust me, I'm the best person for this part of the mission."

"You're the spy," he said with a shrug.

Rachel climbed onto the counter and raised one of the tiles. She pushed her head into the darkened space and let her eyes adjust to the dim light filtering up from the washroom.

Evans's washroom was indeed accessible, but she'd need to be very careful how she supported her weight.

She looked down at Hale. "The overhead beams are sturdy enough to support our weight, but don't trust the slats between the tiles. Hand me my gear when I call for it."

Moving carefully, Rachel reached across the top of the wall and lifted the tile just a crack. Then she listened.

No sounds that indicated Evans was in his washroom, and the lack of light told her it was empty. She hoped he wasn't out. Waiting for him to come back would be a bitch.

She raised the tile a little further and saw that the washroom door was closed. That was a plus. It would serve to muffle any noise she made as she lowered herself down.

The strut over her head was metal and handy. She touched it with the back of her hand. One of her coworkers had found out the hard way that power conduits occasionally leaked energy into their supports. He'd fallen through a roof and landed on a table in the middle of a busy cafeteria. Talk about awkward.

She tugged it to be certain it was strong enough to support her weight. All good.

Rachel set the tile she was holding aside. She then lifted herself up and across before lowering her feet to the wash counter. The lights came on when the sensor detected her movement.

Once she had a solid footing, she dropped to the floor and looked around. This washroom was identical to the other, and it was blessedly empty, as expected.

She listened at the door but didn't hear any voices. That could be good or bad. Only time would tell.

The handheld monitor she'd pulled from her bag had a small, flexible tip that she slid under the door just far enough to see what was going on in the room. Security forces used devices just like this to scout a room before they burst in.

Unlike the empty office, Evans had decorated his with subtle, if expensive, taste. Dark woods and bright chrome meshed surprisingly well. His desk sat between her and his door.

Evans was present, working on something at his desk, his back to her.

She peered at the room as carefully as she could. The desk obscured the far side of the room, and it would be awkward to sneak in while he had someone sitting in her blind spot.

After a minute, she decided that he had to be alone. She'd take a closer look before actually rushing him.

A scuff behind her announced Hale's arrival. He had one of the bags in his hands. His disregard for her instructions was annoying, but at least he'd been right about being quiet.

He set her bag on the wash counter and reached back up for his. He hopped almost silently to the floor as soon as he'd put it down.

"What's the situation?" he said softly, his mouth beside her ear.

His warm breath sent a shock down her spine, causing an unwanted physical reaction. She obviously needed to get out more.

At least he knew that whispers carried. Softly speaking was better for keeping hidden.

She put her lips up to his ear. The scent of his hair was a further distraction. "He's in there, but I'll have to crack the door to be absolutely sure he's alone. We need to get him away from the desk without alerting the guards out front or letting him hit a hidden alarm."

"What's your plan for making him whisper while you question him?"

She smiled grimly. "I have my ways. If it looks clear, I'll open it slowly and then we pounce. You control his arms while I keep him quiet."

Rachel opened the door just a hair. Not enough for someone on the other side of the desk to see a big gap, but plenty to fit the flexible tip through at the top and see that the rest of the office was unoccupied.

Perfect.

She eased the door closed, opened her bag as quietly as possible, and swapped the monitor for a bulky mask suitable for going over someone's mouth and nose.

Rachel killed the lights and opened the door. It was blessedly well oiled. She'd have to send a complimentary note to maintenance.

They slipped up behind Evans together, and she slid the mask over his head and clamped it tight on his lower face.

Hale simultaneously wrapped his arms around Evans's torso and dragged him back in his chair. It obligingly rolled away from the desk as the man struggled.

She was certain Evans was screaming for help, but no sound emerged from the noise cancelling device she'd just put in place.

Once she was sure Hale had a good grip, she let go of the mask, trusting the straps to hold it tight. She pulled a set of cuffs out of her back pocket and locked Evans's hands behind the chair. She made sure they were brutally tight. A set of leg shackles from her bag secured his kicking feet.

Only then did she step back and smile. "It's a pleasure to finally meet you, Mister Evans. I understand you've been looking for me." She kept her voice pitched too low to carry.

The man glared at her, but no sound emerged from the mask.

"Oh, excuse me," she said with bland cheerfulness. "I'll need to grab some earbuds."

She split the pair with Hale. That way he could listen in and they both could have an ear free for trouble.

"That better?" she asked once the earbud was in place.

"You bitch," Evans snarled. "You'll never get out of here alive."

"If you only knew how many dead men have told me that," she said with a wink. "Now, let's get down to business. I have some nice drugs that will make you more than happy to tell us what we want to hear.

"And the good part? If you're half the bastard I think you are, I can give you a nice overdose that will mimic a heart attack and no one will be the wiser."

His eyes narrowed. "You can't win. Even if you kill me, there are too many people looking for you. This station will be your coffin. Give up now and I'll spare your life."

"Like you did for Zane Hale?"

"Exactly."

She opened her mouth to keep at him, but lost her train of thought. "What?"

Evans's eyes flicked to Adam Hale. "Your brother is still alive. He hid something we want. Once we get it, we're going to let him live."

"Why would you do that?" Hale asked, his voice a soft snarl. "Why the hell should I believe you?"

"That's the easiest part of this. I was reading a report on his condition just before you broke in. How the hell did you get in here, anyway?"

Rachel waved her hand in front of the monitor, bringing it to life. To her shock, it had a written report on her partner. It was dated less than two weeks ago. There was an attached video. She played it, making sure the volume was down.

The video came to life, showing Zane in some kind of cell. The lighting was strangely green, but it was him. His hair was long and unkempt, but he had the energy to glare at whoever was holding the recorder.

"Tell your boss he can eat shit and die."

The video ended with that.

Rachel blinked in shock. Holy shit. She'd given him up as dead, no matter what she'd said out loud. He was somewhere, and she was going to rescue him.

"Tell me where he is and I'll promise you your life," Hale said. "If you know anything about me, you know I'll keep my word and see that she does, too."

Evans laughed. "You'd never believe me. It's not somewhere you can just walk in and pick him up.

"Listen closely. Honestly, what he took isn't worth the trouble now. Our plans are far beyond that. In a very short time, it won't matter that any of you are alive, much less what you tell anyone else. You can join him and we'll let you go when this is over."

"Just like that?" she asked.

"Just like that," he said firmly. "None of this matters. Not the shootings on the station. Not the missing FTL drive. Not the people you've killed. None of it. If you want to live, you'd best think before you make a decision you can't take back."

Before she could answer, the main door opened and a guard ushered in a man dressed in an expensive suit. Everyone stood shocked for a split instant and then all hell broke loose.

Hale drew his pistol and shot the guard in the chest. The man went down hard, and the suit ducked back into the hall, screaming.

Two more guards rushed in, weapons up and firing. She shot one while Hale took out the other. A glance showed the guards hadn't hit her new associate.

"Grab Evans while I get the bags," she said. "Time to go."

"He's not going to be very useful."

She turned toward Evans. One of his eyes was missing, and blood covered his face. He wouldn't be answering any more questions.

Despair flooded into her as she grabbed the mask and retreated into the washroom with Hale. How the hell were they going to find Zane now?

29

Adam kept firing at the main doorway to keep the guard's heads down until he could slam the washroom door and lock it. That might hold them a minute. Which was all they needed to get clear.

Price scampered back into the ceiling. She was a lot more agile than he'd imagined. She'd be hell on an obstacle course.

He handed her both bags and followed her up. She put the tile back just as bullets began splintering the washroom door. Time was rapidly running out.

The two of them made it back into the empty office. He noticed she dropped the other ceiling tile back into place. He supposed it might keep them guessing where the two of them had actually gone for a little while.

"We need to get out of the building before they lock down every exit," he said as he holstered his pistol and hefted his bag.

"Walk quickly, but don't overreact," she said as she took the lead. "If someone confronts us, don't touch your weapon. Let me talk us out of it. There'll be a lot of security people moving around, and we can slip by in the confusion."

"I'm not an idiot."

She shot him a little smile. "No, you're not. You're actually pretty good at this kind of stuff. You might even cut it as a RIS agent."

"Pass. I'm happy doing what I do. Then again, I suppose I'm pretty much fired. I might need that job after all."

Two security men with their weapons drawn raced around the corner ahead of them. He tensed, but they barely glanced at Price and himself before they ran past.

Price led the way into the storage area, and he watched for pursuit as she opened the elevator doors. He followed her when she headed up, glad to have a closed door between them and the ruckus.

They made it back to the level they'd entered the shaft. A worker was unloading a pallet of what looked like toilet paper. He gave them an odd look as they stepped out of the empty shaft.

"There's a security alert," Price told him sternly. "You need to get to your designated area."

"What alert?" the man asked.

A loud, hooting alarm sounded in the distance. A woman's voice was saying something, but Adam couldn't make it out. Someone needed to consider tuning the speakers.

"That one," Price said to the man. "Move."

The man scampered off.

Adam pressed the elevator call button. "They'll be rushing people to the exits. If we can't get out before they block us, we're screwed."

"Pessimist. Follow my lead."

The exit looked clear from the inside, but they ran into half a dozen security personnel when they came out. The woman in charge of the squad scowled at them. "What are you doing here? Get back inside to your posts."

"We're assigned to the exterior roving patrol," Price said calmly. "We were in the gym."

She took two steps before the other woman stopped her. "IDs."

Price sighed in apparent exasperation. "My boss is going to be pissed when we're late."

"Uh huh," the woman said as she scrutinized the ID. "Who is that again?"

Adam made note of where people were standing. He could shoot a few of them before they brought their rifles up and mowed them down. This was it.

"Captain Krueger," Price said casually. "Big guy with a scar on his forehead. A real bastard if you piss him off."

The woman stared at Price for a long moment and then handed her ID back to her. She turned to Adam. "Badge."

He passed it over, forcing himself to relax. "Any idea what the alert is about?"

"Nope. Some kind of intruder drill, I think. They'll give us more details shortly. Ask Krueger."

She handed his badge back to him. "Now get out of here before I change my mind about letting you through."

It felt as though he had a target on his back as they jogged away. He knew the woman was watching them leave.

Once they were safely around the corner, Price sped to a full run. He easily matched her pace, and they made it past a number of security guards on the way to the van. All the forces outside were worried about people coming in, not leaving. In fact, there were a lot of security agents running around to blend in with.

He only relaxed when they were driving away from the Janus building.

"I can't believe they killed him before we found out where Zane was," Price said bitterly, her eyes still scanning for trouble. "We'll never save him now."

"I know where he is."

Her head whipped around. "You do? Where?"

"The evidence is right there in front of us," he said. "He's down in Jupiter's atmosphere."

He saw the pieces falling into place in her head, but she didn't seem convinced. "That makes no sense. What the hell would they need some place like that for?"

"So they can build their FTL systems without anyone being the wiser. Think about it. No one would ever know. No worries about spies or industrial sabotage. They've been paying divers like me for the technology to make it easier for decades."

"They use the ship you found to get down there?" she asked. "I suppose it's possible, but it seems really convoluted. Surely, they could make the damned things in a place that was a little more convenient."

Adam nodded. "Probably, but he said Zane was somewhere we'd never find him. That meshes with my scenario. Those coordinates and times you found. Those could be drops to pick up FTL units and leave people and equipment."

"And the FTL drive Zane found in the port? How does that tie in? What are their plans? It has to be about more than just money."

"Probably. There's only one way to find out. We'll have to go take a look for ourselves."

* * *

RACHEL STEWED until they made it back to the warehouse. Then she grabbed her comp while Adam spoke with Grandmother Wu.

The times on the list yielded quickly to her analysis. There was definitely a pattern. One that she could project into the future. That produced a new set of times that had one very close to now. Only a few hours in the future, in fact.

Projecting the coordinates proved more challenging. Her tools weren't suited to that, but she could still estimate where it would be, roughly. She hoped.

That told her nothing of the depth. From what Hale had said, flying down there was akin to diving into a swimming pool filled with soup. They'd be taking a terrible risk, and that didn't even take into consideration getting back onto the station.

Once they stole Janus's dive ship, the company could watch for their return. They'd be easy to spot approaching the station.

Just to be sure, she compared the dates to the report she'd seen on Evans's comp. One of them was just after the date on the report. The most recent one on her just calculated list, as a matter of fact.

That at least made this crazy idea possible.

Hale and Wu came over as she was refining her guess at the coordinates.

"I've isolated the time and rough general area," Rachel said. "We'll need to get a move on. It's this afternoon."

"That makes sense," Hale said. "They're prepping the ship for a reason. So, our timing is tight, but good. Unless things have changed a great deal, a few extra guards showing up at the bay won't cause too much concern."

The old woman smiled. "I will have some men assist you without revealing their identities. Once you get into the bay, you will be on your own. Do not strike until you are certain you can take the ship."

Hale used his com to access the mechanical spy he'd put in place. "It looks like the prep work is done. The pilots are doing a preflight check. I see diving suits on a rack. We have to go right now."

Jason Chang stepped up beside them. "I'm going with you."

His grandmother scowled. "That is not wise. I forbid it."

The Asian man visibly stiffened, but shook his head. "These people are my friends, and I will stand with them. Besides, Janus knows who I am. Do you truly believe they'll just let me go to work tomorrow as though nothing happened?"

"No, but someone must assist me in making their escape possible," she said. "I find myself in the unique position of requiring your contacts to facilitate my plan. I promise you this, Grandson. Without your intervention, they will die."

"What's your plan?" Jason asked.

"We don't have time to listen to it," Rachel said. "If they get too far into the launch sequence, we're screwed. Honestly, there probably isn't space for more people on that ship. Go do what she needs to help us make our getaway."

He looked mulish, but Hale clapped a hand on his friend's shoulder. "She's right. We've got this."

Wu drew Jason away before he could argue.

"Do you think that's true?" Rachel asked as she packed her comp.

"That she needs his help? Probably not, but I don't want him getting killed with us. Besides, I only saw two suits."

"Will they fit us?"

"My personal suit is specifically tailored to me, but those look like they're used for different pilots. We'll manage."

"Now, seriously," she said, hefting her bag, "what's the plan?"

He gestured to their uniforms. "We bluff. If we can't get in with guile, we fight. Wu's people can back us up. If we get in clean, they can distract the security guards while we overpower the crew and steal the ship."

She looked uncertain. "That's taking an awful lot for granted. It's a little shy on details."

He smiled. "We'll have to wing it. Trust me, I've done enough breaches to have an idea how this will go. You talk us past security, and we go with plan A. That's best. Let's mount up."

Rachel sighed. She couldn't blame him for this situation. It was evolving far faster than they'd had any way to adjust for.

In just a few sentences, Hale relayed the plan to Grandmother Wu's people. They were already assembling, better armed than Hale was.

They set out in three different vehicles. She had an earbud linked to Hale and the others so they could communicate once things went down.

Just short of the bays, Hale stopped the van.

She looked around, concerned that someone had spotted them, but no one was paying the vans any attention.

"What's happening?" she asked.

"We just passed a Janus security van," he said, looking into the mirror. "It has to be on the way to reinforce the guards at the bay. We're going to take them out before that happens."

Rachel shook her head. "And alert the others we're coming? Don't be ridiculous. I have a much better plan."

30

Price's tone made Adam's eyes narrow. "Uh huh. What's your plan?"

"When I stop them, head for the back of the van. Team Wu, back us up as soon as they open the doors."

"What makes you think they'll do that?"

She grinned. "Sometimes you have to have faith."

"Well, this ought to be interesting."

Price stepped out of the van and planted herself on the roadway. The Janus van screeched to a halt right in front of her as Adam slid out of the driver's side door and walked toward the back of the other van. The vehicles with Wu's people neatly boxed them in.

The Janus driver lowered his window with obvious irritation written all over his face. "What?"

"Change in plans," she said. "Captain Krueger sent us to join you."

Adam couldn't see the man's reaction as he rounded the back of the van, but that hardly mattered. The sliding doors on Wu's vehicles were opening, so he drew his pistol and did the same with the Janus van's back doors.

Half a dozen men and women in Janus security uniforms stared at him in surprise. They had weapons, but Hale and the men behind him had the drop on them.

"I shoot the first person that moves," he assured them. "And my friends will shoot everyone else. Drop the guns and raise your hands. Slowly."

At first, he didn't think they'd obey, but after the first one did so, the rest followed suit.

Adam climbed in and kicked the weapons out the back. Wu's people dragged the prisoners out, put cuffs on them, and stuffed them in the other vehicles.

Price did the same with the driver before climbing behind the wheel of her new ride. "Hurry up, Hale. The tide waits on no man."

He closed up the back doors and joined her up front. "That doesn't sound like you at all."

"I sail, believe it or not." She started the van and resumed the drive to the bay. "Now we look all official, too. They're expecting us, so that should make this work even better than before."

Adam hoped that was indeed the case.

Price parked the van close to the bay, got out, and brazenly walked right up to the guards. The same woman that had confronted Jason came out to meet her.

"It's about time," the woman said. "We expected you ten minutes ago."

"There was a screwup," Price said with a shrug. "We're still waiting for the rest of my people."

"Perfect," the other woman sighed. "Once they get here, I'll take my team inside."

"Actually, they sent an update for the pilots. Can you take it in?"

The guard blinked but nodded. "Sure."

Price walked to the door before producing a data chip. "They want me to see you hand it off. Said it was burn-before-reading stuff."

"Damned managers," the woman grumbled as she opened the hatch. "Why can't they just let us do our jobs? Come on."

Adam slid in behind them and stopped while the hatch slid closed. He hit the manual lock. That would slow them down.

The two pilots looked as though they'd almost completed the

external part of their preflight. The smaller of the two came over to meet Price and the woman. "We're about to suit up."

"Change in plans," Price said as she brought her shocker out and took the woman down.

Adam drew his pistol and covered the other pilot. "Step away from the ship. Hands where I can see them."

"What the hell?" the smaller man demanded. "Who are you?"

"We're your replacements," Price said. She reached out and took the tablet from his hand. "I assume your final coordinates and times are on this. Where are they?"

"Are you out of your minds?" the man asked incredulously. "This isn't a damned ship you can just joyride."

"You're too touchy," Price said as she used the shocker on him. He dropped into a trembling heap before she turned on the last man. "Give me the time and coordinates. Now."

The larger man looked justifiably frightened. "They're programmed into the controls already."

Adam moved past him and into the open ship. The controls were familiar enough, and he quickly found what he needed. "They're here," he called out.

"Help me escort these gentlemen out," Price said.

"No need," Adam said as he came out. "The bay has an emergency pressurization chamber over in the corner. We can lock them in there."

He aimed his pistol at the man. "Pick up your friend and move him in there. What's down below, and what the hell are you people doing there?"

The pilot picked up his friend. "You wouldn't believe me if I told you. Just say it's a station and be done with it. You'll find out soon enough. You're Adam Hale, the diver everyone's looking for."

"That's right."

"Then I suppose you'll make it. I'm a fan, by the way. I'm sorry as hell that they'll kill you when this is all done."

"We all make sacrifices. Into the chamber."

Price had the female security officer—minus her weapons—over her shoulder. She set the woman down in the chamber.

"We're going to blow the atmosphere in here, so don't come out," she told the pilot after he set his partner down. "We've jammed the main doors and I don't want you getting killed."

"I'm staying right here," the man assured her.

Price didn't seem convinced. She took him down with her shocker. "Yes, you are."

Adam shook his head and sealed the door. "We need to get this going. The guards outside are going to realize something is wrong soon."

"Did you lock the hatch?"

"Yup. They'll need a cutter to open it. Once we dump the atmosphere, they're screwed. We need to suit up. It's time to take you on what I'll loosely term an adrenaline-pumped thrill ride."

He keyed his microphone and told Wu's people to abort the attack. They were committed now.

* * *

Hale suited Rachel. With the unfamiliar gear and the deadly nature of the dive they were about to take, she didn't object before she stripped down and put on the under suit. It had the standard fittings for waste disposal, so she had him turn around while she got that settled.

He strapped the bulky suit on her starting with the torso and then adding the limbs.

"This is designed to keep the blood going to your brain," he said. "That means it's tight. It will also assist your breathing as needed. We're going to be in heavy gravity, so the extremities have a power assist. The ship will provide protection from the radiation."

It took a few tries to get the legs and arms the right length. The helmet went on last. It was thick and had a bunch of information on a heads-up display. She'd used that kind of thing before, so it didn't intimidate her. As long as the suit was working, she'd be fine.

She wouldn't be running any marathons in it, though. Rachel felt like a knight in shining armor as she tried to move. Hale took her into the ship and strapped her into one of the control couches.

The front area of the ship was cramped. The back wasn't empty, either. It had crates of the same size as the one they'd found with the FTL drive. Supplies for the station below, probably. Then they could reuse the containers to send completed drives back up.

He put their bags into a compartment and locked the ship down as soon as he finished. He strapped into the other seat and brought the controls fully online. Holographic windows appeared, no doubt showing the view from cameras on the hull of the ship.

"Systems green," Hale said. "Ready?"

"I'm not sure I have a choice now."

"Believe me, diving in a ship that I haven't thoroughly and personally checked has me terrified. Hell, I have no idea where their course is going to take us. You called me crazy before, well this is nuts. Here we go."

He touched one of the controls. A muffled hooting noise penetrated the hull. The shadows in the room quickly grew razor-sharp as the air bled away.

"I hope there isn't a tug right outside the hatch," he said.

The bay doors dropped, and the ship fell into space. Jupiter hung below them as they plummeted from the station. It was beautiful. And terrifying, considering where they were going. The Great Red Spot was almost out of sight.

It made her feel like an insect.

They'd barely cleared the hatch and turned toward Jupiter when a bright blast of flame came roaring out of the closing hatch. The vacuum abruptly snuffed it. Something had exploded inside the bay. There was surprisingly little debris. She hoped the walls shielding the men they'd overpowered had been strong enough to keep them safe.

"It looks like the guards used a breaching charge," Hale said.

"They used a little too much," she agreed. "I'm not seeing a lot of debris, so the hatch must've finished closing. Thank God. Those idiots might've decompressed the entire area."

"I'm just glad we got out of there in time."

The ship's com system came to life. "Unidentified ship leaving Jove Station, what the hell is going on? Identify yourself and come about."

"I think I'll just let them yell," Hale said as he turned the com off. "We have more important things to consider. We're a little behind schedule according to the numbers, so let's get a move on and make up the time."

The ship turned so the station disappeared behind them. The bands on the planet below started sliding down the screen. They were headed for the north polar region.

"What should I expect?" she asked.

"Take the scariest rollercoaster you can imagine and then crank the dial up to eleven."

"That's not very reassuring."

He laughed. "We dive because it makes us feel more alive than we've ever been. Even more so than combat. Get ready for an experience that you'll be telling people about for the rest of your life."

"If I live."

"Why are spies so pessimistic? Reorienting to begin deorbit burn. Once we leave orbit, you're going to start feeling the G-forces."

"I can handle three Gs. That's what Jupiter's gravity really feels like up here, isn't it?"

He shook his head. "You don't get it. That's only the basic gravity. We'll pull a lot more than that on entry and again on orbital burn. Even more than the old astronauts dealt with on Earth. Here we go."

The ship turned, and she saw space again. The station was nowhere in sight, but if it had been, she was sure it would be rapidly growing smaller.

She tensed as the pressure holding her in her seat rapidly became suffocating. The torso module of the suit contracted and expanded, filling her lungs with air as she became so heavy that movement felt impossible.

It only got worse from there, because her overstrained muscles started screaming. They hadn't had a chance to heal from slamming into Hale's building.

The exterior view switched to the planet below them. The pale band of atmosphere they were over was just expanding to the point it filled the screen. Dammit. How fast were they going?

"Do… we really… need to go… this fast," she forced out.

"Sissy," he said with a laugh.

Even with the suit helping her breathe, her brain felt oxygen deprived as the entry forces crushed her. Her sight narrowed until she had no peripheral vision at all.

The ship shuddered as it bit deeper into Jupiter's atmosphere. The view on the screens clouded until she couldn't make anything out, so she closed her eyes and tried to stay conscious.

She wasn't sure how much time had passed when he spoke again, but the pressure was falling quickly. "Open your eyes or you'll miss it."

Rachel blinked and found herself looking at clear skies. Massive, breathtaking cloud formations hung in the distance as the ship continued to fall.

"Oh, that's pretty," she said. She could speak again, though it wasn't easy. "Are we all the way in?"

"Hardly. The view won't last much longer. This clear area is only about fifty kilometers from top to bottom.

"Welcome to the club. Less than a hundred people have seen this with their own eyes. Metaphorically speaking, since this is a holographic view."

She drank it in until the haze below them rushed up and swallowed the ship. Visibility rapidly fell to nothing. At least the forces trying to kill her were down to levels the suit could compensate for.

"It won't be long until we start feeling the transition to fluid," Hale said. "It's not a clear-cut demarcation, either. Not like the oceans on Earth. That means it's going to be turbulent. You'll need to hold on."

"You mean it'll be rougher than the ride so far?"

He laughed. "You've only felt the king's gentle caresses. Now he's going to slap you around some."

The soup outside continued to thicken. The shocks started out small, but kept growing rougher until it felt as though they were slamming into physical objects. More than once, she feared her restraints would give way.

Eventually, the ride grew smoother until the ship felt like it was floating in a pool.

Hale looked over at her. "We've crossed the boundary. The course is still taking us down. We're up to a hundred bars and climbing."

"How deep can this go?" she asked.

"I've only gone to two hundred before. Anything more would've been outright suicide. Double Dick had the record at 250 bars."

A minute later, he grunted. "Two hundred and still diving." Hale was compulsively checking a number of screens with the air of a very worried man.

Moments later, a loud groan sent her heart into her throat. "What's that?"

"The hull is compressing. It's warning us we're pushing its tolerances to the limit. Two hundred and fifty bars and still diving. Congratulations. We'll have set a new record, if we survive."

The groaning became much louder, and she thought the compartment was visibly smaller. They were going to die.

She opened her mouth to tell him to abort, when she felt the ship leveling off.

"The indicators have us at just over 300 bars," he said. "We're just short of redlining the hull."

A beeping from the panel captured her attention. "That's not bad, is it?"

He tapped the controls with a lot more dexterity than she'd have managed. "It's a beacon. We've found the station. I wonder how they keep it in place in this mess. Hell, I wonder how they built it at all. They're technologically ahead of the stuff we've been selling them."

"Get us there and you can ask them. Frankly, in this gravity, I can't imagine anyone is too mobile. I want to know how they can actually work there. Or survive the long-term effects of this crushing weight."

"Let's go find someone to ask," he said, taking control of the ship and moving them forward into the swirling liquid.

31

Adam turned the ship to the course laid out on the console and brought the holographic cameras to point at where they were going. The destination had to be close.

He was used to seeing the depths of Jupiter, but something looked off. The fluid ahead had a decidedly green tinge. Not what he was expecting at all. Almost an emerald shade. That wasn't natural.

It must be something to guide the ship in. He supposed they needed something to be sure the pilots didn't miss the station in the murk.

The light grew brighter as the signal luring them in became stronger. He finally saw a wide swath of metal in front of them and slowed the ship. The station had a massive hatch that looked strong enough to keep Jupiter at bay. Actually, it looked a lot stronger than that.

A chime from the console brought his eyes down. There was a new control. One for opening the hatch.

"We're going in," he told Price. "The people inside will be in suits similar to these, so they won't be moving very quickly and they won't be able to get a clear look at our faces. We need to find Zane and get the hell out of here before we waste all our strength."

"I've been thinking about that," she said as he pressed the control. "They might be in support systems with treads and mechanical arms. We can't assume anything."

"I'll keep that in mind."

The hatch ahead of them slid ponderously open and he took the ship in. The chamber beyond was a tight fit, but he set the stolen craft down on the marks painted on the floor.

It was hard to make out details in the relative darkness and with the fluid of Jupiter's atmosphere swirling around them.

He jerked a little when the ship started turning. Then he relaxed. There must be a rotating floor plate. That made sense. Backing out would be a bitch.

The fluid bled away. It was time to go meet their new hosts.

Adam released his straps and stood. It was easier for him with all his training and experience, but Price wasn't doing badly. He verified he had his pistol and some spare ammo stashed in a belt pouch before he opened the hatch.

There was a tube snugged up to the side of the ship now. That would lead them to an airlock that made sure no poison made it where people were trying to breathe. It would also let the crew unload the supplies in relative safety.

Two men in suits identical to theirs were coming through an airlock at the other end of the tube. They tromped up to the ship with a clumsy wave. Their helmets, just like his, mostly obscured their faces.

"Welcome back, Tanner," one of them said over a channel the suit automatically accepted. The voice was male.

"Davis," the man said, nodding to Price. "Young wants to see you in his office. Hurry up. We only have half an hour in this window."

Adam nodded and walked clumsily past them. He hoped Price kept her mouth shut. These people would know something was wrong the moment one of them spoke.

The airlock was pretty normal looking, though big enough for cargo. Four large crates waited for the men to load. Probably FTL drives.

He cycled the lock as soon as Price was inside. It was already pressurized, so he wasn't surprised the process went quickly.

What shocked him was what was waiting on the other side. An eerie green glow leaked into the lock as soon as the hatch started opening. The unnatural light seemed to come from everywhere in the room beyond.

Adam stepped out and almost fell over. The suit's musculature was fluctuating.

He grabbed Price and checked his readout. No, the suit was fine. Something was wrong with the environment. Something other than the horrible green light. Something impossible.

Jupiter's intense gravity had abated.

* * *

"WHAT THE HELL?" Rachel muttered softly to herself. The green glow around them wasn't in any way natural, and she was having trouble with her balance. Though her breathing was easier.

That was it. The suit wasn't forcing air into her lungs anymore. She was doing it on her own.

"I have no idea," Hale said. "We're not in high gravity anymore. It's more like 0.8 Gs."

"That's not possible."

"Exactly. How the hell are they doing this?"

A man walked out of the haze and stopped before them. He had something in his hand. Goggles, like the ones on his face.

That's when it hit her. The man wasn't in a suit. He effortlessly stood there in a Janus uniform, as though he didn't have a care in the world.

"We don't have all day," the man said loudly. "Helmets off and get these on. Young is waiting."

Rachel knew it would blow everything wide open if she did, so it was time for plan B. She nodded, reached onto her belt, and grabbed the shocker. The list of people that were going to be pissed at her for using it on them was growing by the hour.

The man never realized what she was holding. He collapsed in a heap when she zapped him.

Hale popped his helmet and sniffed. "Seems breathable, though it smells funny. The damned light is blinding."

Rachel fumbled her helmet off and agreed. It almost smelled like some kind of forest.

She grabbed one of the goggles and slipped it over her eyes. The odd green glare dropped and she could see somewhat normally now. She handed the other set to Hale.

The room they were in wasn't a room at all. It looked like an oddly formed corridor. One that stretched off to the left and right at somewhat awkward angles. A rack with five gravity suits stood nearby, partly blocking the way to the left.

The airlock looked as though they'd set it roughly into the wall. Weird. This didn't seem like something to skimp on.

"Five suits," Hale said. "That means we have this joker, Young, Zane, and two others. I like those odds."

"What is this place? How did they do this? And what's with these idiotic lights?"

"I don't know and we don't have time to wonder. Get your helmet on and let's go find this Young before he comes looking for us."

"What do we do with this guy?"

Hale grinned. "We'll take him with us. That's the beauty of it. Anyone that we come across will worry about him while we deal with them."

With her helmet back on, she helped Hale lift the man and slipped one of his arms around her shoulder. They started back the way the man had come, dragging his feet behind him.

They had to squat a little. The corridor wasn't much more than five feet tall. Why build it so short? This whole place made no sense.

They went about fifteen yards, and the corridor made a hard right turn. They dragged the man between them until they came to a short railing. A shaft opened in front of them. It was large enough for a single person to climb down, but that was it.

The ladder's rungs were too close together, and the grip was stunted. It went down at least ten levels. How did Janus build something like this?

"This is simultaneously too large and too small," she said. "The ladder is made for little people, and I suspect there might be more bad guys here than the number of suits indicates. Why no elevators?"

"I have no idea," Hale said. "This place is spooking me."

A man's head stuck into the shaft below. Only one level down, and thankfully the unconscious man wasn't in plain view from that angle.

"Hurry up. I don't have all day."

He vanished before either of them could have responded, even if they'd wanted to.

"That must be our host," she said. "We'll have to take a chance and leave this guy here. I don't trust my grip with that kind of load, and we don't have room. When Young tells us where Zane is, we get him and leave."

They climbed down to find a corridor almost identical to the one above. The man was nowhere in sight, so she led Hale after him.

Right around the corner, she came to an open iris door. The interior of the room was somewhat trapezoidal. It contained a battered desk that looked wildly out of place. The man sat behind it, his goggles making him seem like a video drama villain.

"Get those helmets off so we can talk," he said curtly. "You're acting like newbies."

Rachel unlocked her helmet and pulled it off, shaking her hair out as she drew her pistol. The man's expression changed to one of deep shock.

"You must be Young," she said. "We're obviously not the people you were expecting. We're on a tight schedule, too, so I'm going to need you to hurry it up. Where is Zane Hale?"

The man visibly flinched when she mentioned Zane's name. This was the right place after all.

"You're not going to get out of here alive," Young said.

"I don't have time to dick around," Hale said. "You have my brother and I'm about to start breaking fingers. Where. Is. He."

"On this level. He's under guard."

Hale smiled. "I'll bet he is. Take us there. Now. Do anything funny and I'll shoot you first."

The man rose from the desk, his hands in the air.

"Put them down," Rachel said. "Walk slowly and stay in front of us. Don't use anyone's name if we meet them. If I get suspicious, I'll let him shoot you."

They put their helmets back on and followed Young into the corridor. She kept far enough back to shoot him if he suddenly turned.

"We know this is where you build the FTL drives, but why did you make it so weird?" she asked. "How did you change the gravity?"

The man shook his head without turning to look at her. "Are you blind? What the hell makes you think we built this?"

She laughed quietly. "Who should I think built it? Little green men?"

"I doubt they were actually green. That's just the lighting."

It felt as though he'd slapped her. "Aliens? Are you kidding me?"

"Believe whatever you like, then."

"Leave that aside," Hale said. "Why is the window so short? We only have half an hour before we have to leave. Why?"

"Because we're at the highest point the station rises to on this pass. In about twenty minutes, we'll start descending again, and you'll be stuck with us for a few weeks. I hope you brought cards. It gets really boring."

He grinned nastily at them. "While it occasionally goes up to the gaseous layers, it mostly stays deep. As in over five hundred bars. It's a miracle Janus found it all those years ago, and we only recently built a landing bay that allowed us to stay here fulltime."

They came around the corner to find another iris door, this one closed. A man with a holstered pistol stood outside it.

He looked over at them, and his eyes narrowed. His hand began creeping toward his weapon. Young must've done something to tip him off.

Rachel shot the man dead. When Young dove for the weapon, Hale shot him, too. Well, this had gotten bloody fast.

The iris controls were a dial, so she twisted it. Left was the only direction that had movement.

The door slid open from the center out. Inside the room, sitting on the cot from the video, was Zane. He wasn't wearing goggles, and his jumpsuit was filthy. He looked even more scraggly than he had in the video.

Based on his expression, he hadn't heard the shots. The room must be soundproofed.

She rushed in, only stopping when he lunged for her. A chain around his ankle yanked him up short.

"Come one step closer," he muttered.

Rachel pulled her helmet off. "Zane! It's me!"

He blinked at her. "Rachel? Holy shit."

"We're here to get you out. Lean back while I shoot the lock."

He flinched at the shot, but the lock came apart. "Who's here with you? You brought backup? Thank God. We're almost out of time."

"Those shots will bring people running," she said. "What are we facing?"

"A couple of dozen people. Maybe a third of them armed."

"We have to go now," Hale said, tossing her a set of goggles from one of the dead men. She handed it to Zane.

Her partner straightened at the sound. "Adam?"

"You look like shit, bro. Our ride won't wait. Let's move."

It was obvious Zane had questions, but he clamped his mouth shut and came with them. He did stop long enough to grab the guard's weapon.

Several men were climbing the ladder when they arrived, but a few shots made them take cover. Adam led his brother up while she kept the men ducking. Then she scurried up after them.

Rachel stayed at the shaft while Adam got Zane suited up. With the high ground, it wasn't hard to keep the Janus people pinned, but that wouldn't last. As soon as the three of them went into the bay, the others would swarm after them.

"We're ready," Hale said over the com.

She fired another volley and waited ten seconds. Then she leaned out and shot the first man on the ladder. He fell into the depths with a scream, taking two other people with him.

That should convince them to wait a bit before they tried again.

Adam already had the airlock open, and she ducked inside. He slid it closed and jammed some equipment into the track. "That might keep them busy for a little bit."

The crates they'd seen were gone, and half the crates of supplies were inside. The outer lock door cycled open, and the two men used hand trucks to bring the remaining supplies inside.

The largest of the pair frowned. "Wait a minute. Who's leaving?"

"It's a secret," Rachel said as she used the shocker on him. It seemed to work well enough through the suit.

The other man backed up, but he had nowhere to go. They tossed him into the airlock just as someone on the other side started trying to open the inner hatch.

"Time to exit stage left," Adam said. "Into the dive ship."

The return to heavy gravity was a blow, but she managed to seal the ship while Adam strapped in. That's when she saw the problem. There were only two acceleration couches.

"Where do we put Zane?" she asked, glad her suit was helping her breathe.

"Strap him to a crate. It won't be comfortable, but beggars can't be choosers."

"He's right," Zane said. "Time is critical. We have to get a message back to Earth. What day is this?"

She told him, and he paled. "God, I hope we aren't too late."

"Price," Adam said. "Strap in."

Rachel finished lashing her partner down and waddled to her couch. Adam helped her lock the restraints.

She couldn't look back, but she could still talk. "Too late for what?"

"The reason I came out here," Zane said as fluid flowed in and the bay doors opened. "Janus is staging a coup against the Republic. It was supposed to have kicked off about now."

32

A dam boosted the ship out of the fluid at the highest rate of speed he could safely manage. The turbulence was more intense than anything he'd ever experienced.

"Coup? How?" he choked out.

"Wait," Zane gasped. "Can't... talk."

He'd always considered his older brother tougher than himself, so that admission surprised him.

Well, they wouldn't be talking until they got above Jupiter's atmosphere, then. He had time to process what he was feeling about this entire situation.

He'd broken things off with Zane for good reason. His brother had chosen his beloved organization over his own blood. Ten years had muted the pain, but not eliminated it.

Adam had thought Zane died coming to prove his innocence. What a joke. It turned out Zane had had the information clearing Adam for God only knew how long. All he cared about was whatever his mission was.

Admittedly, the Republic was important, but seriously, how much chance did a corporation have of taking down the elected government? The people that controlled the military. And then there was the population itself. No way would they stand still for something like that.

He felt torn as the ship rose through the clear atmosphere. He'd probably never see it again. Janus would kill them as they approached the station or when they boarded. Those were pretty much their only options.

Grandmother Wu was resourceful, but Adam just couldn't believe she'd get them out of Jupiter's orbit alive. Janus would search every ship before departure. Not even smuggling them out in a crate would work.

The acceleration they felt finally fell off as they rose into the blackness of space.

"Spill it," Adam said brusquely once he was sure his brother could breathe. "What coup? How?"

"There's more to Janus than anyone suspected," Zane said raggedly. "They're connected with the Disruptors. They control them. They have the RIS thoroughly penetrated. Probably other agencies, too. The people watching the terrorists are in league with them."

"We figured that out," Rachel said. "How does that translate to a coup?"

"The Disruptors are going to stage simultaneous strikes against most of the Republic's leadership. A decapitating blow. Janus intends to step into the vacuum and seize control of the system."

Adam shook his head. "It'll never work. The military is too powerful."

"You'd think so, but not really. Janus has been building warships of their own. Rather, they've built FTL ships, sent them out of the system, and upgraded them. I have no idea how many of the sales they've made are to legitimate companies, but I'm suspecting it's a minority.

"Worse, the FTL drives they provided the Republican military are booby trapped. They won't blow up. The Navy screens them for that kind of thing. But they'll send out a carefully tailored electromagnetic pulse that will cripple the ship's drives, leaving them dead in space."

Rachel didn't seem convinced. "The military shields their ships from that kind of thing."

"They do, but Janus owns the company that's built the normal space drives for decades. This one chink in the armor is all they needed. And, of course, it'll fry the FTL drive, too. The ships can still fight, but they'll be easy targets when they can't maneuver.

"To add insult to injury, the Navy drives have a tracking device that Janus can trigger. They'll know the exact location of every ship the Republic has. No doubt their warships will be shadowing them, waiting to pounce all at the same time. It's going to be a slaughter if we don't warn the Republic."

The ship's radio came to life. "Adam Hale, this is Jove Control. Come left fifteen degrees and proceed to the Janus docks."

He flicked the transmit button. "Negative, Control. I think I'll just circle around out here for a while."

"You have nowhere to go. Don't make this harder on yourself than it needs to be."

"That's the story of my life, Control. Why change now?"

A strange buzzing filled the channel for a moment and then vanished. "Hale, this is Grandmother Wu. Do not respond. We are transmitting on a tight beam that Control will not detect. Tell them you want to speak with the Janus CEO to name your demands, if you can hear me."

He smiled. Yeah, that wouldn't go over well. The CEO was a stuck-up son of a bitch. He'd wait until Adam ran out of air before he negotiated.

"Control, if you want me to come in, you get the Janus CEO on the horn. I'll only give him my demands."

A moment went by with no response. "I'll see what I can do, but I think you'll run out of fuel first."

It was good to see that he'd probably read the man correctly.

"Let me see if I can encourage him," Adam said. "Listen closely."

He'd noticed that the Janus pilots had the automatic transponder and data feeds turned off when he'd started the dive. Let's see how Janus liked the people running the games knowing everything he'd seen and how deep down it was.

A few moments was all it took to enable the equipment. He switched it to the frequency the judges had designated for the games and hit the transmit key. For good measure, he sent it again on the channel used by the local divers. In less than ten seconds, it was done. Good luck covering that up.

Right after he finished, Wu spoke again. "I have made arrangements for your departure, but the window is tight. You've already committed grand theft, but I believe that you can do better.

"My grandson indicates the ship you just turned over to the FTL crew is suitable. I am arranging for a delivery of supplies and people for your crew. You need to go there now. Once I see you change course, my people will disable Control's transmitters. The FTL crew will not be aware of your impending arrival."

"Where the hell will we go if we steal *Javelin*?" he asked Price.

"Anywhere is better than here," Price said. "The RIS can help us."

Zane grunted. "Unless Janus wins. We need to get a message to Earth now."

"No transmitter on a ship is that powerful. We'd have to get closer to Earth."

"Then that's what we need to do."

Wu came back on the line as Zane was finishing. "There is other news. The Disruptors have struck at numerous government leaders. Reports are beginning to flood in. Something is happening with the military as well, though I'm not quite sure what. Details are sparse."

Zane growled and beat the crate with his fist. "Dammit. We're too late. Why did you take so long to come for me? You could've stopped this."

Adam opened his mouth to rip a strip off his brother, but Price beat him to it.

"You know what could've saved time?" she asked harshly. "You telling your partner about this rather than running off to play lone ranger. Or, you could've left enough data for me to know what I was looking for when I got here. Wait, you also could've talked with your damned brother. Don't blame everyone else for your screw ups, Zane."

"You've known I was telling the truth about Mars," Adam added. "How long have you kept that to yourself?"

"Two years," Zane said bitterly. "But I had more important—"

"Screw you," Adam said, cutting him off. "You self-centered jackass. I'm surprised there's enough room in this ship for you and your ego. If I could, I'd dump your ass out for Janus to play with."

He wanted to rub his face. "No, I wouldn't. I'd settle for beating your ass to a pulp and dropping you off at the first place Janus couldn't get you. We're done."

"You were always so damned jealous of—"

"Jesus!" Price shouted. "Shut up. Both of you. We have more pressing business to take care of. Maybe the coup will fail, but we have to assume the worst and get out of here. That means getting a move on, Hale."

She was right. They had all the time in the world to hash this out after they hijacked their ride.

He changed course for the construction area ahead of the station. *Javelin*'s beacon was clear on his screen. It was time for a surprise visit.

* * *

RACHEL WATCHED Hale approach the ship with more than a hint of trepidation. If the ship denied them entry, they'd be screwed.

She could see the fury burning inside Hale. As much as Rachel respected Zane, he'd screwed this up. Badly. If things went the way she feared, they'd need every hand before this was over.

Reconciliation seemed wildly optimistic, but perhaps she could get them to avoid semi-random fistfights if she worked really hard to make her point.

When the ship was large enough on the screens to see the distinctive Alcubierre drive torus, Hale touched a control. "*Javelin*, this is Supply One with your beer." His voice sounded amazingly free of the rage that seemed to grip him.

"Hale?" an unfamiliar voice asked. "What are you doing out here?"

"Kira asked me to make an equipment delivery. The beer was my idea."

He leaned over toward Rachel. "Kira Houston is the construction boss. She's not going to be happy with this. I feel bad. She's good people."

"Really?" the man asked. "That's damned odd, considering she's out here overseeing the FTL install."

"Crap," Hale said. "That tears it. We have to go in hot."

"Go ahead and ask her," he told the man. "I can wait."

Hale boosted their speed, and the ship in front of them grew rapidly larger. Rachel hoped he could stop them in time.

"What will they be able to do?" she asked.

"The external hatches can be locked from the inside. If they haven't changed the override codes, I can get us in. They have some weapons on board, I think. This really all depends on how quickly we can get the upper hand. I don't want to hurt any of these people."

"That might not be possible," Zane said. "This is more important than any of their lives."

"You don't get to make that call," Hale said coldly. "You don't get to tell me what to do anymore."

"Hale," the man on the ship said. "She's on her way up. She says she has no idea what you're talking about. Stand off until she gets to the bridge."

"Copy that," Hale said.

"Holy shit! Divert course now!"

"Sorry, pal. Can't do that."

Hale tapped in a code on the console, and a large hatch at the back of the ship began slowly opening.

"He can't stop it, but he can close it again. Hang on."

The hatch finished opening and immediately began closing. Hale drove the ship through the gap, and the bottom of the hull brushed the deck.

The dive ship spun into the bay and slammed into the rear wall, jarring Rachel badly. She saw the hatch close.

She started to undo her restraints, but Hale stopped her. "I'm blowing our atmosphere."

Their hatch opened, and the air inside the ship roared into the bay. Once the roar died down, she shook him off and got clear of her seat. Zane was already tearing himself loose from the crate.

They floated out into the bay, and Hale waved at the camera high on the ceiling. The ship had settled to the floor, so there must be something magnetic at play that wasn't doing the same for their suits. The airlock didn't respond to him pressing the button.

"Crap!" she shouted.

"Hold your horses," he said, smashing the button with his pistol butt while holding onto a handhold. "This wasn't made for security."

He did something inside the wreckage, and the hatch opened into an airlock.

Rachel drew her pistol and led the way in. She pressed the button to cycle it as soon as they were all inside. It worked.

A very pissed-off woman with a pistol in her hand waited on the other side, two armed men behind her. "Dammit it, Hale! What the absolute hell are you doing? Who are these people? Stand down!"

"Rachel Price, Republican Intelligence Service," Rachel snarled, aiming her weapon right at the other woman's head. "Lower your weapons or we open fire."

The two men behind the woman glanced at one another but didn't shift their aim.

"Kira," Hale said. "You know me. You know I'm ex-military Special Forces. You know I wouldn't play along with this if it were bullshit. Don't make her shoot you. Seriously, I don't want anyone hurt, but we don't have time for a pissing contest."

They all floated there for a long moment before the other woman sighed and lowered her weapon. "Christ. If you're lying to me, I'm in deep trouble. Guns down, boys."

Zane moved past Rachel to disarm them. Once he had their weapons, he made his way back.

"To the bridge," Hale said. "I'll explain it there."

They saw other people on the way to the bridge, but none had guns.

The man on the bridge started to say something at Hale, his expression indicating he was supremely pissed off.

"No time, Jack," Hale said, bringing the controls to life. "Price, explain it to them. Zane, watch the hatch. We have an incoming supply ship. That must be Jason."

Kira Houston glared at Rachel. "What's going on?"

"Someone inside Janus Corporation is staging a coup against the Republican government. Right now."

"Bullshit."

The man who'd been on the bridge cleared his throat. "Ah… maybe not. I heard something about widespread attacks of some kind in the rest of the system. No one knows what's happening."

"And you didn't think to tell me?" Houston demanded. "Jesus, Jack."

The woman rubbed her face. "Say I believe you. What the hell are you doing here?"

"We're leaving the area until we know what's going on. We have most of the plan and if we can get to a large transmitter, we can let everyone know that Janus is behind it. You know a guy named Randy Evans?"

Houston nodded. "Sure. He's a dick. The dick in charge of the FTL program. There was some kind of incident with him in the headquarters building, so they sent me out here to make sure things were okay. Was that you?"

Rachel nodded. "I'm afraid it was more than an incident. He was one of the leaders in the plot, and the guards outside his office shot him dead when we tried to question him."

"Holy shit," Houston said, looking shocked. "This can't be happening."

"It is," Hale said. "That's Jason. He should have enough room in the bay to land. As soon as he's on board, we boost. Where do we go, Price?"

"Ceres," she said. "That's close and will have a transmitter strong enough to hit the rest of the system. We have to get ahead of this. We can drop these people off there, too. Zane, get them out of here. Except Houston. Lock the hatch."

Once he'd cleared the room, Rachel gave Houston a stern look. "If they intentionally screw something up, you won't like the results."

"They won't."

Five minutes passed and then Hale started the ship moving. Rachel could actually feel it.

"Jason is on board and I've set the course," Hale said. "Control is back on the air. We only thought they were screaming before. Man, are they excited."

"Can they catch us?"

He shook his head. "No. FTL ships are fast. The next one in line isn't finished yet, so we're clear. I'm spinning the ship."

He touched a key on the console, and an automated voice began warning of impending gravity.

Rachel put her pistol away and held on as the gravity slowly took hold. "Go get your friend. After you take this dammed suit off me. Take Houston with you."

She looked at Zane meaningfully as Hale began stripping off his dive suit. "We need to talk."

Zane sighed. "That phrase never means anything good."

33

A dam was happy to be out of the suit, even if all he had on was an under suit. He held the pistol in his hand because he had nowhere to put it.

Kira seemed deflated. "Is this all true? Janus is taking over the Republic? That's crazy. Do you really believe them?"

"Sadly, I do. I was there when we questioned Evans. I've seen far too much for this to be faked."

"It was Janus that tried to kill you, then. God."

He snorted. "Actually, that was someone else. I'll tell you the entire story when we have time. What you need to understand for now is that this really is happening.

"Believe me, you're in as much danger as we are. We've seen things that the company doesn't want getting out. Like where these FTL drives come from."

She frowned. "What the hell does that mean?"

"That's another part you'll have a hard time swallowing."

They arrived at the docking bay. Of course Jason had figured out how to cycle the lock. He wasn't alone, either. Their construction crew was with them, along with their families and/or significant others.

He'd also brought some of the storm divers they liked the best and their people. He'd really stuffed the passenger shuttle to the max.

"Bro, you park like shit," his friend said. "I brought friends. Hi, Kira. We've collected your folks' families, too."

They were a welcome sight. People to run the ship he could trust implicitly.

Malcom Enright was another story. The reporter gaped at the ship from his place at Jason's elbow.

"Good God, Mister Hale," the older man said. "Everything Miss Price claimed has come true. Janus really was up to something."

"Told you. Now we have to stop them."

"That may prove more challenging than even you can manage," the man said sadly. "The reports I've seen indicate the coup might have been successful. With the way these things work, it may be some time before we know for certain, but it's too late for anything we do to make a difference."

Adam sagged. "Dammit. We can't have failed."

Jason clapped him on the shoulder. "They started out a dozen moves ahead of us. We're lucky to be alive. We can head somewhere out of the way and see how things shake down while we make plans.

"I'm worried, though. I tried to find Cindy, but she wasn't at her place. She didn't answer the com, either. I'm afraid Janus has her."

Adam grimaced. "They don't. I owe you the full story, but she got off the station before they locked everything down. She's fine."

His friend frowned. "What? Why?"

"No time. I hope you brought a lot of supplies for us," he said, changing the subject.

"Everything my grandmother could beg, borrow, or literally steal. She also sent the FTL drive with us. She said it was too hot to sell and that we owed her. I also have the rest of your friend's spy gear. Did you find your brother?"

"Yes, but it wasn't the joyous reunion you'd expect."

The airlock cycled, and two security officers stepped through. The two patrolmen that had been with Quinn. Adam gaped and started to raise his gun.

Jason grabbed his hand. "They're with us. Once it became clear something funny was going on, they went to guard their boss. Someone tried to kill her again, so I convinced Grandmother to move her to safety. She's in the shuttle with Paul Wong."

The older security man nodded at Adam. Gavin Starnes. "We're not here to cause trouble, Mister Hale. We turned our weapons over to Mister Chang, and we're at your service. Until Detective Quinn says otherwise."

Adam stared at all the people around him and shook his head. "I obviously need to tell this story in a group setting, but for right now, we have to get away from Jove Station. Everyone to your boosting stations. Keep an eye on the FTL crew. I want to trust them, but it's too soon."

Once they'd dispersed, Adam looked at Jason, Enright, and Kira. "Let's go to the mess. We can at least have coffee while I tell you the real story."

* * *

RACHEL WAITED for Hale to leave before she turned on her partner. "You idiot."

"Look," Zane said, his hands held out beseechingly. "I had to cut you out. I didn't want to put you into the position of believing this. Hell, I wasn't sure until I got out here."

"That doesn't cut it," she said harshly. "You didn't trust me. Worse, you got up on that damned high horse and made it impossible for us to get to you in time. Two years. Two. Years."

He sagged into a chair. "You think I haven't raked myself over the coals for the last few months? I know I've screwed up. I did what I thought best. I was wrong."

"Why not bring your brother into this? Surely you trust him."

"Not after Mars."

She felt her eyes widen incredulously. "Seriously? If I can admit I was wrong when I had my face shoved into the evidence, how could you ever doubt?"

"Not that," Zane said abruptly. "His dislike of me made him

unreliable. I've known him longer than you have. He's a loose cannon waiting to go off."

Rachel shook her head in astonishment. "Idiot is too mild a word. Look around you. He more than pulled his weight making this happen. Trust me, he doesn't like me any more than I like him. Though I'm honest enough to admit I was wrong. Absolutely, completely wrong about him.

"More to the point, he's been far more reliable than you. I thought I knew you, but I'm going to have to rethink that. I don't trust your judgment anymore."

"That hurts, but I get it. You'll have to get over it, though. When I finally put together a plan, I'll need you to back my play. Adam won't like it, I'm sure, but together we can keep him in line."

She put her hands on her hips. "Maybe you don't get it. I'll chalk that up to you being a prisoner for so long and everything happening all at once. You're not going to be calling any shots, Zane. I'm in command of this operation."

"Don't be stupid. I'm the senior agent, and I have far more experience than you do. Don't make me force the issue."

Rachel stared at him, too flabbergasted for words. He'd lost his mind.

"You're going to make this difficult, aren't you?" she asked as she grabbed her suit and put it on top of Hale's.

"I'm sorry to quash you like this," he said. "You've done one hell of a job, but it's time for me to take over. You'll understand in time."

"I feel exactly the same way," she said sadly as she brought out the shocker she'd palmed and pressed it to his chest.

Zane had just enough time to twitch his hand toward it before she blasted him into oblivion.

"Breakups are hard," she said over his limp body. "Especially in our line of work."

She'd have to get Hale to lock Zane up. He'd be pissed when he woke up, but she didn't care anymore.

* * *

ADAM FOUND a room that could hold Zane until they decided what they needed to do with him. He was a bit jealous that Price had gotten to shock the bastard. He felt cheated.

The ex-security patrolmen agreed to watch over his brother. After speaking with the still badly injured detective, he was willing to trust the two. They were all in this together.

The next thing he found was a jumpsuit. He tore the Janus emblems off and put it on, happy that it fit.

When he finally stepped onto the bridge, he found it fully manned by his team. The FTL crew was coming around, but he didn't want to chance anything until he was sure of them.

Price sat in the captain's chair, staring at the console in front of her. She looked up as he came in.

"The coup is going to succeed," she said grimly. "They bombed parliament while the president and the senior judiciary were there. They've already blamed the Disruptors and declared martial law."

"What do they have to back it up?" he asked.

"At least some of the Army went over to Janus. Or the officers were in their pay. We may never know for sure.

"The Navy is still fighting, but we're picking up distress beacons. Those go a lot further than the short-range transmitters. Too many of them."

"Show me."

The RIS agent brought up a flat map of the system. Dozens of flashing dots indicated distress beacons. More were appearing at the edges of the map as he watched. She was right. Janus had won.

"I talked with Houston," Price said. "Her people are going to finish installing the FTL drive. Since it wasn't intended for the Navy, it's probably going to be safe. We need to jump out of the system."

He sighed. "No one here knows how to even use the damned things. We're construction people. Normal space operations are about our limit. We're stuck."

"Maybe not." Price tapped the screen. "This one distress beacon is right ahead of us. If we can find a pilot on board, they could help us escape."

He looked at the scale of the display and did some rough math in his head. "We're a few hours away. We'll call ahead. I don't want anyone shooting at us. Move over."

She stood and surrendered the chair to him.

Adam brought the com system online. The other ship was at extreme range, but he could give it a try. The delay in the back and forth wouldn't be terrible.

"Navy vessel, this is *Javelin*," he said into the com when he activated the transmitter. "We are two hours away from your position. Please state the nature of your emergency."

He already knew the answer, but he wanted them to be less suspicious, not more.

The response took a little longer than the travel time for the signal, but not much. The screen came to life. A man wearing a Navy uniform with a nasty cut over his left eye stared back at him. His right arm was in a sling.

"*Javelin*, this is the Republican Navy ship *Hyperion*. We've sustained some kind of engine damage and then another ship attacked us. Rebels we never knew existed, based on the news from the rest of the system. We took them out."

The man leaned forward. "Are you a rebel, *Javelin*?"

Adam grinned. "Hell, no. I'm Adam Hale, and we took this ship from the rebels. I'm sure we'll have to take small steps to build trust, but you need a ride and we need an experienced crew to help us. We used to be construction people out on Jove Station."

The man slowly nodded. "I might be able to believe that. We'll have to build some trust, as you said, but at least you didn't come out of nowhere and start shooting at us. That's a point in your favor.

"I'm Lieutenant Charles Nottingham, *Hyperion*'s tactical officer. The captain and the executive officer died in the battle."

"I'm sorry to hear that, sir. I'm ex-military myself and I know how that hurts." He pursed his lips. "It's better if we share our stories when we meet. We're an FTL ship, but we don't have a pilot. Can you help us out?"

The man smiled grimly. "We *used* to be an FTL ship. The pilot and her backup made it through the fight just fine. I think we might be able to help one another, *Javelin*."

* * *

Rachel rubbed her neck after the tense exchange was over. It had gone much better than she'd dared hope. They'd have the help they needed to get somewhere. Then they had to make plans to turn this around.

Somehow.

She opened her mouth to say something when the com system chimed. Maybe *Hyperion* was calling back.

No, it was an encrypted signal on an open beam. She reached past Hale and brought up the header. RIS encoding. It was from the Inspector General's office.

Talk about being spectacularly late to the party.

"My turn in the chair," she said.

Hale got up and let her take his place. He stared at the screen. "What is that?"

"A signal from the RIS Inspector General. It's encrypted, but going wide. Everyone and their third cousins are getting this. Only someone with the right codes can read it, though."

"It must be important."

She certainly hoped he was right.

Her passcode worked up to a point. It got a video, an executable file, and a large encrypted file with a different key. Hoping the video would give her something to work with, she played it.

A woman in a suit sitting behind a desk appeared. Her expression was grim.

"This message is for all loyal RIS agents in the Earth system. I am Wanda Redding, your Inspector General, and there is a coup in progress. By now, you probably know that, but individuals high in the RIS hierarchy are involved."

The woman smiled coldly. "Unfortunately for them, they didn't realize we've considered the possibility of this before. I've locked them out of the comps and purged all RIS systems and backups.

"They'll get into my office soon, so I don't have time to go into detail, but you need to know that I've included as many covert RIS locations and contacts in the encrypted file attached to this message as I can. I can't give you the code to access it, however."

Rachel frowned. What use was it, then?

"I've culled the roster of active agents and used my best judgment to pick those who are likely to be the most loyal," Redding said. "If you're hearing this message, you're in that group. If you heard about it secondhand but aren't involved in the coup, my apologies, but I can't trust you."

Redding smiled coolly. "The file's access code is based on you, loyal agent. Use your failsafe code with the attached executable program. It will generate a passcode to decrypt the data. Protect it with your lives. The code for this operation is Redemption. If someone claims to be RIS and doesn't know that, be very, very cautious about trusting them.

"The file has the list of agents I chose to get this message. Anyone not on it is hereby suspended as an active RIS agent. Work with them if you must, but be very careful not to trust them too deeply, no matter how long you've known them. The corruption runs deep."

An explosion went off not too far away from Redding's desk. She opened her desk drawer and retrieved a pistol. "I'm going to purge my system now. Do whatever it takes to restore the Republic and stop these bastards. Consider those the last valid orders you're going to get from us. Know that we're proud of you all. Good luck and make them bleed."

The recording ended, and Rachel sat back in her chair. God, she'd never expected it to get this bad. The Republic had really fallen. The RIS was gone. They were on their own.

"Do you have the code?" Adam asked.

"I'll know for sure once I've moved the file to an isolated system, but I'm sure I do. You heard her. Only the most loyal RIS operatives could even listen to her. My code is in there."

"What's the plan, then?" he asked.

Rachel smiled grimly. "We pick up our new friends and get the hell out of here before someone comes looking for us. Then we come back with blood in our eyes. The Republic isn't dead until we say so."

* * *

WANT to get updates from Terry about new books and other general nonsense going on in his life? He promises there will be cats. Go to TerryMixon.com/Mailing-List and sign up.

DID YOU ENJOY THIS BOOK? Please leave a review on Amazon. It only takes a minute to dash off a few words and that kind of thing helps Terry make a living as a writer and gets you new books faster.

WANT MORE BOOKS BY TERRY? Flip to the next page and grab one.

VISIT TERRY'S Patreon page to find out how to get cool rewards and an early look at what he's working on at Patreon.com/TerryMixon.

ALSO BY TERRY MIXON

You can always find the most up to date listing of Terry's titles on his Amazon Author Page.

Note: the links below (ebook only, obviously) redirect you to my website where you can click a button to go to Amazon. This allows me to participate in Amazon's associates program and earn a little more. Sorry for any inconvenience.

The Last Hunter

The Last Hunter

Bonds of Blood

Alpha Strike

The Enemy Revealed

Command Authority

The Grand Conspiracy

Shield of Humanity

Fog of War

Ships of the Line

Operation Liberty

The Empire of Bones Saga

Empire of Bones

Veil of Shadows

Command Decisions

Ghosts of Empire

Paying the Price

Recon in Force

Behind Enemy Lines

The Terra Gambit

Hidden Enemies

Race to Terra

Ruined Terra

Victory on Terra

When Luck Runs Out

Gunboat Diplomacy

The Imperial Marines Saga

Spoils of War

Imperial Recruit

Enemy Action

The Humanity Unlimited Saga

Liberty Station

Freedom Express

Tree of Liberty

Blood of Patriots

Single Novels

Scorched Earth

Storm Divers

The Vigilante Series with Glynn Stewart

Heart of Vengeance

Oath of Vengeance

Bound By Law

Bound By Honor

Bound By Blood

Box Sets

The Empire of Bones Saga Volume 1

The Empire of Bones Saga Volume 2

The Empire of Bones Saga Volume 3

The Empire of Bones Saga Volume 4

Humanity Unlimited Publisher's Pack 1

Humanity Unlimited Publisher's Pack 2

ABOUT TERRY

#1 Bestselling Military Science Fiction author Terry Mixon served as a non-commissioned officer in the United States Army 101st Airborne Division. He later worked alongside the flight controllers in the Mission Control Center at the NASA Johnson Space Center supporting the Space Shuttle, the International Space Station, and other human spaceflight projects.

He now writes full time while living in Texas with his lovely wife and a pounce of cats.

TerryMixon.com

[a] amazon.com/author/terrymixon
[f] facebook.com/TerryLMixon
[P] patreon.com/TerryMixon
[BB] bookbub.com/authors/terry-mixon
[g] goodreads.com/TerryMixon

www.ingramcontent.com/pod-product-compliance
Lightning Source LLC
Chambersburg PA
CBHW052018020726
47501CB00004B/1129